Cut

A Medical

Murder Mystery

Amy S. Peele

SHE WRITES PRESS

Published 2017
Printed in the United States of America
Print ISBN: 978-1-63152-184-3
E-ISBN: 978-1-63152-185-0
Library of Congress Control Number: 2016961146

For information, address:
She Writes Press
1563 Solano Ave #546
Berkeley, CA 94707

Cover design © Julie Metz, Ltd./metzdesign.com
Interior design by Tabitha Lahr

She Writes Press is a division of SparkPoint Studio, LLC.

This is a work of fiction. Names, characters, places, and incidents either are the product of the author's imagination or are used fictitiously. Any resemblance to actual persons, living or dead, is entirely coincidental.

This book is dedicated to:

All the donor families who made the hardest decision in their lives when they lost a loved one and decided to donate their loved ones' organs and tissues.

All the living donors who had the courage to step up and improve the lives of others, thus making a deceased donor organ available to those without a living donor.

All the courageous people who are currently waiting for a second chance at life, and all those brave people who have received a transplant and gone on to honor its giver by making the most out of their lives.

And finally, I dedicate these pages to the imaginative, hard-working, dedicated medical and support professionals who work on behalf of the ethical transplantation of organs and tissues. I am honored to have served among you.

Chapter 1

Sarah Golden didn't remember having left the TV on before she'd passed out the night before, but its loud noise woke her out of a sound sleep. She could tell by the light coming in her window that it was late morning. Sitting up in bed, she watched a tall, naked man drinking from a milk carton in the kitchenette. The studio apartment she'd rented near the Miami Transplant Institute had been all she needed when she'd decided to take the traveling nurse job three months ago, in May. Because of her transplant experience, they'd offered her a $5,000 signing bonus to work a four-month gig.

She struggled to piece together how the prior evening had ended after she had left the bar with her nurse colleagues, but the pounding in her head was too much. She had to lie back down.

"A blonde with a nice, firm body and long legs," she mumbled to herself. Sarah had taken home her share of strong, handsome men but was rarely attracted to blonds. What was his name? What did he do? She watched him playing with the remote and then closed her eyes. She fondly recalled that he was an excellent kisser. She loved to make out. They'd spent almost an hour in his car before she'd asked him up to her place. The thought brought a grin to her sleepy face.

Before she could open her eyes again, he was next to her, kissing her softly on her neck, reaching his hand beneath the smooth sheets. His fingers started to arouse her before she could protest. He kissed her mouth.

"Good morning, you wild woman. I wanted to make you breakfast in bed, but you have no food in your refrigerator. So I thought I'd give you something else for breakfast." With that, she welcomed Blondie as he slid on top of her and they started to rock gently under the covers.

Not a bad way to wake up, she thought, and he was well endowed. She ignored her headache and enjoyed her breakfast.

•   •   •

After they'd both had their fill, Sarah a few times, she kissed Blondie on the head and went into the bathroom. She grabbed some Advil from the medicine cabinet, gulped them down with water, and took a hot, soapy shower. She shampooed her long brown hair and wrapped it in a towel. She was putting on her silky bathrobe when Blondie came into the bathroom, still naked.

"Want to fool around a little more before we go out to eat?" he asked.

"You were amazing, but I need to get ready for work." She didn't actually have to work; she just didn't want a relationship with any man, even though she enjoyed them sexually. She was especially not looking for something here in Miami. Blondie wore a slight look of disappointment when he stepped into the shower.

Sarah went into the kitchen and glanced at the TV. CNN was on, and she spotted her old friend Dr. Bower sitting at a table, facing a panel of US congresspeople. She unmuted the TV. The small print on the bottom of the screen read:"Federal Subcommittee of Investigation and Oversight. Hearings on National Organ Distribution." The camera showed the committee members. The woman chairing the committee was speaking: "Dr. Bower, you can say with absolute certainty that all organs are allocated equitably throughout the United States? There is no way to game the system? You have data to prove this?"

Dr. Bower leaned forward toward his microphone, his disheveled white hair partly covering his soft brown eyes. "Madam Chair and committee members, I am president of the United Network for Organ Sharing, known as UNOS. As you will see when you review your packets, every organ offered is tracked, regardless of whether it is transplanted or discarded. We follow all transplant recipients for the rest of their lives. Public trust is paramount to the success of organ and tissue donation and transplantation. I am happy to answer any questions." With that, he sat back and took a sip of water, appearing calm. His lawyer, sitting next to him, whispered into his ear.

Sarah was shocked to see her old colleague. It had been over four years since their paths had crossed. He looked dapper, as always, but he'd clearly aged. She had worked with Bower when he was a transplant fellow and recalled how handsome he was and how passionate he was about anything that had to do with transplantation. She'd known then it was only matter of time before he'd be leading one of the biggest programs in the country, and then was elected to be the president of UNOS.

Just then, Blondie emerged from the bathroom, fresh and dressed, and jolted her out of her thoughts. What a handsome man he was; his blue eyes sparkled as he looked at her. "I'd like to take you to my favorite hole-in-the-wall breakfast joint right near the hospital. Best coffee and waffles you'll ever taste." He put his hand on her shoulder and gently kissed her cheek. She muted the TV again but had trouble keeping her eyes off the screen.

"Sounds good, but I really do need to finish up some work here and then head straight out. Sorry about that." She stood up, pecked him on the cheek, and ushered him toward the door.

"I'd really like to see you again—sooner, rather than later," he insisted. "When's your next day off?"

"How about you give me your number and I'll call you when I get my schedule?" Her cell phone began to ring from her bedside table. She ran back and answered it when she saw on the caller ID that it was Marty, the nurse manager from the hospital.

"Hi, Sarah. I hope I didn't catch you at a bad time, but I really need you to come in today. They did two liver transplants last night, and they're having to transfer more patients out of the unit than they expected. Betty and Jill called in sick with the flu. I know it's your day off, but you'll get overtime pay."

Betty and Jill looked just fine last night at the bar, Sarah thought. This would be her fifth twelve-hour day in a row. But she needed the money, so she took a deep breath and said, "Sorry to hear Betty and Jill are sick. Sure, I can come in. What time?"

"As soon as you can get here. How about in an hour?"

"I'll need to get a quick bite; then I'll be in, Marty."

"Thanks. I really appreciate it. Bye."

Sarah ended the call and looked at Blondie, who had followed her into the bedroom and was smiling. "Shit, I have to go in early." *That's what I get for lying,* she thought.

Blondie handed her a piece of paper with his name and number written on it and said, "I'll be waiting for your call, Beautiful." With that, he reached in for a final hug and left.

She glanced at the paper: Ned Brook. Nice to know. Sarah looked at the TV again, but the screen was now showing weather reports, so she turned it off. She opened her laptop on the kitchen counter and sent Dr. Bower a quick e-mail praising his excellent testimony. She opened the tiny cabinet next to her refrigerator and pulled out a jar of crunchy Jiffy, grabbed a tablespoon from the utensil drawer, and ate one big scoop of peanut butter, then another. She tossed the spoon in the sink, leaving the peanut butter jar on the counter, grabbed her purse and keys, and headed downstairs.

• • •

As soon as she got in the car, an ugly brown rental, her phone rang again. It was Jackie, her best friend since nurses' training.

"Hey, Jackie, perfect timing."

"Hey, Sarah. Thanks for texting me that picture of the tall blond and those two women in scrubs. Looked like a real serious work meeting. I assume you were drinking rum."

"I think I drank enough for both of us. I don't think there's any left in Miami. Those two whores called in today, so I have to go in on my day off." Sarah leaned over, opened the glove compartment, and took a Reese's Peanut Butter Cup out of a bag.

"That sucks. What were you doing with the blond? He had his hand on your boob—speaking of whores."

As Sarah was unwrapping her candy, she responded, "He was a souvenir and a mighty fine one, if I say so myself." She took a bite of the peanut butter cup; she liked to eat the chocolate off the sides first and then squish the top and bottom and lick the peanut butter as it oozed out the sides.

"Wow, you don't waste any time—you've been there three months, and you're already getting laid. You go, girl. Was he any good?"

"Right up there, Jack. I'm going to put you on speaker-phone. I need to start driving to work. How are that sweet son and rocket-scientist wife of yours?" Sarah finished the peanut butter cup, threw the wrapper on the passenger-side floor, started the car, and drove toward the medical center.

Whenever she and Jackie had gone out to bars in nursing school, Jackie had had a way with bumping into all the cute guys—literally. Only five feet tall, with a wide frame, she commanded a lot of attention. Sarah had then apologized for her friend, and that had always turned out to be a good conversation starter, so they had never had any problems meeting men willing to buy them both drinks, even though Jackie played for the other team. Jackie's motto was "a free drink is a free drink."

Now, Jackie was a wife and a mother, and was saying, "Wyatt misses his aunt Sarah and wants you to take him to a Giants game. You spoiled him, not me."

"Well, someone has to be Ms. Disciplinarian. Tell him I'll be home soon and we'll have an overnight so his moms can have a date."

"Yeah, at this point I'm lucky to see Laura once a week. She gets home long after Wyatt and I are in bed and leaves before we get up. She should just get an apartment in the city."

"Now, don't get dramatic. You knew when they offered her the assistant medical examiner position that it was a park-your-life-at-the-door job. Remember, you guys made a deal. Besides, this will give you the perfect opening to ask her if you can meet me here in Miami and we can go to Cuba."

"Yeah, I know I made the deal, but this suburban-mom thing ain't all it's cracked up to be. I miss her."

"Get a sitter and go in to the city to surprise her and take her out for dinner. Find that romance again. You can do it."

"Good idea. I'll work on it. Listen, I've been researching

our Cuba trip and I found really cheap airfare. It turns out my aunt Millie is going to be in Cuba around the same time we're planning to go. The Cuban national ballet asked her to come coach their troupe and teach the costume staff how to make tutus. Like, for real." Jackie paused.

Sarah started to laugh. "And to think, all these years we thought it was crazy that she was a ballerina, and now, in her old age, she's still working full-time. She's our ticket to Cuba. You sure pulled that one out of your ass."

Jackie chimed in, "Yeah, well, she's going to tell the US government that we're her assistants. She said we'll need to do some paperwork and be sure our passports are current. She even offered to let us stay in the apartment she's expensing. We'll only have to pay for our airfare, and the rest of your bonus money can go toward pure entertainment."

"I hear the music is off the charts and the food is amazing, and I love Cuban cigars," Sarah said. "You know me—when I'm off work, I unplug. It'll be all about the food, the fun, and the sex. And boy, am I ready to unplug. You promised to find me a wild Cuban, too, and I'm holding you to it." The only person Sarah trusted implicitly to share this adventure was Jackie.

"I'll find you more than one," Jackie assured her. "How's the assignment, anyway? Are you going to make it to the end so we can spend your bonus?"

"You better believe it. I'm working my ass off, but I can handle it."

"I am so ready to party. I'm about to eat one of these fucking soccer moms. I'll take your advice and take Laura to dinner in the city. She has to know I'm getting crispy around the edges. I'll introduce the Cuba idea slowly."

Sarah turned down University Street, which would take her right to the medical center.

"If anyone can get her to say yes, you can. You haven't

had a vacation with me since we went to Mexico and we both almost got arrested. That was two years ago, and we've both been on our best behavior since then. Hey, do you think there are any comedy clubs in Cuba?"

Jackie started laughing. "I'll do some research; I know you like your comedians. Brush up on your Spanish so you'll know what you're laughing at. I really need a Sarah fix, and a side of rum would help, too."

Sarah pulled the car over under a huge palm tree across the street from the hospital so she could finish her conversation without distractions. "I'm so excited. I can't wait. We have one more month until I'm out of here."

Jackie said, "You be careful down there. I know you're a big girl, but no one has your back like I do."

"I know, Jackie. And I appreciate it."

"Call me tomorrow so we can talk about exact dates and details. What should we call this one—our Ricky Ricardo getaway? That's R and R, right?" Jackie asked.

"Love it. I'll call you tomorrow. Give Wyatt a hug and kiss from me, and tell Laura hello. Love you."

"Love you, too."

Once Sarah hung up, she quickly checked her e-mail and found a response from Dr. Bower to the message she'd sent him that morning. He was inviting her to go interview for a senior transplant coordinator position at the San Francisco Transplant Institute. She responded with a maybe and asked him to send her the job description. Then she pulled her car back onto the street, turned left into the hospital parking lot, and found a space.

. . .

Sarah made her way to the transplant floor, changed into her blue scrubs, and wrapped her stethoscope around her neck. As was customary, the nurse going off duty would give a verbal report to the nurse coming on duty. Then the nurse who was coming on would check the shift's electronic medical record to confirm medications and treatments. Sarah would be taking care of a deceased-donor liver transplant recipient who had just been transferred from the surgical intensive care unit to the transplant floor; a living liver donor; and the recipient of a liver transplant, over a week ago, from a directed donor—some gang member, the nurse thought. Sarah took the necessary notes and checked the computer records to confirm all the medications and review the comments the nurse had written at the end of her shift.

As the day nurse was leaving, she motioned for Sarah to follow her back to the report room. "That woman who got the directed liver from a gang member, Amanda Stein, I think she's some bigwig from one of those huge tech companies in Silicon Valley."

Sarah asked, "Do you know what company?"

"I don't, but I'm sure her boy toy would tell you if you could get him off his cell phone. He's a real looker—tall, dark, and *handsome*. He looks like a younger, taller version of Antonio Banderas. His name's Sergio Torres. I had to tell him three times to turn off his cell phone or go down to the family lounge to take his calls. You know that shit doesn't cut it around here. Anyway, you've got your hands full. I told him next time I'm calling security. By the way, Amanda likes her pain meds. Good luck."

"Thanks for the heads-up. I'll take care of him," Sarah said. With that, she went into Amanda's room. Sure enough, there was the Antonio Banderas look-alike on his cell phone. With one glance, Sarah knew she would take him home if she met him in a bar. He was much more her usual type than Blondie from that morning.

She walked up to him and snatched the phone out of his

hand. "This is a hospital, and we have patients who need their rest. You can deal with security regarding your cell phone."

She turned on her heel, marched right to the nursing station, and called security. Sergio was right behind her. "Excuse me—I need my cell phone back right now. Who do you think you are? That's my private property!" The only thing between him and Sarah was the tall nursing station counter, and he was reaching over it, toward the cell phone in Sarah's hand.

Sarah backed away, creating more distance between them, just as two hospital security guards approached him from behind.

"Sir, you're going to have to come with us now. We can make it easy or hard," declared the taller guard.

Sarah leaned over the counter and handed the security guard the phone. "He needs to be escorted off this floor now and educated about where and when he is allowed to use his cell phone, or he is not welcome back to this unit."

The guards bookended him and moved him toward the elevator doors at the end of the hallway. Sarah stood for five seconds she didn't really have to spare, watching Sergio protest against his escorts, as he spouted bilingual curses and threats to sue the hospital, get the guards fired, and call the CEO of the medical center. The hefty guards didn't even look at him.

Sarah shook her head and went into the medication room to confirm that the pharmacy had delivered her patients' medications for the day. "Why do all the really handsome ones have to be such assholes?" she mumbled to herself. She was about to dismiss Sergio as just another good-looking jerk, but it was more than that—he cared more about his cell phone than he did about his sick girlfriend. All the other patients' families hovered over their loved ones, who had just been given a second chance at life. Because of an organ shortage, most of the patients were at death's door before they received a liver, and many died while waiting. Sergio was more than the usual brand of handsome, pampered prince who strolled through this floor now and then. There was something really off about him.

"Oh well," Sarah said aloud to the unoccupied meds room. "Too much rum will get you talking to yourself."

Chapter 2

When Sarah went back to Amanda's room, she could still hear a loud discussion going on between the security guards and Boy Toy down the hall as she closed the door. The combination of not having gotten much sleep the night before, her hangover, and her five consecutive twelve-hour shifts had left her exhausted, and her patience and compassion were on empty. She knew she had to muster up enough energy to get through this shift, but things hadn't started out well.

Amanda was awake. "I need something right now for pain!" she cried out. "Where is Sergio?"

Sarah watched Amanda thrashing back in forth in bed and could hear that Amanda's breathing was shallow and rapid. She approached the head of the bed and gently put her fingers on Amanda's wrist to check her pulse, which was steady and fast.

"Hi, Ms. Stein," she said. "I'm Sarah Golden, and I'll be your nurse. I can get you something for pain as soon as I take your vital signs and check your dressing. I read your chart, and you're due for pain medication in about thirty minutes."

"Thirty minutes! I can't wait that long," Amanda shrieked.

"Ms. Stein, please try to calm down. I need to be sure that everything is okay, and then I'll go and get your medication from the narcotics cabinet." Sarah quickly took Amanda's blood pressure and temperature and counted her respirations. Her blood pressure and pulse were slightly elevated, but everything else was fine. Her abdominal dressings were clean, and her intravenous lines were flowing well.

"Now!" Amanda screamed. "I need it *now!*"

"All right, I hear you, Ms. Stein. I'll go get your medication right now." Working on a transplant floor had made Sarah well aware that the first seven to ten days after a liver transplant was a painful time for most patients.

"Hurry." Amanda was starting to cry.

"I'll be right back." Sarah left the room, got the keys to the narcotics cabinet, and asked another nurse to cosign for Amanda's morphine, a highly regulated drug. She drew up the appropriate dose and promptly returned to Amanda's bedside. "I'm here with your medication. Per hospital procedure, I'll need to ask you for two patient identifiers before I administer it to you." Big mistakes had been made in the past when the wrong patient had gotten the wrong drug, so now, asking for two patient identifiers was a mandatory step for medical professionals everywhere in the United States.

"What is your full name?"

"For Christ's sake, can't you read? Amanda Stein." Amanda was holding her abdomen with both hands.

Sarah checked the records. "Thank you. And your date of birth?"

"My birthday is none of your fucking business. Just give me the drugs!" Amanda tried to push herself up in bed but collapsed back onto the bed in pain.

"I am required to ask you these questions, Ms. Stein. If

you're uncomfortable telling me your date of birth, then how about what city you were born in?"

"San Francisco, California."

Sarah confirmed the information and administered the medication directly into Amanda's IV.

Amanda let out a sigh of relief as the morphine entered her bloodstream. Sarah could see her body visibly relax and her breathing slow down. She positioned Amanda's pillows to ensure that she was comfortable. She reminded herself that a liver transplant was major surgery; they had to take out the entire diseased liver first, then transplant a healthy one. The patient was in the operating room for almost six hours from start to finish.

"I'll make sure we stay ahead of that pain, Ms. Stein, so you don't get to that place again. Can I get you anything else before I leave?"

Amanda gently shook her head back and forth. "No, I think I need to rest for a little while. Where did you say Sergio went?" She was starting to doze off, which happened when the morphine first kicked in.

Sarah didn't think it was a good time to tell her that security had escorted him away. "He went downstairs."

"Okay." Amanda was slurring.

"I'll be back in a little while to help you sit on the side of the bed, and then we'll go for a walk. Dr. Santos would like you to walk up and down the hall at least three times before bed tonight." Amanda acknowledged Sarah's comments with a nod. Sarah left the room and headed to the nursing station to chart on Amanda's status.

As Sarah walked toward the nursing station, she glanced into the rooms of her other patients; they all seemed to be resting comfortably. She would go check on them after she charted on Amanda. She remembered why she liked working on a surgical floor: once the patients had their pain under control and could get around, they were discharged and she usually never saw them again. When Sarah had worked on a medical floor right out of nursing school, the same patients had come back repeatedly. They usually had a condition like hypertension or diabetes and didn't take care of themselves, so they had come in with the same issues over and over again.

Sarah went to the nursing station, completed the charting, and scrolled down to review Amanda's history and physical while things were quiet. The intern's notes on Amanda revealed that she was thirty-six. Only child. Both parents healthy, no preexisting diseases; died in a private-plane crash in France when Amanda was twenty. BA in history from Vassar; MBA from Columbia. Contracted hepatitis C when she was working in China for Cisco two years earlier. Single; no children. Kept hepatitis C in check for some time with the help of a hepatologist in San Francisco and new drugs. Had a history of using cocaine and alcohol but stopped when diagnosed with hepatitis C. Her disease had stopped responding to the drugs about six months before, so she had been listed for a liver in Miami.

Interesting, Sarah thought. *She must know someone who knows the deal about waiting times for livers in the United States.*

Before Sarah could dig any more deeply into Amanda's chart, she heard the patient call lights buzzing and had to log off. She wanted to check who was listed as Amanda's emergency contact but would have to do that later.

Sarah's head was spinning with the facts about Amanda as she walked into Mr. Grant's room. She could tell he was physically in pain from the grimace on his face.

"Looks like you need something for pain, Mr. Grant. Can you tell me what number you are, from one to ten, on the pain scale?"

"I'm at a nine. I think I waited too long to ask. Sorry about that." He put out his arm as Sarah quickly took his blood pressure and checked the rest of his vital signs. She reviewed his chart, then went to the medication room and drew up some morphine.

Sarah returned to Mr. Grant's room and administered the drug. "There—that should make you comfortable, Mr. Grant. You're one of our heroes, you know—donating a lobe of your liver to your ten-year-old son is the most generous and brave thing you could have done. James is so lucky to have such a healthy and loving father." Sarah checked his dressings and drainage tube; everything looked clean and dry. They would probably pull the drainage tube in the morning, as it didn't seem to have anything coming out of it anymore.

Mr. Grant had visibly relaxed from the medication. "You'll do anything to save your child's life. Do you have little ones at home?"

Sarah was charting the medication in Mr. Grant's record, using a portable computer on wheels, and glanced up at him. "No, no kids. Still single and happy," she said, adding silently to herself, *Not having any kids. Never getting married.* Jackie's son, Wyatt, was plenty for her to love up and then drop back home.

"Pretty girl like you, I bet you have plenty of these handsome doctors running after you, trying to put a ring on your finger." Mr. Grant was sitting up in bed now.

Sarah ignored his comment and said, "Now, Mr. Grant, let's get you moving around a bit. I know you want to walk over to the pediatric floor to see James. Maybe tonight, if you're up for it. I did get a call from the unit he's on, and the charge nurse said he's doing great. What's your pain level now?"

"It's a two. And James *is* doing great. My wife stopped

by this afternoon on her way back from the cafeteria and was going to take him for a walk. "

Sarah went to help Mr. Grant stand up and walk to the bathroom with his IV pole. "Your surgery is actually more complex than the liver transplant James had, so it's normal for you to be in this much pain. We'll get you moving around and off the IV fluids by tonight if you hold your dinner down. I saw in your chart that you had a light lunch. Did that feel okay?"

"Yes, lunch was actually pretty tasty. Who knew hospital food could actually be good?" he said, as he shut the bathroom door.

Sarah straightened Mr. Grant's bed linens and placed a soft white blanket on the chair next to his bed so he could sit up for a while. She organized the beautiful assortment of roses and carnations on his bedside table and glanced at the card. It read: "Thanks for saving my life, Dad. Love, James." There was a red heart drawing under James's signature. Sarah sighed deeply and smiled. This was part of why she was addicted to transplant patients: their families' love and commitment were often so intense and emotional. She'd seen the flip side of the coin, too, where time ran out and little kids died waiting for a deceased-donor organ. Even though the national sharing system favored kids, sometimes the right-size donor never came in time. Many transplant programs had even taken to splitting deceased-donor livers so two small recipients could benefit from a single liver. Still, the fact remained that there were far more patients waiting than there were organs available.

Mr. Grant came out of the bathroom, wheeled his IV pole over to the chair, and sat down. "How about I watch a little TV and then we take that walk to see James?"

"Sounds like a plan. I'll be back in about an hour. I put your call light and some water for you on your bedside table.

If you need anything, just press the bell. You look much better. Got some color in your cheeks." Sarah did a quick visual assessment of the room and, once she felt comfortable leaving Mr. Grant, gave him a thumbs-up. He returned the gesture, and she walked out.

Sarah was about to return to Amanda's room, when she heard Sergio Torres's voice. "Don't worry, honey, you're almost at the finish line. No problems with anything. You'll be back to your fabulous self, full of energy, in no time at all. All my planning has paid off."

Sarah wasn't quite sure what to make of his statement and needed to get Amanda up, per doctor's orders. She walked into the room, but before she could say anything, Sergio stood up.

"I want to apologize for my bad behavior earlier. I have turned off my cell phone and will not even take it out of my pocket until I'm outside. Please accept my apology."

Sarah watched him bend down to read her name tag.

"Sarah Golden."

"Thank you, Mr. Torres. I appreciate your understanding. I need to get Ms. Stein up for her walk. Could I ask you to step outside for a few moments?"

"You can call me Sergio, and yes, I was just going on an errand for her."

Sergio looked over Sarah's shoulder at Amanda, now propped up in bed. "I'll be back soon, if I don't get lost. Anything else I can get you from Saks, other than your face cream?"

Amanda was looking much better than she had when Sarah had left her half an hour earlier. "Yes, get me the Sisley night cream and their serum. Thanks, Sergio. Hurry up— Saks closes at nine. You're such a dear."

Sergio closed the door behind him on his way out, and Sarah coached Amanda on how to support her incision and move herself to the side of the bed.

"Take your hands and press them gently over your incision, as if you're holding on to something fragile. One on top of the other," Sarah instructed.

Amanda paid careful attention and did exactly as Sarah directed.

Sarah placed her hand on Amanda's back and carefully helped her stand up.

"That really helped. I feel a little dizzy." Amanda took a deep breath.

"Take a few more deep breaths, and then let me know when you're ready to start walking. Do you have a robe, or would you like me to put a hospital gown around your back?"

"A hospital gown will do for now. I don't want to get any blood on my robe. My slippers are under the bed." Amanda took another deep breath.

Sarah bent down and retrieved the fancy pink satin slippers and placed them in front of Amanda. Amanda slipped them onto her feet. Sarah took a clean, folded hospital gown off the chair beside Amanda's bed and covered Amanda's back.

This broad must be loaded, sending Sergio to Saks for million-dollar facial products and wearing these Gucci slippers. Must be nice, Sarah thought. "You're doing great, Ms. Stein," she said aloud. "How is your pain?"

Amanda responded, "I'm at about a three. And you can call me Amanda."

Amazing how morphine makes people friendlier, Sarah thought.

"That's good. I'll be taking you on a slow, steady walk around the corridor three times if you can tolerate it. Then we'll come back into your room and have you sit up in the chair for a little while before you get ready to rest for the night. Does that sound okay?" Sarah had started to move Amanda toward the door.

"Yes, I think I can do it; I walked earlier today. I will definitely need something for sleep. It's so loud here at night, with all the beeping and the hall noise. I don't know how anyone can sleep. Thank goodness I have a private room."

Amanda's five-foot-eleven-inch frame towered over Sarah, who was only five-foot-six, as they walked slowly down the hall. Amanda's long blond hair was tied in a ponytail; she had high cheekbones and large blue eyes with bags under them—appropriate, given the major surgery she had just had. Her lips puffed out much more than normal lips should, so Sarah was pretty sure Amanda had had some work done on her face.

"Yes, I will be giving you something for sleep and possibly for pain, should you need it," she replied to Amanda's request.

"Oh, I'll need both. Just count on it."

As the two women slowly made their way around the nursing corridor, Amanda stopped and stared at a wall with handwritten notes and letters pinned on it, along with photographs of patients with their arms around some of the nursing staff and transplant doctors. Sarah had seen this type of wall created at many of the transplant programs she had worked for. She watched Amanda pause to read what looked like a letter with a big "thank you" written on it.

"What are all these thank-you letters?" Amanda asked.

Sarah moved in closer. "These are copies of notes the patients have written to their donor families. They also thank the staff and doctors for their wonderful care. You're welcome to write a letter to your donor family, and we can send it along to the procurement program that recovered your liver. They will decide if and when it's appropriate to pass it along to the donor family. It does take a while for the donor families, but they are truly comforted by knowing that the senseless death of their loved one helped others live. Some donor families actually want to meet the recipients."

Sarah watched Amanda's face, expecting her to offer to write a letter to her donor family, but Amanda remained expressionless as she started to move down the corridor again. *How odd*, thought Sarah; almost every recipient of a deceased-donor organ immediately thought of the person who died and wanted to thank the family.

The silence between the two of them was deafening as they finished the walk. Once they returned to Amanda's room, Sarah helped her sit in a high-backed chair while she straightened Amanda's bed and bedside table.

Amanda asked, "Would you get me my laptop? I haven't checked my e-mail since I was admitted, and I know there are a million people who want to know how I'm doing. It's in the leather briefcase in the closet."

"Please" might be nice, Sarah thought. This lady gave new meaning to the word "entitled." She opened up the closet and saw another Gucci product, a lush, expensive-looking maroon briefcase with the initials "AS" embossed on the top.

"Here you go." Sarah placed the case on the bedside table.

"That's perfect. Now, if you'll just plug in the charger and get me some ice water, I'll be good." Amanda dialed the combination to open the case and handed Sarah her laptop charging cord.

Sarah knelt down on the floor and plugged in the cord behind the bed. *Would you like me to kiss your ass while I'm at it?*

Amanda opened up her laptop and turned it on. "I hope there's Wi-Fi in this room."

"Yes there's free Wi-Fi throughout the hospital." Sarah handed Amanda a glass of ice water. "I'll be taking care of other patients, so press your call light if you need me." With that, Sarah left Amanda staring at her computer screen, the words "thank you" nowhere to be heard.

Sarah went by the nursing desk to let the charge nurse know she would be leaving the floor with Mr. Grant and then went to his room. He was already standing up, with his hospital robe around his shoulders.

He greeted Sarah with a smile. "I'm ready to go see my boy. Would you like to be my escort?" He bent his arm without the IV toward her. *What a change in energy*, Sarah thought; she needed to clear the toxic feelings she had from being with Amanda. She escorted Mr. Grant slowly to the pediatric unit several floors below, and her heart burst as his son saw his dad walk into his room. James's big brown eyes were the size of half dollars as he left his chair and went to gently hug his dad. After a few minutes, father and son walked to the playroom with Mom.

"I'll be back in about thirty minutes to take you back to your room, Mr. Grant. Take it easy, now." Sarah took the elevator down to the coffee shop on the first floor and sat down to have a quick cup. The strong aroma wafted up her nose, and she slowly sipped it after she added cream and sugar. It was just the boost she needed.

Mr. Grant was waiting in James' room when Sarah got back. He looked tired. "I'll see you tomorrow, James." Mr. Grant embraced his son and winked at his wife as he and Sarah left the room. Sarah put her arm around his back and held on to the IV pole to help Mr. Grant navigate the hall and get into the elevator.

Sarah pressed the ninth-floor button. "Your son looks amazing, Mr. Grant. Did you have a nice visit with him?"

"Yes—he's already back to his old self. He asked if he could play soccer again and wants to join the swim team this summer. I can't tell you how happy we are that he's doing so well. You have an amazing transplant team."

"I will be sure to share that with the team. You may want to tell them yourself when they make rounds tomorrow morning. In the meantime, let's get you back in bed and ready for a good night's sleep. How's your pain level?" Sarah could see by the way he was walking, leaned over a bit, that he was in more pain than he had been when they'd left.

"It's about a six, so I think I may need something once I'm back in bed. Don't want to be chasing that pain again." Mr. Grant sat down in his chair and rested as Sarah got a warm washcloth for him to wipe his face with.

"Here's a washcloth. I set up your toothbrush, too. Then get in bed, and I'll be back with your nighttime medications and a pain shot."

After finishing Mr. Grant's care and getting him settled, Sarah charted his progress in his record, washed her hands, and headed back to Amanda's room. As she got close, she saw Sergio walk in before her with a large Saks Fifth Avenue bag. A strong odor of alcohol trailed behind Sergio.

As she walked into the room, Sarah saw Amanda give Sergio the evil eye as she asked him, "Where the hell have you been?" Then Amanda looked at Sarah and said, "You were gone too long, too. I need pain medication and a sleeping pill."

"I was taking care of another patient, Amanda. I'll get your nighttime mediations and something for pain. What number are you at?" Sarah retorted.

"I'm at a ten at least. I'd appreciate it if you could get my medications immediately."

Sarah finished adjusting Amanda's various lines and walked toward the door. "I'll give you two some privacy," she said. Sarah closed the door and was about to walk to the nursing station, when she heard Amanda yelling at Sergio. "You reek of alcohol. What took you so long? Were you out with some Cuban whore while I was here, suffering?"

"I have worked hard to be sure you got everything you needed, so don't start bitching at me for having a few drinks and relaxing. You shouldn't be saying anything about a Cuban whore, when you have no idea where your liver came from."

Amanda yelled, "I told you I didn't want to know anything! No details! Your job was to get me a liver; now get the fuck out of my room!"

With that, Sergio came barreling through Amanda's door and almost knocked Sarah over.

Chapter 3

After working five twelve-hour shifts in a row and dealing with Amanda and Sergio, Sarah decided to fly to the Bay Area for three days to see Jackie. She had been working as a traveler for over three years but had kept an apartment in San Francisco as a home base.

Sarah called Jackie the next morning to let her know she was coming.

"Hey, Sarah, what are you doing up so early? Don't you have another twelve tonight?"

"I need a home fix, so I decided last night I'm coming back for a few days. I'm so excited to see you. We can plan our Cuba trip. Can you pick me up at the airport?" Sarah was feeling relieved already.

"I would love to pick you up. When are you getting in?"

"I get in to San Francisco Thursday night at seven. Let's go to that great Burmese restaurant, and you can spend the night at my apartment. Can you get a sitter?"

"I can do better than that. Wyatt has a Boy Scouts camping trip this weekend, and Laura is going to a state medical examiners' conference in San Diego, so we're free, sister! Let me grab a pen so I can write down your flight info." Jackie sounded beyond excited.

"I'll just text it to you. I plan on meeting with Dr. Bower Friday afternoon about a possible position. I think this is going to be my last traveling job. I need to stay home, watch Wyatt grow up, and be with my BFF."

"Man, have *you* been doing some serious thinking, girl. What prompted this new change? Did you say *the* Dr. Bower? The Dr. Bower you declared would be the only transplant surgeon you would ever consider sleeping with? *That* Dr. Bower?" Jackie was speaking quickly.

"Yes, *that* Dr. Bower, and I never did close the deal, so just relax. He's still happily married to Mrs. Movie Star, and their two kids are perfect. Blah, blah, blah. Don't get your panties in a bunch. I saw him on CNN and e-mailed him to congratulate him, and he responded and asked if I was interested in a senior coordinator position. I thought, why not throw my hat in the ring and apply?" Sarah paused as she walked into the kitchen to pour herself a cup of coffee.

"Well, we certainly have some talking to do and some Cuba trip planning to figure out. We still have to go there before you sign on the dotted line for any new job. I'll see you at the airport. I have to go to a stupid Boy Scout troop meeting to finalize the camping trip. Some of these moms make me want to throw up—so worried about little Billy not having a night light. They're out in the fucking woods. I'll see you Thursday," Jackie said.

"Can't wait, Jack. Tell Laura and Wyatt thanks for loaning you to me for the weekend." Sarah hung up, then cleaned up her studio and sat at the kitchen table, working on her laptop. She updated her resume and sent it off to Dr. Bower to review and send on to human resources. She reviewed the job description he sent her and believed she was definitely qualified for the senior transplant coordinator position.

When Sarah got to work, the charge nurse assigned her the same patients she'd had the night before. Wednesday nights were usually a little quieter, as the big operating day was Thursday. There were a few fresh deceased-donor kidney transplant patients and one new liver recipient transferred out of the unit. The twelve-hour evening shift, 7:00 P.M. to 7:00 A.M., gave her a little downtime after all the patients were settled.

Amanda Stein had begun to improve and was scheduled to be discharged in the next couple of days. When Sarah walked in to check on her, Amanda was on her cell phone, apologizing to someone about not being able to attend a big fund-raising event in San Francisco that weekend. Sergio was nowhere to be found, and that was just fine with Sarah. Mr. Grant was scheduled to be discharged the next day and was thrilled to get his whole family home to heal together and begin their new life.

When Sarah's shift ended, she reported off to the day nurse and let her know that she was going home but would be back for her Monday-afternoon shift.

• • •

Jackie was waiting by the curb at the San Francisco airport and gave Sarah a big bear hug as soon as she walked through the sliding doors.

"Are you ready for some great food? I thought we'd go to Burma Superstar and chow down." Jackie got behind the wheel of her bright-red SUV and steered out of the airport.

"I am so ready for their rainbow salad and clay-pot chicken. I slept all the way here. No one was in the seats next to me. I can't wait to have some fun. God, it's so good to see you," Sarah said.

"So good to see you, too. What's it been? Two, three months?" Jackie asked, as she merged onto Interstate 280.

"It's been three months. I have only one left, and then we're cashing my bonus check. Did you bring all the brochures on Cuba?"

"They're in that blue canvas bag behind my seat. Wait until you see some of these spots; I think the place is frozen in the 1960s. I spoke with my aunt Millie, and she's so excited we're going with her. She feels safer knowing we'll be staying with her."

Jackie merged onto Nineteenth Avenue, heading toward San Francisco's Richmond district, where the restaurant was.

"We couldn't have organized this better," Sarah said. "She is so amazingly talented. I can't wait to plan our R&R adventure."

• • •

After spending two hours sipping cold beer and cleaning every morsel off every plate, they drove to Sarah's one-bedroom apartment, a couple miles from Burma Superstar. They pored over all the Cuban materials that Jackie had collected from one of the soccer moms she liked, who was a travel agent. Jackie made a list of all the places they wanted to see and eat at so she could work out the details.

"Tomorrow I'm going to go meet Laura for brunch. She's heading to the airport, and I want to send her off with a smile. Why don't we meet back here around three? That will give you enough time for your interview with Dr. Bower. Watch yourself, sister. You know the rule: don't sleep where you work," Jackie warned, as she started to make up the pull-out coach in Sarah's living room.

Sarah smirked. "Let me write down that rule; I've never heard it before. I told you, Jackie, that chapter is closed. I love my life. No more falling in love, no more romantic attachments. No man breaking my heart and telling me what I can and can't do. No kids to worry about. Going to Cuba with my best friend. Don't worry." Sarah walked into her bedroom and flopped down face-first on her bed.

Ahhhh. There's nothing like your own bed, she thought. *Fresh sheets, a down comforter, and my own pillows. Thank goodness I had Stella come clean the place this week. Everything smells of lavender.* Sarah lay there as Jackie washed up in the bathroom.

When Jackie came out, she grabbed the extra comforter out of the bedroom closet and finished making her bed in the living room. Then she called out to Sarah, "Let's get some coffee in the morning and go for a walk before I leave to meet Laura. I promised her I would walk a little each day to see if any of this weight falls off. I'm not going on a diet. I may always be this size, and so what?"

Jackie was already under the covers when Sarah went into the living room to respond. "Sounds good to me. Jack, you've been the same size since I met you, five years ago. You're healthy, so who cares? Is Laura giving you a hard time again?"

Jackie sat up. "She thinks I should be more active with Wyatt. He plays outside all day after school, doing soccer or basketball. He's so skinny and tall, you're not going to recognize him. I did find this yoga video where you can sit in a chair and get a great stretch. I ordered it and will start doing that."

"If anyone can find a chair-yoga video, it's you. Wake me up when you get up, and we'll go for a stroll. See you in the morning." Sarah turned off all the lights on her way to her bedroom, snuggled down, and fell asleep within minutes.

• • •

After their morning walk and coffee, Sarah and Jackie parted ways. Sarah decided to continue on foot to the medical center, but she still arrived early at Dr. Bower's office.

His secretary led Sarah into his office and said the doctor was just getting out of surgery and would be down shortly.

Sarah sat opposite the large maple desk and scanned the bookcases, loaded with awards, transplant journals, and books. Dr. Bower's desk was a mess, with piles of papers stacked all over it. *A typical surgeon's desk*, she thought. Surgeons spent most of their time in the operating room, where they belonged.

Dr. Bower startled her out of her thoughts. "Well, how nice to see you, Sarah. It's been a long time. You look wonderful." He gave her a big hug and then sat in his chair behind the desk. Sarah still felt a pang of attraction for him in her gut but planned to ignore it, as she always did.

"It's great to see you, too, Dr. Bower. I can see by that smile on your face that you're doing what you love. Did you just finish a liver transplant?"

"I did indeed. A living related liver transplant. Started early this morning. So, tell me, what have you been doing? Are you still living in San Francisco?" He grabbed the cup of coffee his secretary had put on his desk and started to slurp it.

"I'm working as a traveling transplant nurse at the Miami Transplant Institute. I have one month left on a four-month contract, and then I've decided to settle down in San Francisco. I've been traveling as a transplant nurse for almost three years; I've seen the inside of most of the major transplant programs. How about you, Mr. CNN? Sounds like you're knee-deep in the national organ-sharing media frenzy." Sarah sat back in her chair and watched Bower's eyes scan her from the feet up, stopping at her crossed legs a little too long.

"The media has blown the whole thing so far out of proportion that it's gotten ridiculous. We have to prove that we have the most equitable organ-sharing system possible, but it will always be a work in progress. You know our community, always fighting about the perfect allocation system. It keeps me busy, as you can imagine. What about you, Sarah? Are you really ready to settle down? What did you think about that job description?" He got up and walked toward the door and motioned for his secretary to get him another cup of coffee. "Would you like anything to drink?"

"No, thanks, I'm good. I did review the job description. I was hoping you could tell me what your expectations are and show me a copy of the organization chart. Was there someone in the job already?" Sarah took out a piece of paper and a pen from her purse.

"I'm looking for someone who can lead this group of coordinators. I think we should be doing twice the number of living-donor kidney and liver transplants. I need standardized protocols that each nurse will follow. They all give lip service to the doctors, and I need someone like you, who knows the business and is respected by nurses." Bower took a gulp of his coffee.

"You hire very bright, independent nurses, train them well, and then wonder why they give you a hard time? Basically, you want someone to boss them around because all you doctors are intimidated by them. Is that about right?" Sarah looked straight into Dr. Bower's big brown eyes.

He batted his eyelashes right back at her and smirked, showing his dimples. "I guess you could say it that way. We just received a huge NIH grant and have several protocols that need patients. The coordinators have to sign up their patients. There are a few older ones who really need to either retire or leave. The young ones are really technologically savvy and are running circles around the old ones. None of the transplant coordinators like administration, so you would be riding a bronco. They threw off the last manager we hired."

Sarah loathed management and rolled her eyes. "I hate administration. Why would I want to be one of them? I think I'm a better coordinator than I am a boss. Do you have any coordinator positions open?"

Dr. Bower stood up. "I need to go back to the OR to start a new case. How about you think about the senior coordinator position? I've seen you work well with coordinators in the past; you're a natural. I also happen to have a couple extra tickets to the big Liver Foundation gala tomorrow night at the Mark Hopkins, and I'd like you and your boyfriend to join our table. They're honoring one of our hepatologists, Dr. Bosco. We'd be honored if you'd join us."

"Having trouble filling a table again? Sure, I'd love to come, but I'll be bringing my best friend, Jackie, if that works," Sarah said, as she stood and started walking out with Dr. Bower.

"That would be fine. It's a black-tie event. Cocktails start at six." He glanced at his secretary and said, "Jessica, would you give Sarah two tickets to the gala Saturday night? I'm off to the OR." Dr. Bower reached over, gave Sarah another long hug, and then headed out the door. "Seriously, think about that job, Sarah—I could really use you around here. You can teach us what you learned in your travels at other centers."

Sarah said, "I'll think about it, but don't get your hopes up. It may be easier to work at San Quentin. Let's talk on Saturday."

Jessica smiled at Sarah and handed her an envelope. "Good luck turning him down; he usually gets what he wants."

"We'll see about that, Jessica. Thanks for the tickets." Sarah walked out and took the elevator down to the street level.

· · ·

"You're in town less than a day, and you've got me going to a black-tie event. Remind me again: Why are you my best friend? I hate, *hate* dressing up." Jackie was standing outside the Mark Hopkins, handing a valet the keys to her prized SUV.

"You look amazing, Jackie. That black suit with a pink silk blouse—who knew pink was your color? Just pipe down. Let's go get a martini at the bar. These tickets are a hundred and fifty dollars apiece. At least we'll get a good buzz and a meal out of this." Sarah led the way through the doors, held open by smartly dressed doormen, who seemed quite aware of how well her tight-fitting, short black dress accented her figure.

Jackie walked next to her in her flat black dress shoes. "Honey, that dress has 'come and get me' written all over it. And those fuck-me heels are insane. Do you want Bower to nail you in the lobby or what? We are *not* getting into trouble tonight. We have to save our trouble points for Cuba—you got it?"

Sarah turned and smiled at Jackie. "You know his glamarama wife will be all dolled up, so don't worry about Bower. You just never know who we'll meet at these soirees. Let's find the bar and get this party started. You do look great, by the way. I have to take a picture and send it to Laura."

Jackie shook her head. "No, no, no. Laura sees me dressed up like this, she'll make me go to all those rub-ber-chicken dinners with her, and I absolutely refuse to. They're boring, and the food always sucks. No picture. You owe me big-time on this one."

Sarah led the way to the elevator, following the flow of all the evening gowns and tuxedos. She nudged her way up to the bar and returned with two large gin martinis. Jackie had located seats near a window; the San Francisco skyline glimmered.

Sarah handed Jackie her drink and sat down across from her. "Here you go. Hendrick's gin, just the way you like it: a little dirty, with a twist of lemon. Cheers! Thanks for coming to this penguin party with me."

They clinked their glasses delicately, careful not to spill a drop. After they finished, they got refills and found their way to the main ballroom, which was dripping with crystal chandeliers and satin curtains. They located their table and walked over. Dr. Bower and his wife were already seated. Dr. Bower stood up, looking very handsome in his James Bond tuxedo, and said, "Sarah, I am so glad you decided to join us. This is my wife, Kristin Gerard."

"Nice to meet you, Kristin. You certainly look stunning tonight." Sarah scanned her quickly from head to toe. Her wavy, shoulder-length blond hair framed her flawless complexion, and her green eyes sparkled almost as much as the pear-shaped diamond drop earrings she was wearing. Her turquoise silk gown clung to her tall, trim body.

"This is my best friend, Jackie Larsen. We've known each other since nursing school." Sarah stepped back so Jackie could shake hands with Dr. Bower and his arm candy.

Looking away from Dr. Bower, Jackie nudged Sarah and mumbled, "Are you sure you can restrain yourself from Dr. Fancy Pants?" Sarah elbowed Jackie in her side and smiled as they both sat down.

Their table quickly filled up with faculty members and their wives. The executive director of transplant, Bart Lincoln, and his wife sat right next to Sarah. Throughout dinner, he shared that Dr. Bower really wanted Sarah to join their team and that if there was anything he could do to persuade her to accept the offer, he was at the ready. Sarah asked him to go get her and Jackie two more martinis, and he jumped on it.

Jackie was giving Sarah a "let's get out of here before the lectures and awards start" look, but the lights went down and the emcee for the evening welcomed everybody. Bart came back to the table with the drinks just in time for Sarah and Jackie to keep their buzz going.

Some glamour girl and a guy in a tuxedo welcomed everyone and thanked them for their generous donations to the Liver Foundation. They showed slides highlighting all the amazing research that the donations would fund, and the many children and adults whom the foundation's services would help.

Sarah was enjoying her martini and glancing at the slides while quietly speaking to Jackie. She did a double take and almost spit out her drink when she saw a huge picture of Amanda Stein projected on the ballroom screen.

Jackie gave her an intense look and leaned over. "What is wrong with you? Are you okay?"

Before Sarah could respond, Dr. Bower's wife told the people at their table, "That's my best friend, Amanda. She just received a liver transplant in Miami. She almost died from hepatitis C, but my husband and his team of wizards got her viral load down, and then she flew off to Miami and received a liver transplant. She has done so much for the Liver Foundation over the past five years. She was the mastermind of this entire gala. I'm so excited she'll be back to her old self. She's coming home soon."

Everyone nodded and smiled, but Sarah merely stared at Kristin in shock, until others at the table began to notice. Jackie kicked Sarah under the table and said, "Drink up. We're going. I don't know what's wrong, but we need to leave *now*."

Sarah took the last swig of her martini, then glanced over at Dr. Bower and said quietly, "Thank you for inviting us, but we need to leave. Jackie has to get home."

Bart Lincoln followed them out to the hallway and tapped Sarah on the shoulder. "It was a pleasure to meet you, Sarah. Here's my card. I hope to hear from you soon and look forward to having you join our team."

Chapter 4

Jackie followed Sarah into the elevator; she hadn't seen Sarah this upset in a long time. "Talk about a buzzkill—I thought you were gonna fall off your chair. What happened in there? You looked freaked out."

"I *am* freaked out. Something's wrong. I don't know what, exactly, but we need to talk. Let's find a table in the back of the bar." Sarah exited the elevator on the first floor and made tracks to the far side of the space.

The cocktail waitress came over immediately. Jackie looked at Sarah and asked, "Is this a one-drink story, or do we need to order several cocktails?"

"At least one to start." Sarah bent over, removed her high heels, and started rubbing her foot as the waitress left.

"Did you see the photo of that blonde they showed on the screen?" Sarah leaned toward Jackie.

"The one that Bower's wife started jabbering about? Yeah."

"I just took care of her in Miami. She was my patient, and she had a seriously handsome but self-absorbed boy toy with her. She was an odd one. Every other transplant recipient who gets an organ from a deceased donor asks about the donor immediately. They feel so grateful, and usually remorseful because someone had to die in order for them to get their organ."

The waitress brought over chilled martini glasses with two silver shakers. She carefully strained the gin into each of their glasses and then recapped each large shaker. "Vince over at the bar said he'd be happy to refill those whenever you're ready." They looked toward the bar, and the bartender gave them a brief wave.

Sarah and Jackie waved back. Sarah took a sip of her drink, then put her glass down. "When recipients are ready, they write a letter to the donor family, thanking them for their heroic gift and letting them know that it changed their life. When the time is right, the procurement agency sends the letter to the donor family. They actually check to see if the family wants to receive the letter—"

Jackie interrupted, "I know all this. You've told me this story a million times. That's why you stay in this specialty. Remember, you made me go to that donor-family celebration with you, and my eyes were bloodshot for days. Those stories broke my heart. The generosity people find at the worst time of their life is more than inspiring. I'll never forget it."

Sarah looked at Jackie. "I remember. When I took Amanda for a walk around the transplant floor, she saw all the thank-you notes patients had written to the transplant team and asked about them. I told her about writing a letter to the donor family, and she wanted no part of it. She didn't seem to even care that someone had died. Very detached and callous."

Jackie refilled Sarah's glass. "Maybe she's just a self-centered bitch and once she gets what she wants, she doesn't care about anyone else. There are a lot of those out there, especially among entitled rich people."

Sarah took another sip and said, "Her boyfriend said

some things about the donor. I heard them fighting. He was drunk, and she laid into him about being with some Cuban girlfriend, and he responded by saying something about her liver donor. There's no way he could have known about her donor." Sarah looked seriously concerned to Jackie.

"They got the liver in Miami, right?" Jackie asked.

"Honestly, I never checked, because at the time, I was swamped. I guess I could have called the local procurement agency. Those two were acting weird, and now I'm starting to wonder why."

As Jackie studied Sarah, she was becoming more curious as well. "Why would Amanda go to Miami if she's best friends with Bower's wife? He's a bigwig in transplant, based on everything you've said. Couldn't he just move her up the list, like they did for Steve Jobs?"

Sarah finished her martini and stood up. "Let's settle the bill and get the car. I'll explain how people get organs when we get home. I don't want to run into any of those stuffed shirts. You okay to drive, Jack?"

"Yes. I've been filling your glass with all the leftovers, so, sadly, I'm sober. Let's pick up a bottle of Pusser's rum on the way home, and then we can hash out the rest of this mess. Sound good?" Jackie walked over to the bar and gave Vince her credit card. He looked past her to see if Sarah was still there. Jackie saw Sarah wink at him, and he winked back.

Back at the apartment and in their pajamas, Sarah opened the rum and they sat at Sarah's kitchen table.

"I am so glad to get out of my monkey suit and relax. Don't ever make me wear that disgusting outfit again. You're pushing your luck, Golden." Jackie squeezed some lime into her glass and took a sip. "Now we're talking. So, educate me on this organ-sharing system."

Sarah started, "There's a national algorithm for how

various organs are shared. Basically, every liver is given to the sickest patient. So if a liver in San Francisco is recovered but there's a sicker patient in Los Angeles, then the liver goes to the patient in LA. There are parts of the country where there are more livers available than there are patients listed in that area. We call those procurement-rich basins. When every patient is evaluated for a transplant, they sign a form that they can multiple-list at other programs. Most patients don't have the resources to move somewhere else and wait. Even though Steve Jobs lived in the Bay Area, he went to Tennessee, because there were more livers available there than patients waiting. Here in the Bay Area, there are three large, competing transplant programs." Sarah took a sip of her rum.

"You're telling me no matter how rich you are, you can't buy a liver? I'm not buying that," Jackie responded.

"It's true. There were times when there may have been some gaming, but I believe those programs got slapped with serious fines, if not closed down. Every organ is tracked from the time it's recovered until it's either transplanted or discarded." Sarah clarified.

"Discarded, as in thrown in the garbage? That sounds like a waste." Jackie was staring at Sarah.

"Sometimes the liver or other organs have a problem you wouldn't know about until you take them out or even start to transplant them. Then you have to discard them. But don't worry—we don't throw them in the garbage. If an organ is transplanted into someone it was not matched to, the surgeon has to write a letter to the United Network for Organ Sharing, a national organization composed of transplant professionals from all over the country: surgeons, physicians, nurses, tissue typers, and administrators."

Jackie burst out laughing. "No! Not tissue typers, whatever the hell they are. Sarah, this is starting to get too complicated for me, and I don't want to have to concentrate any more than I have to while I'm starting to reboot my buzz." Jackie could tell Sarah was dead serious, but she had to lighten things up.

"Fair enough. My point is that gaming the system, moving someone up on the list, just doesn't happen. The transplant program can get shut down if anything like that happens," Sarah said.

"So, what rich people like Steve Jobs and Amanda can afford to do is find a place that has a surplus of livers and move there. Doesn't sound fair, but life's not fair for poorer people who have to get their liver where they live because they can't afford to travel. Here, have some more rum. Enough of this transplant stuff." Jackie refilled their tumblers. Sarah was still visibly upset.

"How about we do a little homework on the web tomorrow and see what we can learn about Amanda Stein and the Miami Transplant Institute? For now, let's have some fun, talk Cuba, and watch a good movie." Jackie saw a slight grin on Sarah's face. She trusted that if Sarah was worried, there was something to worry about. Sarah had saved Jackie's ass more than once in nurses' training. Jackie trusted her completely.

"I'll go check my DVD collection in my bedroom and find something funny for us to watch. Be right back," Sarah said, and disappeared into her bedroom.

While Jackie sipped her rum and waited for her friend to return, she remembered that back in nursing school, Sarah had saved her—twice—from being expelled. One time, she and Sarah had brutal hangovers, and all Jackie wanted to do was sleep through class. A teacher, BUHA—short for Bug Up Her Ass, as Sarah and Jackie fondly referred to her—kept calling on Jackie to answer questions about the pathophysiology of hypertension. Jackie stood up and declared in front of the whole class that BUHA was the classic example of a person with hypertension: someone with an intense need to control people and their environment, unable to relax (which resulted in constipation), and a virgin at the ripe old age of forty-five. The class lost it, and BUHA escorted Jackie straight to the dean of nursing. Thankfully, Jackie was only put on probation, but she was warned that one more infringement would be grounds for dismissal.

Several weeks later, the housemother and the dean inspected Sarah and Jackie's dorm room after a tip-off from a "faculty member" that the girls had stolen operating-room gowns in their closet.

BUHA escorted Jackie into the dean's front office, where Sarah was already sitting. Behind closed doors, the dean, an older woman with a tightly wrapped bun, glared at Jackie and began the inquisition. "Ms. Larsen, do you have any property in your dorm room that belongs to the hospital? Anything at all?"

Jackie had stolen a lot of items; how was she supposed to know which one the dean was referring to?

Before Jackie could respond, Sarah barged into the dean's office.

"I can't let Jackie take the blame for what I did," Sarah declared. "I took those operating-room gowns and robes. If you need to expel someone, expel me." Then she walked out of the dean's office and closed the door.

Jackie knew they would never expel Sarah, who was top in the class and never got in trouble. "I don't feel comfortable answering that question. I do believe that I have been wrongly accused and that this instructor here," Jackie pointed to BUHA, has it out for me. I plan on lodging a formal complaint to the president of the hospital for being harassed by faculty."

At the end of the day, the dean, not wanting the president of the hospital to know anything about this issue, agreed not to put Sarah on probation but demanded that she pay for the "mutilated" operating-room robes and gowns.

•   •   •

Sarah came back with three DVDs for Jackie to choose from: *The Ref*, *Best in Show*, and *The Heat*. Jackie picked *The Heat*, a comedy starring Melissa McCarthy and Sandra Bullock.

Sarah popped in the movie, and they both sat back on the opened-up sofa bed. Sarah lit up a joint to relax a little, but Jackie preferred the buzz of the alcohol. They sipped their drinks, laughed at the movie, and munched on their favorite salty-crunchy combo snack: Ruffles potato chips with onion dip. Sarah always made sure she had some when Jackie was coming over.

During the movie, they also talked about Cuba—how much fun it was going to be and what hot spots they were going to hit.

"Only one more month, and we'll be there," Sarah said.

•   •   •

The next morning, Jackie woke up first and made a pot of coffee. Sarah's bedroom door was still closed, so Jackie googled Amanda Stein on Sarah's laptop. She sipped her coffee as her eyes raced over all the hits Amanda's name got. She was currently on the board of directors for Google and Hewlett-Packard. In 2010, she was one of the top one hundred most successful businesswomen in the United States, according to *Forbes*. She had never married but was all over various society pages dating back to the late 1990s, when she had worked as a fashion model while she was in school at Vassar. Jackie found some *Town & Country* photographs of her and Bower's wife, Kristin, from some fancy party. Briefly, she wondered if they were gay or bisexual; of course, she wondered that about most women. Clearly, Amanda was running with the rich and famous, so it made sense to Jackie that Amanda could get anything she wanted, regardless of price or ethics.

One picture was of Amanda with a stunning Latino man who was even cuter than Antonio Banderas. Jackie read the caption: "Amanda Stein and Sergio Torres, enjoying opening night of the New York Opera with close friends Dr. Harris Bower, well known transplant surgeon, and his wife, model-actress Kristin Gerard, from San Francisco. The four flew to New York on Stein's corporate jet."

"Must be nice," Jackie muttered to herself.

Sarah opened her bedroom door. "Coffee smells good, Jack. You already talking to yourself?" She poured herself a cup, then walked over and glanced over Jackie's shoulder.

"That's Amanda and her boy toy with our very own Dr. Bower. When was this taken?"

"Her boy toy—Sergio—is a showstopper. If I weren't gay, I would consider having sex with him, or maybe just making out. This photo is from 2010."

When Jackie stood up to pour herself more coffee, Sarah sat down to look at the picture more closely. "I never took Bower for an opera guy; I bet his wife made him go. Quite a handsome foursome. What else have you found, Detective Larsen?"

"No question your friend Amanda is a big-time gal— rich, famous, and connected. I did check the Miami Transplant Institute website, and they do advertise that they can get anyone a new liver in four to six months. I e-mailed the coordinator listed on their website and requested that information be mailed to my house. I think this is simply a case of rich people getting what they want when they want it."

Sarah sat across the kitchen table and looked at Jackie. "You may be right, but there's just something weird going on here, and it's bugging me."

"If it's bugging you, then it's bugging me, too. Let's go for a walk. Do you want to grab a bite before I take you to the airport?" Jackie walked to the front door and began tying her walking shoes.

"That would be great. Let's go to that dim sum place Yang Sing. I haven't eaten there for ages, and there's nothing like it in Miami. Don't you want to do some chair yoga before we go for our walk? Then you can tell Laura you're doing yoga and walking, banking those Cuba points big-time." Sarah put on her jacket.

"You just go ahead and laugh at my chair yoga. I already went on the Chopra Center website and ordered the video; it'll be at my house when I get home." Jackie grabbed her coat and followed Sarah out the door.

It was a typical, cold and crisp morning in San Francisco. As they exited Jackie's building, Sarah picked up the *San Francisco Chronicle* from the stoop. Jackie looked over her shoulder as she turned to look at the Datebook section, which covered social and entertainment action. There on the first page was a big picture of Amanda Stein with the caption "Liver Foundation hosts biggest fund-raiser ever, over $2 million. Amanda Stein runs the event from Miami after getting a liver transplant herself. Ms. Stein will be flying home this week to recuperate with family and friends."

Sarah handed the paper over to Jackie, who quickly read the headline and asked, "Do you think if there was something really off here, Amanda would allow this type of information in the newspaper?"

Sarah shrugged. "Maybe I'm just being overly sensitive. Let's focus our attention on Cuba."

Chapter 5

Sergio helped Amanda down the steps of the Learjet that had just landed at the San Francisco airport. Her private duty nurse and physician walked ahead to open the door to the black Cadillac Escalade awaiting her on the tarmac.

"I need something for pain," Amanda demanded, as she cautiously got into the backseat.

The doctor ran around the other side and, once Amanda was settled, gave her a shot of morphine. Amanda let out a deep sigh of relief. The nurse put a soft pillow under her feet and one over Amanda's abdomen.

Sergio watched to make sure that everything possible was being done to comfort her, then said, "Thanks, team. We'll meet you in an hour at Amanda's penthouse. I want to get her settled in and confirm that we have everything we need. There's a car waiting for you outside at arrivals." Sergio looked past the medical team and saw a few photographers approaching the SUV. He closed both doors and walked toward them.

"May I help you?" he asked sternly.

Two photographers walked briskly up to Sergio. "We'd like a quick photograph of Ms. Stein. We're from the *San Francisco Chronicle* and *San Jose Mercury News*."

"I don't think she's really up for photos right now." Sergio got in the backseat and closed the door.

In a morphine daze, Amanda looked over at him and asked, "What's all the racket out there?"

"It's the press. They want a quick picture of you. I told them no." Sergio tapped the driver to move.

"I can let them take a quick picture through the window. Hand me my lipstick and hat." Amanda looked at her compact, then put on red lipstick and powdered her nose. "I feel much better than I look right now." She put on her wide-brimmed hat and large sunglasses and rolled down her window.

The driver stopped the car, and the photographers moved toward the open window. "Ms. Stein, how are you feeling?" one asked. "Welcome home."

Amanda gave them a smile and nodded. "Tired, but wonderful." With that, she rolled her window back up and the driver moved toward the exit.

"I wonder who tipped them off that I was flying in today," she slurred, laying her head back against her seat.

Sergio glanced over at her. "It must have been Molly at the Liver Foundation when they called about the fund-raiser. I saw something in the *Chronicle* this morning but didn't get a chance to read the whole thing, because we were rushing to get you home."

Amanda didn't answer; she had already fallen asleep. Now that the morphine had worked its magic, Sergio opened his briefcase and began to read the entire article in silence. The driver made his way out of the airport and inched along in the usual traffic headed toward San Francisco on Route 101.

Sergio kept reading his paper and glanced at his cell phone: four missed calls from a Miami area code. *They must be from Maria*, he thought. He texted her that he'd call in a couple hours, and she promptly responded, "Need to talk to you NOW."

Sergio called Maria and spoke very softly so as not to wake Amanda. "Hi there. Can't really talk right now. What's the emergency? Are you okay?"

"I miss you already, and I'm not feeling well. I had to call in sick today. Can you come back earlier? Pretty please?" Maria's soft voice, with its Spanish accent, really pulled at his heart. It sounded so much like his mother's and was such a nice contrast with Amanda's shrill and demanding tone. Plus, whenever he talked to Maria, he couldn't help but think fondly of his first time making love to her. When she had confessed that he was only her second lover, Sergio had made a point of being extra gentle and caring with her. His approach had been almost the complete opposite of what he did with Amanda, who was extremely seasoned in the bedroom.

Now, he said, "I'll see if I can come down this weekend. I may be able to hop the corporate jet. I'll call you back tonight."

"I love you, Sergio. Talk to you tonight."

"Me, too," Sergio whispered and ended the call as the driver pulled up in front of Millennium Tower on Mission Street. The doorman gathered the luggage while Sergio gently nudged Amanda.

"You're home safe and sound, my love. Let's get you upstairs." Sergio tapped her shoulder and then exited the car and came around and opened Amanda's door.

"Home. I am so ready to be in my own bed with my own things around me. Where is Victoria? I told her to be ready for me." Amanda took the pillow away from her stomach and moved sideways to get out of the SUV.

"Victoria is upstairs. She has everything ready for you, just as you asked. She has to be the most dedicated maid, coming in on her only day off. You know Sundays are her family days." Sergio took Amanda's arm and walked her through the gold-latticed doors the doormen were holding open.

"She was off while I was in Miami. She should be well rested." Amanda retorted.

The elevator stopped on the thirtieth floor. Amanda's was the only penthouse and its glass windows surrounded the entire circumference, giving onto a breathtaking view of San Francisco and the bay.

The double doors were open, and Victoria was waiting there in her black dress and white lace apron. "Welcome home, Ms. Stein. We missed you. I have your bed all ready."

Amanda and Sergio walked past her and directly toward the bedroom. "Thanks so much, Victoria," Sergio said. "Ms. Stein is in pain, and I want to get her to bed."

Amanda walked directly to her king-size bed. As Sergio helped her slide between the luscious sheets, he paused briefly to recall many a wild evening on and off this mattress.

"I want to sit up for a while, until I get myself settled," Amanda said.

Victoria was right behind them, making sure that Amanda was supported with pillows. Amanda put a pillow over her stomach, just as the nurse had taught her to do in Miami.

The doorbell rang, and Victoria left to go answer it. When she came back, the nurse and doctor who had been at the airport were following her.

"How are you feeling?" the nurse asked, as she took Amanda's blood pressure and vital signs.

"My pain is about a four. I am so tired. Too much activity today." Amanda lifted up her sheets so the nurse could check her abdominal dressing.

"Everything looks great, Doctor. Her vital signs are normal, and the dressings are clean and dry." The nurse handed the doctor the piece of paper she had written everything on.

"Well, then I think we just need to let Ms. Stein rest. Everything looks to be in order." He took another glance at the dressing. "I'm going to leave two more doses of the morphine for the nurse to administer, and then I want you to start taking oral pain relievers, Amanda. You'll heal faster that way, and soon you won't need any pain medications." The doctor stepped back and looked at Amanda, then at Sergio.

"I need more morphine than that. At least for a few more days. I just had a liver transplant, for God's sake!" Amanda said. "I don't pay you all this money for nothing."

"How about we talk tomorrow and see how you're feeling?" The doctor started walking out of the bedroom.

"As long as I have your home number and your beeper, that seems reasonable," Amanda snapped.

As the nurse followed the doctor out, Sergio sat on the end of Amanda's bed and said, "You should rest now. Long day of traveling and moving around. I'll leave you in Victoria's capable hands, and don't forget, we have the nurse right outside your bedroom door. She's going to check on you throughout the rest of the afternoon and tonight." He leaned over to kiss Amanda on the forehead, and she straightened up.

"Who were you talking to in the car on the way over here? I heard you whispering."

As if sensing an argument coming, Victoria excused herself, saying, "I'll go get some tea and soup ready for you, Ms. Stein."

"I thought you were asleep. I hope I didn't wake you." Sergio had been hoping to dodge this conversation for a couple of days until Amanda was feeling better, but he could tell by her tone that she was gunning for a fight.

"I wasn't asleep. Just resting my eyes. Where do you think you're going this weekend?"

Sergio tried to keep it simple: "I need to go back to see my friend. I'll be back in a couple of days."

"Your friend! You mean your *Cuban whore* friend. I can't believe you. We just got home! No. You're not going anywhere, you insensitive bastard," Amanda yelled.

"Amanda, I know I don't need to remind you that we agreed on an open relationship when we first started dating, it was you who insisted on it. Don't get yourself so upset, you'll just set yourself up for more pain. I am going and I will be back. That's all you need to know right now. I need to take care of some unsettled business," Sergio said.

"You tell me what's going on right now, Sergio. What do you mean, 'unsettled business'? I need you here with me. People will be stopping by to visit. They'll want to know where you are. You need to just wait on whatever 'unsettled business' you have for a couple of weeks at least," Amanda demanded.

"It can't wait a couple of weeks. Maria is pregnant, and I'm taking her for an abortion, if you must know. All those trips I took to Miami, you didn't expect me to go without sex, did you? While you were sick and unavailable, I needed some attention, too. I probably got a little closer to her than I should have, but it'll all be over by next week. I thought she was using protection, but apparently not, and now I have to be responsible. I'm not asking your permission, Amanda; I'm telling you," Sergio said, adopting his best macho-Latino stance.

"You got her *pregnant*? Okay, get the fuck out of my house and don't bother coming back. Go be with your precious Cuban slut. I can't believe you're so stupid and insensitive." Amanda was sitting up straight now and pointing toward the bedroom door.

Sergio stormed out and slammed the front door behind him.

Chapter 6

As Jackie waited outside Sarah's apartment, her cell phone rang. She looked at the caller ID and answered when she saw that it was her aunt Millie calling. They spoke for a few minutes, and as she was saying good-bye, she looked up and saw Sarah walking toward her SUV.

Sarah opened the back door, threw her carry-on in the backseat, and hopped in the front.

•   •   •

Jackie put the car in gear and drove toward Nineteenth Avenue, in the direction of the airport. "Looks like our Ricky Ricardo getaway may have a slight delay. Aunt Millie just called, and they postponed her trip. They want her the first two weeks of October. I'm going to have to check Wyatt's schedule and do some fast dancing with Laura if this going to happen. What do you think?" Jackie glanced over at Sarah, who looked disappointed.

"This sure has turned out to be an interesting morning. I just got off the phone with Dr. Bower, of all people. He called to see if we were all right. He noticed we bolted before the dancing and auction. He also said if I'm interested in the job, he wants me to start as soon as I'm done in Miami—end of August."

Jackie glanced over and saw Sarah watching her face for a reaction. "Why don't we stop at Bill's Place and get a greasy burger and fries on the way to the airport? We can look at our calendars there. Are you really sure you can work that closely with him? Daily temptation. When is your last official day of work in Miami?" Jackie turned off Nineteenth and onto Twenty-Fifth Avenue.

"My last day of work was going to be August twenty-ty-third, because I told them I had a two-week vacation in Cuba planned in September. I wanted to give myself a week at home to get organized. I can work as many days in a row as I need to in order to get to the finish line faster. As long as I put in the time, I get the bonus."

Jackie parked in front of Bill's, and they headed inside. After they ordered burgers and diet sodas, Jackie leaned in toward Sarah. "We have some decisions to make here. Do we still want to go to Cuba? Do you really want to take the job at the San Francisco Transplant Institute? And if you do take it, when would you want to start?"

Sarah furrowed her brow and paused before she answered. "First of all, I think I'm going to take the job. They want me and are willing to put together a good compensation package. The benefits are great, and Dr. Bower said there was a signing bonus, which will add to our travel fund." Sarah took a sip of her drink.

"You're sure you can work with Bower without wanting to go to bed with him?" Jackie studied Sarah's face.

"Bower is not my cup of tea—maybe when he was younger, but when I do decide on my next sleepover, it'll be with someone younger and, hopefully, another comedian.

So, yes, I can work with him, as much as I'll see him, anyway. You know those surgeons are always in the operating room. It's the coordinators I'm worried about. Some of them are really intense control freaks."

The waitress placed a patty melt and fries in front of Jackie and a double cheeseburger and onion rings in front of Sarah and asked, "You girls need anything else?"

"Nope, this looks delicious. Thanks." Jackie reached for the ketchup.

"I really want to go to Cuba, Jack. I say we figure out a date, so when I talk to Bart Lincoln, Bower's administrative handler, I can tell him I already have vacation plans."

When they had finished eating, Jackie said, "Let's look at our calendars and see what we can come up with." Once they had established the tentative dates for their trip, she continued, "I'll pencil these in and let you know as soon as I confirm everything with Laura. Her mom has been asking for months to come spend some time with Wyatt, so as long as I'm not home when she's there, this may work out perfectly. The backup plan would be for Wyatt to stay with his best friend." Jackie threw her calendar in her backpack, and they walked back outside to the car.

When they were nearly at the airport departures terminal, Sarah said, "I'm going to call Dr. Bower once I get through security and let him know I'm in, and he can work out the details. Sounds like we got us a plan, Jack."

"I'm excited you're coming home earlier than we thought. That'll give us some time to plan our adventure and have a few playdates ourselves." Jackie pulled her SUV over to the curb, and Sarah reached over and gave her best friend a hug and a kiss on the cheek. "Thanks for the lift. Call me as soon as you have the thumbs-up, and let Aunt Millie know she's got escorts to Cuba. Love you." Sarah hopped out of the car.

Jackie rolled down the passenger-side window and hollered, "Text me when you get to Miami, and then get your ass back here. I miss your ugly face already. I'm burning those stupid clothes from last night when I get home, too."

Jackie could hear Sarah laughing as she pulled away from the curb. She was looking forward to going home and baking some of her world-famous brownies for Laura and Wyatt. Maybe she'd do a little more research on Amanda Stein before Wyatt came home from school.

Chapter 7

Once Sarah was at the gate, she called Dr. Bower's cell, and he picked up. "Bower here."

"Hi, Dr. Bower, it's Sarah Golden. How are you?"

"Great, Sarah—just about to walk into a meeting. I hope you're calling with good news. I could really use your help around here. The inmates are running the asylum."

"On a scale of one to ten, just how bad are those inmates?" Sarah knew he was referring to the transplant coordinators.

"I'd give most of them a twelve; there are a few around five."

"If the job includes some type of combat pay, then I think I'd like to join your team. I did look up your transplant outcomes online—they look amazing."

"I'll tell you what: I'll have Bart Lincoln—the guy you sat next to at the gala on Saturday—give you a call. Let him know what you need, and if he gives you any flak, page me. Gotta run." Dr. Bower hung up.

The airline gate attendant announced that her flight would be delayed by an hour, so Sarah went to the nearest bar to watch the Giants game. Her cell phone rang just as she sat down. She didn't recognize the number, but she answered anyway. "Hello, this is Sarah."

"Hi, Sarah. This is Bart Lincoln from the San Francisco Transplant Institute. I just got off the phone with Dr. Bower. Sounds like we may be lucky enough to have you join our team. He sure thinks the world of you."

"Hi, Bart. I would love to be part of your team if we can come to some type of agreement." Sarah was holding her cards close to her chest; she knew once she was in the door, they would do what they always did: cry poor-mouth when it came to giving her more money. While she didn't really like her mother, she had taught Sarah the art of financial negotiation and Sarah had always done well for herself on that front.

"I think we'll be able to work something out. Why don't you send me your resume and your current salary, and we can go from there?"

Ah, Bart's a card player, too, she thought. "I'll send you my resume, but I'm not really comfortable sharing my salary. Why don't you give me a call or e-mail me after you review my resume? Listen, I have to go—my plane is boarding. I look forward to hearing from you, Bart. And thanks for calling." Sarah's plane wasn't actually leaving yet, but she wanted to watch the game.

"Sounds great, Sarah. I'll be in touch. Travel safely."

Sarah ordered an Anchor Steam beer on tap and cheered along with some of the other patrons as Buster Posey, the Giants star catcher, hit a grand slam and won the game. Sarah had learned to love everything about baseball from her father. He had been a die-hard Cubs fan and had taken Sarah to every game he attended when he wasn't working long hours as a CPA. He had died of a heart attack when Sarah was only twelve, leaving a void that still hurt her when she thought of him.

She grabbed a copy of the *Chronicle*, reviewed the baseball stats, and then turned to the Datebook section. It included a picture of Bower and Kristin dancing—*perfect-looking couple*, Sarah thought—along with a photograph of Amanda and a feature article on the Liver Foundation fund-raiser. The coverage of Amanda was vague. It mentioned that she was head of international business development of Cisco and that she had left for health reasons, then had gotten a serious golden parachute that included fifty thousand shares of stock and a paid seat on the company's board of directors once her health had improved. There was only one sentence on Amanda's successful liver transplant in Miami.

This whole thing still didn't sit well with Sarah, but she was too excited about her future to dwell on it. Maybe Jackie was right—maybe Amanda really was just another entitled, rich bitch who could get whomever and whatever she wanted. Maybe.

Chapter 8

Sarah looked around at the full room of all the various team members sitting at the liver-selection meeting. No patient got on the San Francisco Transplant Institute's liver waiting list unless every team member agreed to it. Sometimes the social worker would trump a transplant surgeon's vote or the financial counselor had to stop things because the patient didn't have the money or insurance to pay for the drugs after transplant. The hepatologists had to present every patient, and then, after an in-depth discussion, either the patient would be listed or rejected—which usually meant death from liver failure—or additional tests would be required before the team made their final decision.

The surgical team at the institute consisted of eight transplant surgeons, who performed all the abdominal transplants: liver, kidney, and pancreas. The institute had the largest waiting list on the West Coast for all three organs, so the surgeons were always busy transplanting, lecturing, or doing research. Many held prominent positions within national and international transplant societies, in addition to doing their clinical work.

As Sarah was studying the faces around the room, a

woman's voice startled her: "Well, well, look who's joined our team. Think you might stick around for a while, Sarah Golden?" The chair of the department of surgery, one of the most talented and brightest transplant surgeons Sarah had ever observed in the operating room, had her gaze locked on Sarah. Dr. Jane Goldberg was her all-time-favorite transplant surgeon; she always told it like it was, she wasn't afraid of anyone or anything, and no one wanted to cross her, ever. Once you got on her bad list, she was done with you.

Sarah grinned. "Dr. Goldberg, how nice to see you. You look as elegant as ever, and even thinner than you were the last time I saw you. Was that three years ago?"

"I can see you've gained a few, Sarah, but now that you're working at a real transplant program, you won't have time to eat. How many livers did they do in Miami—fifty, sixty?" She sat in her high-backed leather chair with a smug look on her face.

"They do fifty at most, and their outcomes don't hold a candle to your programs," Sarah was all too familiar with Dr. Goldbergs direct and playful manner.

Dr. Bower interrupted the banter: "All right. First patient please."

One of the hepatologists, Dr. Gaines, directed everyone's attention to the large computer screen at the front of the darkened boardroom. Eight to twelve patients were usually presented each week, each story sadder than the next. The horrible things that people did to themselves or that had happened to them always gave Sarah pause and made her appreciate her own good health. In addition, many of the cases inspired heated ethical debates. For example, should an alcoholic get a liver transplant? Was alcoholism a disease like any other, and, as such, shouldn't alcoholic patients be given a chance if they stayed clean and sober?

Dr. Gaines put the next patient up on the screen. "This is Hector Rodriguez, a thirty-five-year-old farmworker from Salinas who was diagnosed with hepatitis C four years ago. He used heroin in his twenties and has been clean for six years. He underwent medical treatment, which was successful for a while, but now he needs to be considered for a transplant."

Dr. Gaines then reviewed all of Hector's labs, including his current MELD score, a combination of several clinical lab values that determined how sick a patient was. The higher the MELD, the sicker the patient. A MELD between thirty-five and forty meant the patient was in the intensive care unit, knocking on death's door.

"How long does a patient with hepatitis C wait for a liver?" Sarah asked.

"Depends," Dr. Gaines said. "Usually eight months to two years, unless they get so sick that they trump all the other patients in our region with the highest MELD. When they're that sick, sometimes the outcomes aren't as good."

Sarah thought about Amanda Stein. *She had hep C and got a liver in just three months after she was listed in Miami.* Then Beth, the social worker, piped up: "Since Mr. Rodriguez is here illegally and has no family support, I don't recommend him to be listed."

In the discussion that followed, Mr. Rodriguez was declined. He would be transferred to Salinas hospital, where he would receive comfort care while he died of liver failure. Sarah always felt badly for these types of patients. There was just no way everyone was eligible for a liver, and no guarantee that anyone would get one in time.

Dr. Bower was talking quietly on his cell phone as Dr. Gaines presented the next patient. Based on the questions Dr. Bower asked, Sarah could tell he was getting an organ offer.

"This is Jessica Ramirez, a forty-year-old female, married, with five children," Dr. Gaines said. "She has hepatocellular carcinoma. The tumor will need to be ablated, and we'll need to follow up with her every three months in order to increase her MELD score. She is stable, with a current MELD of twenty."

Beth chimed in, "Mrs. Ramirez has a very supportive family. Her oldest son is twenty and living at home, helping with the other children, while Dad works as a landscaper. She's here illegally, but because she has three children under the age of eighteen, she's eligible for Medicaid and Medicare. I would recommend her for listing."

"Oh, here we go. Another anchor-baby story—just have kids, and we'll foot the bill," one of the surgeons at the table commented.

Bob, the liver transplant coordinator, spoke up. "You want me to list her with follow-up CT scans every three months. I'll submit a petition to UNOS for an increased MELD score. When do you want to see her in clinic?"

"Let's see her in two weeks. Where does she live?" Dr. Gaines asked.

"She lives in Fresno."

"Let's follow her there until she gets sicker, and then we'll bring her up to the city," Gaines said.

"What about a living donor? Did you ask her about her twenty-year-old son?" Goldberg looked at Gaines.

"I didn't, but, Bob, will you follow up with her and get his work-up started if he's interested?" Gaines directed

"We have to be more aggressive about asking these patients if they have a living donor; otherwise, they're likely to die waiting," Dr. Goldberg said.

Dr. Bower was off his phone and looked across the board table at the other hepatologists sitting there. "Do you routinely ask all the patients you evaluate if they have a potential living donor? You manage their liver failure until we transplant them."

Sarah saw some of the younger hepatologists moving around in their chairs. The latest addition to the group, Dr. Reilly, looked at Dr. Bower and said, "We don't really have a lot of time to discuss this with them after we've spent forty-five minutes on their history, physical, and evaluation. I'm not sure it's the right time. They barely understand they have terminal liver failure and what a liver transplant is. Maybe we should have the independent living-donor advocate come in and speak with them at their follow-up appointments."

Shirley Mildsen, the independent living-donor advocate, leaned forward. "I'd be happy to do that. I just need to be notified when they come in, and I'd need to coordinate with the living-kidney-donor clinics."

Just then, the in-house pediatric transplant team walked into the standing-room-only boardroom. Dr. Jacobs, the pediatric hepatologist attending, walked to the front of the room and said, "Sadly, we have two children to present today. They were transferred in from Oregon. The parents took the whole family to pick mushrooms and proceeded to cook and eat them. The parents are in Oregon, being worked up, and the kids were transferred here. All are in fulminate liver failure. The team has one liver offer for the mom." He reviewed the children's records; there was a five-year-old girl and her seven-year-old brother. Both kids were in the pediatric intensive care unit, with a PELD of forty. "As soon as we get your approval to list, we should get offers," he said.

Bob looked at Sarah and responded to the question she hadn't asked, "PELD is the pediatric version of the adult MELD," in a condescending tone.

"Thanks, Bob," she responded curtly.

The pediatric social worker, who was standing in the back

of the room, offered the family's social history: "This is a Korean family who live outside Portland and own a restaurant. There are three older kids, twenty-two, twenty, and fifteen. The aunt is down here with the kids, and the older kids are back in Portland, running the restaurant and checking in on their parents. They have excellent insurance coverage, so that's no problem."

Goldberg looked over at Dr. Jacobs. "Has anyone asked about the older kids being living liver donors up in Oregon?"

"Not that I know, but I can call the attending up there and check. I don't think we'll have time to work them up; these kids are really sick. Both of their livers have shut down. They need to be transplanted within twenty-four hours, or they won't make it."

"Let's list them immediately, Bob. Since all pediatric patients get top priority in the country, we'll likely get calls right away," Dr. Jacobs said.

Dr. Bower added, "We may be able to do a split liver. Are the kids the same blood type?"

"Yes. They're blood type A," Jacobs said.

"I'm not familiar with split livers," Sarah said. "They didn't do them at the programs I worked at in the last couple years."

Dr. Goldberg responded, "Not everyone can do them. We've been working on the technique for some time, and we've done about twenty over the last two years. The number of deceased donors has been flat, so we have to figure out other ways to get our patients transplanted."

"I'd love to observe one, if you don't mind," Sarah said.

"We'll page you when we do one. You *are* taking call, aren't you?" Goldberg glanced over her glasses at Sarah.

Sarah nodded yes. Goldberg expected them all to carry their weight, and taking call was part of being in the world of transplant. Sleep was a luxury most transplant staff simply didn't get.

The pediatric team left to go up to the pediatric intensive care unit to draw the necessary blood, and their nurse-practitioner, Bianca, and Bob coordinated who would do what, as the pediatric patients and their families required more one-on-one care.

Selection ended after a few more patients were presented, and then all the doctors in white coats or surgical scrubs left to go to either the operating room or the transplant unit. Dr. Bower's pager was buzzing away, so he got up and went outside. Sarah's head was swirling with all the intense activity. She looked over at Bob and asked, "What can I help you with? You have about ten things you have to do all at the same time."

Bob gave her a scowl and barked, "You can hire some more transplant coordinators to help. I'm quitting if you don't get me some help."

This was the part of the job Sarah dreaded most; getting administration to pony up for any positions usually took an act of Congress.

Sarah looked at Bob and said, "I can see you've got more than one person could possibly handle, which is why I offered to help. How about we meet tomorrow about staffing?"

Bob glared at Sarah. "If I'm still alive tomorrow!" With that, he stomped off, carrying a load of charts in his arms.

Sarah just shook her head. *What a drama queen.*

Chapter 9

Sarah walked out of the meeting room and saw Dr. Bower pacing in the hallway, having what appeared to be a heated exchange on the phone. He might be fighting with his wife. She wondered if they even had much of a relationship, given that he was always at the hospital. She certainly knew of numerous transplant surgeons whose spouses had cheated on them out of neglect.

When Sarah caught the doctor's eye, he motioned for her to come over and ended his call, saying, "We can discuss this when I get home, Kristin. I have a donor."

He was about to speak, when his beeper went off. "Just a minute, Sarah," he said. "It's the local organ procurement program. Let me call them back. Walk with me."

Following his brisk steps, Sarah listened as the doctor responded to the page. "It's Bower," he said. "Yes, we just listed the two kids, and we'll take an adult liver and split it if that becomes available before a pediatric liver donor. Thanks, Denise. I'll be on call with Dr. Forrest, so don't hesitate to contact me."

When he hung up, he said, "Sarah, let's go make rounds on the peds floor and see how these kids are doing. What's going on? You looked a little upset when you walked out of selection."

"You were right. The coordinators are already at it. Bob said if I didn't hire another coordinator to help him, he was going to quit. Very sarcastic and unprofessional. I'm going to have to counsel him after he simmers down." She let out a sigh.

"We're understaffed, and we haven't added any new coordinators for over five years. Our transplant numbers have continued to increase, so we have the same amount of staff doing a lot more work. There's a breaking point, you know." They got into the elevator, and Bower pressed the button for the pediatric floor.

"I just started. I need to get the lay of the land before I start barking for more resources. You and I are supposed to meet with Bart tomorrow afternoon at four. Will you still be able to?" Sarah asked.

Bower waited until they exited the elevator, then said, "I should be able to be there. Even if we get a liver offer, which I think we will, the fellow wouldn't be back with it until after midnight. We'll be done with the transplant by morning."

Bower swiped his name badge over the square black box outside the double-locked doors to the pediatric intensive care unit on six north. The doors swung open, and Sarah followed him to the bedside of the little girl whom they had discussed in selection.

Bianca, the pediatric nurse-practitioner, was at her bedside. "Hi, Dr. Bower," she said softly. Then she looked past Bower and added, "Hi, Sarah. Welcome back. It's great to have you on the team." Sarah had worked as a staff nurse on the transplant floor before she'd started the traveling nurse job, so she knew many people there already.

Bianca returned her attention to the little girl and said,

"She's not doing so well. They're having trouble stabilizing her bleeding, and her encephalopathy has gotten worse. Bob listed them both right after selection, so you should be getting calls soon. They just gave her some Lasix to try to decrease the brain swelling."

"I already got one call from the organ procurement folks," Dr. Bower began, but before he could continue, a loud announcement over the hospital intercom system interrupted him: "Code blue, six north. Code blue, six north."

Sarah saw Bower exchange a glance with Bianca and say quietly, "It must be the brother." Sarah followed Bower as he rushed to the little boy's bedside, where Dr. Jacobs and the rest of the ICU team were trying to resuscitate the child. He was already intubated, the monitor over his bed had flat-lined, and the pediatric intensivist team was working on him, calling out drugs to push through his intravenous lines.

As Sarah stared at all the people trying to save this little boy's life, Dr. Bower's beeper went off. He called back the number and said, "This is Bower."

Sarah watched as he listened intently to the voice on the other end of the line. When he hung up, he said, "That was Carol from the procurement agency. She says they got a call about a six-year-old who drowned and was resuscitated at the scene. Declared brain-dead about two hours ago. The family decided to donate all his organs. All the labs are normal, and the blood and sputum cultures were drawn and are cooking now." Bower paused, then continued, "The donor hospital operating room can't accommodate us until maybe ten or eleven tonight, because of all the trauma cases they got this morning. Carol will let me know once we get an OR time, and I'll speak with our transplant fellow to arrange the recovery."

With that, he glanced over at the code team and then put his hand on Sarah's shoulder as the lead pediatric intensivist began shaking his head, saying, "We're calling the code at fifteen hundred." Calling the code meant that they had done everything they could and still had no response. The little boy hadn't made it. The sadness on the faces of Dr. Bower, Dr. Jacobs, and the rest of the ICU staff was acute. Losing a kid never got easier for anyone on the unit.

Dr. Jacobs walked out of the room and motioned for Dr. Bower to go with him. They were going to have to go tell the boy's aunt, who was in the waiting room. Dr. Bower looked over at Sarah and said, "Why don't you and Bianca come with us? We need to talk to the aunt, and I'll need you to sit with her afterward."

"Sure thing," Bianca said. "I'll go ahead and put them in the patient counseling room."

A few minutes later, Sarah followed Dr. Bower and Dr. Jacobs into the room and sat next to the boy's aunt. Dr. Jacobs took her hand, and she started to cry as he explained, "I'm so sorry, Mrs. Kim. We tried everything we could to save Jimmy, but his little body just couldn't take the amount of poison from the mushrooms." Bianca was on the other side, with her hand on the Mrs. Kim's back, rubbing it gently as the woman sobbed heavily into Dr. Jacobs's shoulder. Everyone sat in silence and allowed her to cry.

Finally, she raised her head and asked, "How is my niece?"

"She's extremely sick, but my friend Dr. Bower here is going to do his best to get her a liver, maybe even tonight."

Sarah looked over at Dr. Bower, who appeared deep in thought. He said, "I believe we may already have a liver available for your niece. I'm going to ask my coordinator, Sarah, here to have you sign a consent for a liver transplant and help you understand what all that means. You'll be meeting with our pediatric social worker, who will have a lot of questions for you, too. I know this is a hard time for you, and I'm sorry for your loss, but we will need to move quickly if we're going to be able to save your niece." Dr. Bower stood and moved toward the door, and Sarah walked with him to the nurses' station.

"Sarah, I need you to page the social worker and be sure she meets with Mrs. Kim. Bianca can help you with the consents and education materials. You'll need to be sure you get an interpreter so we know she really understands what this is all about. I have to follow up on this possible donor. Do you have any questions before I go?"

His beeper was going off.

"I think Bianca can help me with all this. It's just so sad when a kid dies—I don't know how you deal with it," Sarah said.

"You just have to remember that we're able to save some patients and not others. I decided early in my transplant fellowship training that I can't dwell on patient deaths. If I did, I would never be able to stay in the field I love. Page me if you need me. Let's still plan on meeting Bart in the conference room at four." With that, Dr. Bower walked out of the unit.

Chapter 10

Sergio pulled his rented Cadillac up in front of Maria's house. She was living with her parents until she got married, as was their custom. Her parents were old school Cubans and, Maria had told him, were very strict Catholics. The only way Sergio and Maria could be alone was if Maria lied to her parents and told them she was staying with her best friend, who lived on the other side of Miami.

Sergio was still working on how he would have to let Maria know he was heading back to San Francisco in a couple of days. She thought he would be staying in Miami for a while. The lies he had told Maria had started the day he'd met her, three months earlier. At first, he'd wanted only to befriend her so that he could find Amanda a liver, and had told Maria that he was Amanda's brother and a big business tycoon. It was one lie after another, and Maria was naive enough to buy every one of them, so taken was she with his charm and good looks.

Sergio walked up to the simple, three-bedroom house and rang the doorbell. Maria greeted him by throwing her arms around his neck and giving him a long kiss. "I've missed you so much," she said.

She grabbed his hand and walked him into the kitchen, where her parents were sitting, drinking coffee. *I hope Maria hasn't told them about the pregnancy*, Sergio thought.

Her dad stood up and extended his right hand. "Nice to see you, Sergio. I'm sorry we missed you when you were here a couple days ago. Maria said your sister was able to go home from the transplant hospital. I hope she's doing well."

Sergio shook Maria's father's hand and said, "Yes, she's doing great. Her new liver is working perfectly, and she's so glad to be back home and in her own bed. She sends her regards and can't thank you enough for all you did to save her life."

"Marco's death was so sudden that it's still a nightmare for us, but we feel fortunate that we could make some sense out of it this way. Please sit down. Can we get you something to drink?" Maria's dad asked.

"I'd love a glass of water." Sergio could see that Maria's mom was withdrawn; she held her coffee cup and stared at it in a daze.

Maria got a glass of water and put it down in front of Sergio, and he said, "By the way, Maria, I made us reservations at Versailles, that famous Cuban restaurant I heard about. It's gotten amazing reviews. They had an opening at eight tonight."

"I would love to go out to dinner. With my brother's funeral and all the relatives in town, I don't think I can cook anymore."

Sergio saw Maria looking at her mother for a reaction, but Maria's mom still seemed not to be taking in the conversation. After a few moments of silence, her dad interceded and said, "Maybe when you two get home tonight, Sergio and I can have a little talk, man to man."

"Dad, we'll be home pretty late. How about you guys go for breakfast tomorrow and I'll take care of Mom?" Maria said.

"Sounds good to me, Mija. You two had better get going, or you'll miss your reservation. Traffic will be bad. Mama and I will be having a light dinner and turning in early." Her dad stood up behind her mom and gently rubbed his wife's shoulders.

Maria walked toward the hall that led to her bedroom and said, "I'll change into something for dinner and be out in a minute, Sergio."

Sergio winked at her and smiled. *She's so beautiful and sweet*, he thought. Letting her down was going to be harder than it had been with any other woman, but it needed to be done. He wasn't a family man and never would be.

When Maria came out, she was wearing a striking royal-blue dress that accentuated her firm hourglass figure and high heels that made her legs look long and sleek. Her black hair draped over her shoulders in loose curls.

"Wow," Sergio said, as he stood up. Maria smiled at him, then kissed her mom on the cheek and hugged her dad. "*Adios, mi familia.* See you in the morning."

Sergio followed Maria out to the car and opened her door. He walked around and let himself into the driver's seat and headed toward the freeway.

"You look stunning tonight, my love. How are you doing?"

"I'm so glad we'll have some time alone together tonight. I want to talk to you about my pregnancy. I hope you know I didn't do this on purpose. I don't expect you to marry me, but I need you to know that I will not be getting an abortion. I just can't do it. I don't expect you to support the baby or me. I've given it a lot of thought, and I won't change my mind. I know this baby will bring disgrace and shame to me at first, but after that passes, it will bring love and joy to my family." Maria looked over at Sergio.

"I hear that you've given this a lot of thought, Maria, and I respect your feelings. It's your body. But this is not what we agreed on. I don't want to be a father or get married. I would be terrible at both those jobs. Your family can't afford to take care of a baby. They're barely making it now. You know your mom and dad are here illegally, and it would be terrible if they got deported to Cuba." Sergio hated to play that card, but he needed to nip this situation in the bud.

"Is that a threat, Sergio? I can't believe you would even say such a thing. They have been nothing but kind and generous to you and your sister," Maria exclaimed.

"You're right, honey. Let's not fight. We'll work something out—I know we will," Sergio said, as he pulled the car up in front of Versailles. Valets opened up both doors and welcomed them to the restaurant.

"My family has been through too much pain already. I need you to support my decision and be patient. I'm not trying to make you marry me—really, I'm not."

Sergio put his arm around Maria's shoulder, leaned in, and kissed her deeply before they went through the brass double doors. "I love you, Maria," he whispered in her ear. The sweet smell of her perfume filled his nose and softened his tone. He was accustomed to telling women he loved them, leaving out the part about "at this moment." Sergio had said he loved many women to get what he wanted and then had disappeared, just as he planned to do with Maria.

"I love you, too, Sergio. No matter what happens with us, I will always love you."

They had an amazing dinner; the waiters were all over Maria. Sergio could tell how much she was enjoying all the attention from them and him. They ordered the *ropa vieja*, a house beef specialty. Sergio ordered an expensive bottle of red wine, and Maria sipped club soda. Dessert was a tableside delight: Bananas Foster severed over ice cream. He loved seeing the excitement in Maria's eyes when their server lit the flame. She told him that in her twenty-three years, she had never been to a restaurant like this.

Sergio put his hand on Maria's hand and said, "Maybe we *should* get married, Maria. I know I've said I'm not the marrying kind, but you're such a wonderful person, I know we could have a happy life together." He had no idea how he was going to work his way around or out of this situation, but he had always managed in the past. He was just going to go with this for now.

He stood up, and Maria came around the table and embraced him. "This is a dream come true, Sergio. I love you so much. I know we will be wonderful together."

Once they had finished their dinner, they went back to Sergio's suite at the Four Seasons and made love. Sergio was always happy to get laid, and since Amanda had been sick for some time, his lovemaking sessions with Maria, while simple, kept him satisfied. After he indulged her with some sweet pillow talk, Maria got up and went into the luxurious shower, and Sergio followed her. Maria's small frame fit perfectly inside Sergio's tall, strong body, and he could wrap his arms all the way around her.

"I love you, Sergio," she repeated, as she put her head on his chest.

This works for me for now; I'm not going to rock the boat, he thought.

Afterward, Sergio drove Maria home and walked her to the door. After a long kiss, she went inside and Sergio drove back to his hotel. It was three hours earlier in California, so he called Amanda's cell. She picked up immediately. "Where are you, you asshole? I can't believe you left me here alone. Everyone who has visited has asked where you are. It's embarrassing. I hate you!"

It was the same argument they'd always had in their

intense, love-hate relationship. If Sergio didn't do everything Amanda wanted him to do, she threw him out or hung up on him. Then they always had a postfight yelling match, usually followed by wild makeup sex.

"I told you I was going to Miami, and that's where I am. How are you feeling?" He put Amanda on speaker as he walked around his suite.

"I'm miserable. They're taking me off the morphine and giving me some lame pain pills. The nurse is a bitch—she reminds me a little of you." Amanda sighed.

"You need to watch it with the pain pills. You don't want to get addicted to them. Remember your cocaine days?" Sergio said.

"I was never addicted, and you know that. Once they told me to stop, I stopped. So don't give me that shit. You make me crazy! I'm going to New York with Kristin this weekend. My old company called and offered me their Learjet. We're taking her daughter shopping for a dress, and I'm going to relax. I reserved a suite at the Ritz."

"Are you sure you should be traveling so soon after the surgery? You're still healing."

"I asked Bower, and he said as long as I don't exert myself, I can go. I can relax even better in New York than I can in San Francisco. Plus, I'm bringing my nurse, so don't worry. Don't hurry home this weekend, because I won't be here, and I'm mad at you anyway."

"Okay, have it your way, Amanda. I was going to come home tomorrow, but I'll see you when I see you. Have fun with Kristin." Sergio hung up and thought, *Some things will never change. Anyway, I'd rather be with Maria and play at being engaged for a while.*

• • •

The next morning, Sergio arrived at Maria's house and found her dad outside in the carport.

"Good morning, Sergio. You just missed Maria and her mom; they're off shopping. Let's go have some breakfast."

Sergio looked at him and walked back down the driveway. "Let's take my car." Jose had a serious look on his face, and Sergio hoped, once again, that she hadn't told him about the baby. Sergio was usually good at charming women, but he'd never had to deal with their fathers.

They went to a local Cuban restaurant where her dad knew everyone. The owner came by and shook hands with Jose, who then introduced him to Sergio. "So, this is the handsome young man Maria has been talking about, eh?"

"I guess I am," Sergio responded.

They ordered fried eggs, rice, and plantains. They enjoyed their meal in silence, and then Jose looked directly into Sergio's eyes and said, "Maria told her mother and me that she is pregnant and that you have proposed to her. Is that correct?" Jose took a sip of his *café con leche*.

Sergio finished chewing his food. "Yes, Maria is pregnant, and I did ask her to marry me last night. I must apologize for not coming to you first for your permission. Please accept my apology." He could feel his face turning red and hoped Jose was not the violent type.

"After everything our family has been through the last two weeks—our son murdered in a gang fight, and then the whole organ-donation thing—this is good news. Don't get me wrong, I am not happy that Maria is pregnant before she is married—it's not our way—but I'm glad you are doing the right thing by marrying her, and the news has made her mother come alive. I trust you will have the wedding very soon."

I'm going to have to do some quick thinking here, Sergio thought, then said, "I'd like to discuss the wedding plans with

Maria first, and of course I'm sure the sooner, the better. I was planning to take her out this afternoon to buy her engagement ring—if I have your permission, that is."

The truth was, Sergio had gone online and found a Kay Jewelers in downtown Miami and had called to see what type of inventory they had in his price range. His plan was to pick out a fancy ring, then go to the bank, open up a checking account in Maria's name, and put $30,000 in it. They would call it a wedding account, but Sergio had no intention of coming back to Miami after all the silly celebrations. That money would take care of Maria and her baby for however long it lasted. He would be sure she was set up, and then he was out of there. *Not a family man, not a marrying man,* he kept saying to himself. He'd had more than his share of friends and family get married blissfully, only to end up in court for bitter divorces and ugly custody battles. It always started out wonderfully; then someone cheated on someone and the games began.

"Sergio." Jose snapped him out of his reverie. "You have been very kind to our family, and I will welcome you into it. Of course, I understand you have a small family, your parents dying when you were young and all. I am very happy for my little girl to have such a fine young man as a husband. There is so much to talk about."

After Sergio and Jose embraced, Sergio's mind went into overdrive. He needed to set Maria up, then get a new cell number and disappear into the sunset—leave this family alone to welcome a new life while grieving their recent loss. The less interaction he had with any of them, the better. This was never going to be one of those happily ever after endings.

Chapter 11

Sarah's cell phone rang as she was walking into the hospital. She'd had a tough time sleeping after the little boy had died, but Bower had gotten a liver for the little girl and she was now in critical condition in the pediatric intensive care unit.

It was Jackie calling. "Hey, how the hell are you?" Sarah said when she answered. "I feel like it's been months since I saw you, but it's only been a week."

"I know, Golden—last time I saw your mug was at the airport."

Sarah stopped outside the hospital entry so she could finish talking to Jackie. She knew once she walked through that door, the transplant world would consume all of her energy and attention. "I got the bonus in my savings account, safe and sound. Got what I wanted from Bart, too."

"Did you mention that you already had vacation plans?" Jackie asked.

"Yes, I did. I didn't ask; I just told him. I even got a little signing bonus and some moving expenses. When he offered, I didn't have the heart to tell him all my stuff was already in San Francisco. That check is in the same account as the Ricky

Ricardo funds, just waiting for us. Can you meet me tonight for dinner?"

"Absolutely. I'm dropping Wyatt off after school at his best friend's house. The kid's mother will feed the boys and take them to their Scout meeting tonight. Where do you want to go?"

Sarah thought about the question for a minute, then said, "How about the Clement Street Bar and Grill?"

"I love their food. Sounds good. You want me to come grab you outside the front of the hospital?" Jackie asked.

"That would be great. Text me when you're about ten minutes out. We have a lot to talk about, my friend. I have the day from hell coming up. I have to meet with all the angry transplant coordinators, so buy some Kleenex stock, because there's going to be lots of crying." Sarah started to walk toward the entrance.

"See you tonight, Attila the Hun. Give 'em hell. Stay strong. I have a surprise for you, too. Bye, Golden."

After she hung up, Sarah double-checked her schedule. She was booked back-to-back, as was the case many days. There was a meeting with the kidney coordinators on how overworked and underappreciated they were. Then the liver coordinators were demanding to meet with her because they claimed they were severely understaffed and were going to quit. To top it off, she had a meeting with Dr. Bower and Bart at the end of the day. She'd be drinking hard alcohol that night for sure. Maybe, just maybe, she'd get to the transplant floor to see a patient or two—to honor the real reason everyone was working there, although it was hard to tell some days. She did have a young woman, a living liver donor, coming in to get all her tests done. Her brother was in the intensive care unit and was deteriorating quickly; if her work-up went well, she could donate a lobe of her liver within the next couple of weeks.

At four o'clock, Sarah plopped down in a chair across

from Bart and Dr. Bower. "Well, it's been a roller coaster ride, fellas. I hope your day has been better than mine. You want the good news or the bad news first?"

They both looked at her intently. Then Bart said, "Dr. Bower and I have a few things we must get to before you start, Sarah." Bart sat back and looked at Dr. Bower. "I just met with the COO, and he wants to know why your numbers are so low this month. You did only four livers and eight kidneys?"

"Well, Bart," Dr. Bower started, "we can transplant organs only when there are deceased donors, and there just weren't that many of those. You know we're aggressive about accepting all the viable organs we can."

Bart leaned in and asked, "What about the living-donor programs? Weren't they supposed to yield transplants each month? We just hired a new coordinator and paid sixty thousand dollars for that new software. The COO is not happy. When he's not happy, I'm not happy. Sarah, you're supposed to get these coordinators in shape."

Sarah snapped, "Well, Bart, I've now been here a whole two weeks. I'm not a miracle worker. The bad news is that the coordinators are threatening to quit unless we hire more staff. They say they just can't work any harder or longer."

"What'd you say to them?" Dr. Bower asked.

Sarah said, "I told them all that they should do what they need to do and that I would speak to you and Bart to see if there's any way to get them more help—"

Bart interrupted her: "I know you're doing a good job, Sarah. You just need to get this living-donor program up and running soon, or we're going to have to start looking at cutting positions if these numbers don't start going up."

Sarah shook her head. "I told the coordinators that I would ask both of you if we could at least hire a temporary secretary for both liver and kidney coordinators. That's what

I'm asking now. I think it would be a good move, because they're doing secretarial work and we're paying them a nurse's salary. Not smart."

"You know I get upset when the nurses do secretarial work," Dr. Bower said. "Bart. I think we should give them some help and also talk to them about ways they think we could increase the number of transplants."

"That's exactly the discussion we had this afternoon, Dr. Bower. I think they have some good ideas. First, I want to get them some much-needed help, and then I want to have them present their ideas to all of us. Sound like a plan?"

"Sounds reasonable," Bart said. "Was that the good news or the bad news, Sarah?"

"It was both. They said they'll quit without help, and if we get them some help, then they want to discuss ways they think they can work more efficiently and that should yield more living donors."

They all sat quietly in the small conference room for a few minutes, until Bart broke the silence: "How about we hire one temporary secretary for both of them to share, and go from there?"

Dr. Bower said, "Let's try two temps for six months. If they don't make a difference, then we'll get rid of both of them and start back at square one."

"I'll have to sell it to the COO, but I think that's fair. I have to run to another meeting. If you need me for something else, just shoot me an e-mail. Thanks, guys." Bart grabbed his briefcase and left.

Sarah and Dr. Bower remained where they were, sitting across from each other. Bower reached across the table, put his hand on Sarah's, and said, "How you doing? I know it's been a tough entry. First we lost a kid, and now the coordinators are unhappy."

Sarah could feel the energy in Bower's hand and pulled hers away before she spoke. "It has been harder than I would have expected this early. I guess I don't blame the coordinators for getting upset, but they have to be patient with me. Losing a kid—I don't know if I'll ever get over those things."

Just then, her cell phone pinged. She had a text from Jackie: *Ten minutes away. Get your ass outside.*

Sarah looked over at Dr. Bower. *Damn, he's handsome.* "I need to go—dinner plans." She got up and walked toward the door.

Bower stood up, too. "I'll walk to the elevator with you. You're doing a great job, Sarah. I'm here for you. I know you have tough stuff to deal with."

"I appreciate your support, Dr. Bower; it's really important. I can see that it's Bart's job to keep you happy, so I'd appreciate anything you can do to get him to give us those temps sooner, rather than later."

Jackie was out front in her SUV with a big smile on her face, waiting for Sarah.

Sarah got in and reached over to hug Jackie. "Man, am I glad to see you. I really need me a dose of Jackie right now. What was I thinking, taking this stupid job?"

"Stop right there, Golden. Stop and just give me some 'fucks,'" Jackie said.

"Fuck those fucking coordinators, fuck Bart Lincoln, fuck the COO, fuck kids dying, and fuck fuck fuck." Sarah took a deep breath and felt some immediate relief. This was something she and Jackie had been doing together since nursing school—just a quick release, no questions asked.

"Good job, Golden. That's my girl. I didn't hear 'fuck Bower.' Is that a good thing or a bad thing?" Jackie pulled out of the circular driveway and headed toward the Clement Street Bar and Grill.

"That's a different 'fuck.' Let's go have a cocktail, and I'll fill you in," Sarah suggested.

"Sounds like a plan."

When they arrived at the restaurant, Jackie ordered for both of them. "We'll take two Hendrick's dirty martinis, up, ice on the side." The bartender went about his business and quickly placed the cocktails before Sarah and Jackie.

After they took a few sips in silence, another one of their rituals, Jackie began, "Where do you want to start?" She turned her barstool toward Sarah.

"I don't waste my Jackie time on the little bullshit, so here are the CliffsNotes. The coordinators want more money and more help, are whiners, and are a pain in the ass."

"Takes one to know one," Jackie said.

"Okay, that's fair, although I never whined like they do. We lost a little boy. His parents thought it would be a good idea to pick wild mushrooms and eat them, so the whole family is in liver failure."

"That's a big ouch. I know you can't deal with those little ones dying. You bailed out of Peds as soon as you passed your exams." Jackie took a sip of her drink.

"At least Bower was able to save the sister if the liver works. And, yes, Bower—you were right: I'm attracted to him. It's not as bad as before, but it's still there. I overheard him fighting with his wife on the phone. Things aren't good at home, so you can figure it out from there." Sarah sat back on her barstool and took a long sip.

"I have a surprise for you after dinner that may help with that." Jackie was grinning from ear to ear.

"Uh-oh. You have that trouble's-a-brewin' look on your face, Larsen. What is it?"

Jackie smiled back at Sarah. "I'm not telling you until we get there, but I promise you'll love it. For now, let's go eat. Oh yeah—Laura's picking Wyatt up after Boy Scouts, so slumber party tonight."

"I have to work in the morning, so we have to behave tonight. Can't face those people at work with a hangover." Sarah took the last sip of her martini.

"That's up to you, Golden."

After they ate dinner, Jackie steered her SUV toward Fisherman's Wharf, parked in a nearby garage, and led Sarah in the direction of Cobb's Comedy Club. "I got us two tickets to the early show. I figured you could you use some comic relief," Jackie said.

"Perfect. I am so in." Sarah followed the hostess to a table, with Jackie trailing behind her.

Once they were seated, they ordered the obligatory two drinks before the show started. When the emcee came onstage and announced the first comedian, Sarah's face froze.

"Tonight we have someone special here from New York. He's out here filming a movie, and we're lucky to have him. Please give a warm welcome to Mo Platt," the emcee shouted, and the audience clapped.

"Are you fucking kidding me?" Sarah said to Jackie.

"Nope."

Mo got onstage and started his routine and glanced down to see Sarah. "We must be lucky, folks, because my old girlfriend is sitting right in the front row. Hello, Sarah Golden; wave to the audience."

Despite her embarrassment, Sarah waved graciously. "Holy shit!" she whispered to Jackie.

Before Jackie could say anything, Mo started telling jokes and the crowd loved him. Thankfully, he left Sarah out as the brunt of the jokes, and after the show was over, he came over to their table.

Sarah stood up to greet him, and he gave her a big bear hug. She noticed there was no wedding ring on his finger.

"Mo, you were hysterical. I am so glad to see you. Aren't you a big movie star? Movies, comedy clubs, wow." She smiled as she took in his sandy brown hair, blue eyes, and skinny frame.

"Great to see you, too, Sarah. Last time we saw each other was in Chicago after you graduated from nursing school and I ran off and married that pharmaceutical rep," Mo recounted.

"What happened to that chuckle slut?" Jackie loved that term; Mo had told her and Sarah it was the comedy world's equivalent of a groupie.

"Good to see you, too, Jackie." He leaned over and gave her a hug.

"We were together for about three years. She wanted kids, I didn't, and she didn't like me traveling, so that was that."

"You broke my heart. It took me five comedians to get over you, but I'm all good now." Sarah smiled at him again.

Jackie's cell started to buzz, and she took it out of her pocket and studied the screen. "Shit! I have to head home. Laura got called in for a double murder. Shit!" Jackie got up and gave Sarah a quick hug good-bye. "I didn't even get to tell you what I found out about your friend Amanda Stein. I think your concerns may be valid. Not sure what's going on, but something isn't right. Let's talk in the next couple days." Jackie waved at Mo and left.

"Who's Laura? Who's Amanda Stein?" Mo asked. Sarah explained Jackie's life, Laura, and Wyatt, but she wasn't about to say anything about Amanda. All she had was weird feelings about her and Sergio Torres.

They sat and talked until Mo was tapped to go backstage

for the second show. He leaned over and whispered in Sarah's ear, "I'm only opening for this next guy. I'm doing twenty minutes. Wait for me, and then lets go get a drink."

Sarah could feel her old emotions stirring. She and Mo had really been in love, but after he'd broken her heart, she'd promised herself she would never let another man get that close. Enough time had passed, though, that she knew she could handle him now. So she said, "Okay. After you get off-stage, I'll meet you out front."

Sarah listened to Mo's twenty-minute routine, which was even funnier than the first show. Then she went outside to wait for him. When he came out to find her, he said, "Damn, you are still gorgeous, and you've got a body that won't stop."

"Calm down, Platt. Let's go get a nightcap."

They had a couple of drinks, and then Sarah decided she would invite him back to her place, so they ordered an Uber. As they sat on the couch in Sarah's apartment, Mo gently took her chin and kissed her on the lips. "Is that okay?" he asked quietly.

Sarah felt the comfort of his kiss and put her arms around him. "It'll do, Platt." With that, she took his hand and led him into her bedroom, where they disrobed each other. Mo kissed every part of her body and entered her slowly, and Sarah moaned with delight as they rocked back and forth. It was if they had never been apart from each other.

When her alarm went off at six, she hit the snooze button. Mo snuggled up to her, and they started all over again. At seven thirty, Sarah got up, showered, and dressed. When she walked into the living room, Mo was holding a Tiffany crystal heart he had given her when they'd first fallen in love.

"I'm glad to see you kept this and didn't throw it at the wall when we broke up. Let me walk you to work."

"You can hop a cab with me, but I really have to get in. I can't be late for my morning meeting."

They caught a cab to the hospital, and when Sarah got out, Mo walked her to the front entrance and asked the cab to wait. He gave Sarah a long, passionate kiss. "Let me take you to dinner tonight. Please," he pleaded. "What time do you get off work?"

"I'm off around seven, since I'm coming in late." Sarah glanced over Mo's shoulder and saw that Dr. Bower was also in front of the hospital, talking to an intern and looking in her direction. He had seen Mo kiss her; she felt embarrassed but was relieved that her time with Mo had satisfied her, so she didn't have to feel quite so attracted to Bower. Maybe she just needed to get laid on a more regular basis; that would keep her hormones more balanced.

"Sarah," Mo said now, "I'll make reservations and pick you up at your apartment around seven thirty. Sound good?"

"Sounds wonderful. See you then." She walked toward the hospital entrance.

Chapter 12

Sergio went back to his room after breakfast with Maria's dad. The whole conversation had gone well, considering that some fathers got out a shotgun when their daughter got knocked up. It was good thinking on his part that he had befriended Maria's entire family three months ago, when he had first come to Miami.

His cell phone rang, and he saw Maria's name on the caller ID. "Hello?"

"Hi, Sergio. My dad said you wanted me to call you when we got back from shopping. Did you have a good talk with him?" Maria sounded so happy.

"After he hit me a couple of times for having sex with his daughter and getting her pregnant, we had a fine discussion. Everyone in the restaurant is coming to the wedding," he joked.

"He did not hit you."

"No—luckily. I'm going to come pick you up. We need to go shopping for something," Sergio said, already walking out of his suite.

"Shopping for what?" Maria asked.

"When you get married, you need an engagement ring, don't you?" He heard Maria yell with delight. "I'll be there soon." He hung up, got his car, and drove back to her house, but when he pulled up, he saw Maria sitting on the front porch with a concerned look on her face. "What's wrong, honey?" he asked as he approached.

"Sit down." She patted the lawn chair next to her.

Sergio sat and took her hand. "What's going on? You look worried."

"My mother and father have insisted that we have an engagement party soon. We have a big family, and they want all my relatives to meet you and get to know you," she said.

"That sounds fine. Maybe next time I fly down—say, a couple of weeks," he said, all the while thinking, *I'm not planning on coming back again, ever.*

"That could work, but they've already invited everyone to come to our community clubhouse tomorrow night. They want to have the party while you're here this time. I told them it was too fast, and they said I should have thought of that before I got pregnant."

"That's really too soon. *Tomorrow?* How could they possibly plan something that fast?" *In that case, I really do need to start planning my exit,* he thought.

"It's my cousin's son's first communion tomorrow, and they had to rent the hall for the entire afternoon and evening anyway. My dad called my cousin, and they want to keep the party going. My dad is calling in lots of favors for this, Sergio. I think we should just go for it. My mom already bought a new dress today." Maria said.

"Boy, you people don't waste any time," Sergio let slip out.

"'You people'—what's *that* supposed to mean?" Maria stood up and walked inside the house.

Sergio followed her, pleading, "I didn't mean it the

way it sounded, Maria. Come on—let's go shopping for that engagement ring. This is no time to fight." He pulled her toward him and held her close to him, then kissed her until she softened.

"I'll go let my parents know we're heading out. My father wants to take us out for a celebratory dinner tonight. He wouldn't take no for an answer." Maria walked toward the back bedroom to tell her mother she was leaving.

Once they were on their way to Kay Jewelers, Maria looked over at him and asked, "Why so quiet? Is everything okay?"

"Everything is wonderful. Have you thought about what type of diamond ring you want?" Sergio asked as he parked.

"I can't believe this is happening so fast. It's like I'm in a dream. I hadn't even thought about a diamond engagement ring. I thought we'd just get simple matching wedding bands." Maria leaned over and kissed him on the cheek.

Inside the store, an older gentleman approached them. "Are you Sergio Torres?" He held out his hand to shake Sergio's. "I'm Arthur Edwards, the manager."

"Yes, I am, and this is my bride-to-be, Maria." Sergio glanced her way. Maria held out her hand, and Arthur shook it gently.

"First, thanks for calling, Mr. Torres. We have a room set up in the back and several lovely rings for Maria to look at. We're not sure of her preferences, but we do have a wide array of diamonds. Please follow me." Maria and Sergio trailed Arthur to a closed conference room, where there was a bottle of champagne and a swatch of black velvet fabric laid out on one side of a wide desk.

"Please, please, make yourselves comfortable. May I pour you a glass of champagne? On the house, of course."

"That would be lovely," Sergio responded. Then he added, "It turns out we'll need to make a purchase today, Arthur, so I hope you'll have something suitable. I'd like you to size Maria's finger and then bring in some options."

"I like a man who knows what he wants. May I measure your finger, Maria?" Arthur took out an assortment of sizing rings and held one up to Maria's hand, then immediately placed it on her finger, "Just as I thought: a size five. You have beautiful hands, Maria."

Arthur pulled the ring off Maria's hand, then said. "I will be back in a few minutes. Maria, would you prefer a pear-shaped, square, or round diamond?"

"I'd like something simple that will match a set of gold bands. I want Sergio and me to have the same band."

"I won't be wearing a wedding band, honey—I don't believe in them. The men in my family never wore a wedding band. I want to spend all the money on your engagement ring." Sergio made sure his voice was clear and stern, no room for discussion.

"I'll bring in an assortment of engagement rings, and we can go from there," Arthur said.

After Arthur excused himself, Maria turned to Sergio. "Do you really want to get married? I don't want you to say I forced you into something you don't want. I've never heard of a married man not wearing a ring."

"Maria. I know this has been a bumpy start, but yes, I want to marry you, and I want you to have a beautiful ring to look at every day for the rest of your life. You can show it off tomorrow night at the party." Sergio poured himself some more champagne and held up his glass. "To us." Maria lifted her glass and took a tiny sip, and they toasted.

They passed the next hour admiring an array of beautiful diamond engagement rings and wedding bands for the bride. Finally, Maria chose a one-carat square-cut ring and a matching diamond band. Arthur polished the ring and brought it back in a black velvet box. Sergio handed him his credit card, and Arthur excused himself again.

Then Sergio looked directly at Maria. "Maria Chavez, will you marry me?"

Maria started to cry. "Yes, Sergio. Of course." Sergio opened the box and put the sparkling ring on her dainty finger, then kissed her softly.

He stood up and put out his arm for Maria to hold as he escorted her out of the room. Arthur gave Maria a gift bag containing the wedding band and handed Sergio the receipt. "You can come back as often as you like. We will check the prongs and polish the stone. On behalf of Kay Jewelers, I would like to congratulate both of you. We are honored to be a part of such an important life event." Arthur walked the couple to the door.

"Thank you, Arthur. You have been most kind," Maria said, as she gave him a hug. She held out her hand, and all the bright lights in the jewelry store made her ring sparkle. "It's beautiful, Sergio. I'm so happy."

Sergio was genuinely pleased that he had given her some joy. Actually, he thought, this part of getting married was really fun; he could see why it drove people to the altar. But then, he reminded himself, it always went downhill after all the hoopla was over.

Sergio took the scenic route, along the ocean, back to Maria's parents' house. He rolled down his windows and let the sound of the waves fill the car. The evening air was slightly cool. He played some soft jazz on the radio, and they both listened in silence, enjoying the blissful moment.

The rest of the evening was filled with "oohs" and "aahs," as everyone at the Cuban restaurant came by to congratulate the couple and look at Maria's ring. The owner sent over a bottle of complimentary Dom Pérignon, and Maria and her parents told Sergio about all the relatives he would meet the following night. Sergio sat back and let Maria and her mother discuss the details of when and where they would get married, while he and Maria's father enjoyed the fine wine and Cuban cuisine. When questions about where the couple would live and raise their family came up, Sergio was quick to assure Maria's parents that they would work things out, then redirected the conversation.

After Sergio dropped Maria's parents off at home, he took her back to the Four Seasons where they made love and then fell asleep in each other's arms.

They spent the next day running around, collecting liquor and supplies, and before Sergio knew it, the engagement party was upon them. What seemed like hundreds of relatives flocked to Sergio, asking him the same questions that he had already answered repeatedly. Many of the men convened outside to enjoy Cuban cigars, while Maria's same-age cousins whisked her away to goggle at her engagement ring. A salsa band played, and the couple slow-danced in front of a crowd of onlookers. It was well past two in the morning when Maria and Sergio got back to the hotel. After a sweet lovemaking session, they fell fast asleep.

The loud sound of the room telephone woke them both.

"Hello," Sergio answered.

It was Maria's father. "Good morning—almost after-noon—Sergio. How are you and Maria doing today?"

"We're fine, just tired after all the festivities. This is an unexpected surprise. What can I do for you?" Sergio asked.

"I'd like to have some private time with you before you leave for the airport. I'm downstairs, and I thought maybe you could come down and meet me for a cup of coffee."

Sergio looked at the clock on the dresser; his plane wouldn't leave for three hours. "That would be fine. I'll come down now."

"That would be great," Jose said, and hung up.

Sergio was hoping everything was okay. So far, there had been no hiccups; all he had to do was say his good-byes and get back to San Francisco.

"Who was that?" Maria asked, as she sat up in bed.

Sergio took in her beautiful face, glowing and fresh. He did have strong feelings for her, but this needed to be over. Way too much family. He was already tired of playing the fiancé.

"Your dad wants to speak with me before I fly home. I'll be back up soon, honey. Relax and order room service." Sergio kissed her.

He found Jose downstairs in the dining room. He shook Jose's hand and then sat down. "Good to see you this morning. I'm sorry, but I have to leave early. Something has come up at work, and I need to attend to it. What's on your mind?"

The waiter poured Sergio a cup of coffee and left a menu.

"I understand that you need to leave today. My wife and I had a long talk this morning, and we have a special request." Jose sipped his coffee.

"Anything, Jose. What can I do for you?" Sergio watched him intently.

"My wife, your future mother-in-law, wants to meet your sister, Amanda, before the wedding. She feels once she meets Amanda, then she will know that it was right for us to donate Marco's liver to her. We need to put her heart at ease so she can truly enjoy the wedding. Would you be willing to bring Amanda down here so we can all get to know her before the wedding?" Jose asked.

Sergio's mind was already racing. He hadn't expected this. It did seem like a reasonable request, but there was just no way he could convince Amanda to come down to Miami, especially not to meet Maria's family. It would be a disaster. Amanda would eat Maria alive.

"Jose. Amanda is still recuperating at home. I don't know if she'll be able to fly back down to Miami so soon, or if she'll be able to come to the wedding, given her health," he said.

"It is very important to us, Sergio. We called the agency that helped with the organ donation, and they said they would help us with the reunion. They said many donor families meet their recipients. My wife begged me to come ask you this, Sergio. I can't go back and tell her no. It will break her heart," Jose pleaded.

"I understand how hard this must be for you and your wife and Maria. I'll tell you what: I will go home and bring Amanda back in a month if she's feeling well enough. How does that sound?" Sergio asked.

"That would be a wonderful gift for all of us. Then the wedding will take place in two months. Thank you, Sergio. I knew I could depend on you."

Sergio stood up and said, "Sure thing, Jose. I'll be dropping Maria off on my way to the airport. Thank you again for everything you and your family have done these past few days. I am very grateful." The men quickly embraced, then shook hands, and Jose left.

"What did my dad want?" Maria asked, sitting up in bed, enjoying breakfast.

Sergio kissed her and said, "Get ready, and I'll tell you about our whole conversation while I'm driving you home."

Once they were in the car, he shared her mother's wish and relayed his commitment to get his sister down to meet Maria's family. It was the least he could do, he told her.

Sergio walked Maria inside the house and hugged her mom and dad goodbye after thanking them again for everything. He promised her mom that he would bring Amanda to Miami in a month.

As he headed to the airport, he thought, *How am I going*

to pull this off? Amanda needed to find one grateful cell in her body, for once, he decided. Sergio had no idea how he would make it happen, but he would. Best of all, he would have one more interlude with Maria before he disappeared from her life for good.

Chapter 13

Sarah thought about Mo throughout the day and how great being with him had been. She would never forget the heartache he had caused her, but enough time had passed since their breakup that she had forgiven him. By now, she had also learned how to enjoy a man sexually without getting emotionally attached to him. When they'd been a couple, Mo had made her laugh so much that after him she'd decided she would focus on sleeping with comedians whenever possible, so that she got laughs *and* sex out of the equation. Even though she would never let herself get caught in his web again, she planned to enjoy every morsel of him while he was in town. He was a known commodity to her, simple as that.

Dr. Bower jolted her out of her daydreaming. "Thanks for reviewing that living liver donor work-up for me. Give me the highlights." He sat back in his desk chair.

Sarah opened her laptop and brought up the donor's record. "His history and physical were unremarkable. Very healthy, a little on the lean side; he's six feet tall, with a BMI of twenty-eight. He's got a high-powered job with Charles Schwab, no problem taking off work. The independent living-donor advocate cleared him. She wrote a note expressing a tiny bit of concern about the fact that he's single at forty and has no history of a serious relationship—bit of a loner. He states he is heterosexual. All his labs are negative; no sexually transmitted diseases. Sounds like a smart guy to me." Sarah closed her laptop.

"Sounds like a real smart man, still playing the field at forty. Good for him. Kinda like you, Sarah," Bower said.

Sarah saw the smirk on his face and realized, *It must be because he saw me kiss Mo this morning.* "The single life has its benefits—that's for sure," she retorted, but she felt herself blushing.

"The donor sounds ready to go. Are they going to present him at our living-donor conference tomorrow? I've already reserved an operating spot, assuming all goes well."

"Yup, they're going to present him. Looks like a green light. I'm so glad to see that your screening process for living donors is so conservative, after what happened on the East Coast. The death of that living liver donor got media coverage all over the country. You know, when something like that happens, all organ and tissue donations decrease nationwide. Did you know the surgeon?" Sarah asked.

"Yes. We were in medical school together. Excellent technician. No way he could have known. It could have been any one of us. There but for the grace of God go I. I was asked to review the records and all the operating-room notes. The donor was stable when he was discharged from the OR. I can't say much more at the moment; the case is under review and will likely involve ligation."

"I understand. On a different note, I wanted to thank you for the tickets to the gala. My friend Jackie and I had a wonderful time. I didn't know you and your wife were so actively involved," Sarah said.

"I'm involved only when they want money or a speaker. Kristin and her friend, Amanda Stein, really run the show. They generated over two million dollars in donations that night. Their grants fund some amazing research. One of my fellows got a grant to prove coffee is actually good for the liver—in moderation, of course. I think the title of his paper was something like 'Does a Latte a Day Keep the Doctor Away?'" With that, Bower started flipping through one of his journals, which was his way of saying the meeting was over.

"I know Amanda Stein," Sarah said.

"How do you know her?" Bower briefly glanced up.

"I took care of her after her liver transplant in Miami. She was not an easy patient. Her boyfriend—I think his name is Sergio Torres—was quite a handful, too." Sarah watched Bower's face for a reaction.

"Sergio is a character. Extremely wealthy man. His parents owned a lot of prime real estate in Mexico and, unfortunately, died in a car accident when he was twenty. He sold off most of it and kept one small parcel near Mexico City. Left him a billionaire. He barely made it out of Yale, bought his way in and likely out. He's done some modeling for Ralph Lauren, which is how he met Amanda. They were modeling a new line in New York."

"I could see him being a model; he's probably one of the most handsome men I've ever seen. I did have to have him escorted out by security, though, because he wouldn't stop using his cell phone. He didn't like that very much," Sarah said.

"I'll bet he didn't. He doesn't let anyone boss him around besides Amanda, and I think she makes up for everyone. I can only imagine how she's running him around after her liver transplant." Dr. Bower snickered.

"Did you tell Amanda to go to Miami for the transplant?" Sarah asked.

"She was listed with us, too, but I told her she'd get a liver faster in Miami. There are more available livers than there are recipients waiting down there, so it was really her best bet. Anyone can go online if they're smart enough and find waiting times across the country. Just takes a little digging at UNOS.org. But you already know that," Bower said.

"Did you know she got a directed donor?" Sarah asked.

"That's interesting. I didn't know she knew anyone down in Miami. I know Sergio had business down there this year. He was investing in a restaurant, I think. Hmm," he mumbled.

"I must say, she was none too grateful for her gift," Sarah said, not bothering to conceal the disgust in her voice.

"That's Amanda. She's not a very grateful human being."

"How did your wife and Amanda get to be best friends?"

"They both studied fashion design at Vassar. Same sorority, too. My wife went on to act in New York, and Amanda got her MBA at Columbia. They shared a snazzy flat in Manhattan. They were inseparable back then. Amanda was *not* happy when Kristin and I met and got married. That wasn't in Amanda's long-term plans at all. Made things a little bumpy at first, but we all came to an agreement. The girls get their getaways, and we spend every Thanksgiving with them. Kristin loves Sergio. He'd do anything for her, too." Bower shrugged his shoulders and stood up to walk out. Sarah got up, too.

Outside, they went their separate ways. Bower was off to make patient rounds on the transplant floor, and Sarah needed to go back to her desk to answer her endless e-mails. As she walked back to her office, she thought about the fight she had overheard between Amanda and Sergio in Amanda's Miami hospital room. She recalled something about Amanda's organ donor and Sergio's Cuban "whore" girlfriend.

Sarah gave Jackie a quick call when she got back to her desk. Jackie picked up. "Hey, Golden, did you get lucky last night?"

"What do you think? Nice job arranging that outing. We're having dinner tonight." Sarah could feel herself smiling.

"I was reading the *Chronicle* and saw that Mo was opening at Cobb's and thought, why not get you together to have some fun? I know you're so over him, but you did tell me he was the best lay you ever had. Plus, I don't want you getting too close to Bower. Everything go okay? You're not mad, are you?" Jackie asked.

"Not mad at all, Jack. Great idea. It really was just what I needed."

"So what's up? Don't you know I'm busy, too? I have smelly boy clothes to wash and errands to run, and it's almost time for soccer practice. Don't get jealous."

"I wanted to talk to you about Amanda Stein. I got some info from Bower about how she got to Miami. How about dinner tomorrow night?"

"Sounds good, although I'll need to make it an early evening. How about I pick you up around five in front of the hospital?" Jackie asked.

"That should work. Text me, and if I'm in a meeting, I'll excuse myself. I'd really like to forget about this whole Miami-Amanda thing, but something about it is still bugging me. I figure we can talk it out and see if there's anything there, or whether I'm just too protective of donor families or hate really rich people. But right now, I gotta go."

"Sounds good. Have fun with Mo tonight. Don't let him break your heart again. Just get yourself serviced," Jackie teased.

"Don't worry, Jack. I've got my permanent armor up, as always. We like each other in and out of the bedroom, but it's just a drive-by. He'll be moving along tomorrow. Bye."

• • •

Sarah left work a little early that afternoon to get dressed up for her date. When Mo came to pick her up, his jaw dropped. "You look amazing. Have you been working out?" Sarah watched his eyes scan her legs, hips, and waist, stopping for a good long look at her breasts.

"I don't have time to go to the gym around here. But I never stop moving, and I take the stairs all day. Where are we going, handsome?" Sarah glanced at Mo's cute smile and dimples. "You look pretty dapper yourself."

"I got reservations at Spruce. Have you ever been?" Mo held the Uber's door open for Sarah as she hopped in the back. The San Francisco fog had rolled in, and the temperature had dropped into the fifties; she was thankful she had brought her cashmere pashmina.

As the car made its way to Spruce, Sarah and Mo talked about the restaurant. "I went once, but I haven't been since they won that prestigious award from *Wine Spectator*."

"You're in for a real treat," Mo said, then leaned over and gave her a long, passionate kiss.

Over a three-hour, five-course, chef's choice meal and wine pairings, Sarah and Mo talked nonstop about what they had each done over the past five years. Sarah told him all about Jackie and their upcoming Cuban adventure and their last adventure in Mexico, when they had almost gotten arrested. As he laughed at her stories, she thought, *Maybe I shouldn't be so quick to dismiss him after all. People can change.*

The evening ended as the evening before had: they disappeared into each other's arms. Nothing had ever felt more comfortable to Sarah's heart and body than the times when she was with Mo.

Chapter 14

Sergio took Amanda's abuse when she got back from New York, and they settled into their usual mean relationship: yelling, throwing things, all the standard stuff.

Still, four weeks after Amanda's liver transplant, Sergio agreed to escort her to her first formal outing since the surgery: a black-tie event for the de Young museum that they attended every year, at which all the rich and famous of San Francisco convened to brag about their private art collections and donate a few hundred thousand dollars. Amanda had gotten an amazing gown when she was in New York with Kristin. She'd lost weight, so she was looking very slim, and she wasn't yellow from her liver failure anymore.

The night of the gala, Sergio left his beautifully appointed loft at the Infinity, which overlooked the Bay Bridge, and had his driver take him to Amanda's. He went upstairs, let himself in, and poured himself a couple fingers of Macallan scotch. He checked himself out in her hallway mirror. His Armani suit fit perfectly, and his silk bow tie was just right.

"Hello, my love," he called out. "I'm in the front room. No rush. I poured myself a scotch."

As he sat in the Eames chair that faced the long glass windows overlooking all of downtown San Francisco and the Golden Gate Bridge, his cell phone rang and he saw it was Maria. "Well, hello there. How are you?" He was careful not to use any romantic words, in case Amanda heard him. Maria had been calling him almost every day with updates about the wedding plans. It was a breath of fresh air to hear her sweet voice describe what he thought of as his "pretend wedding."

As soon as Maria had told him where they were having the reception and all the various companies they would be using, Sergio had called them and bought insurance, just in case the wedding had to be canceled or postponed. Maria had no idea, and Sergio, stating that her health was fragile, was clear with each vendor that she should continue not to know.

"I miss you so much, Sergio," she said now. "You've been gone too long. I have to plan this wedding all by myself. My mother thinks I'm being way too extravagant but I told her you insisted it be high class and would accept nothing less."

"Do you want me to call her and let her know you're just following my orders?" Sergio took a sip of his scotch.

Amanda walked into the front room, looking elegant beyond words.

"Okay, Jim, I'll call you tomorrow after I check out the stock price. Have a good evening." Sergio hung up on Maria and turned his cell phone off.

"Well, you were sure worth waiting for. You look gorgeous, my love." He stood up to gaze at her from head to toe. She was wearing a black Prada gown with a deep neckline, brushed by each of her firm breasts, a solid sapphire necklace, and matching, pear-shaped earrings. Her blond hair was pulled up; a few strands hung loose on either side of her exquisite face. The slit in her dress revealed a shapely long leg. She stood taller than Sergio in her four-inch Jimmy Choo stilettos.

"Don't kiss me and mess up my makeup now. Get me a glass of champagne, and then we'll go. I want to be fashionably late, but not too late." Sergio could see her look at herself in the mirror and smile as he went to bar to pour the champagne. *We're the perfect looking couple,* he thought. *Who cares if we hate each other half the time, as long as we look good in the media?*

"I could rip off your clothes right now and make love to you on the living room carpet," he said, as he poured champagne into a Waterford flute. He knew she wasn't supposed to drink any alcohol, but a little bit wouldn't hurt.

"Don't be silly. We still need to proceed with caution a little longer, until I'm totally healed. I told the Bowers we'd meet them there. Kristin hates to go places with Harris. Everyone makes such a big fuss over him because he's a transplant surgeon and saves lives, blah blah blah. He has no fashion sense and will probably have on the same ugly black suit he always wears. Poor dear." Amanda took the champagne and had a sip. "Cheers." They clinked glasses.

Sergio's driver took them to the de Young and dropped them off in front. Sergio reveled in the knowledge that he and Amanda turned every head as they walked the red carpet. "What a stunning couple," he heard several people whisper as they passed. Once they were inside, photographers from the *Chronicle* and *Town & Country* snapped picture after picture of them.

"We're back," Amanda said to Sergio, and kissed him on the lips amid camera flashes.

Sergio could see that the Bowers had spotted them and were walking over to greet them. "Hello, Amanda. You look very healthy," Harris said.

"Thanks, Harris. I owe it all to you. I would have never known to go to Miami had it not been for your wise advice." Amanda gave him a peck on the cheek.

"Hello, Kristin," Sergio said. "You look stunning tonight. I can see you did some damage in New York, too. So sorry I wasn't able to join you girls. You know how I love it there." Sergio gave Kristin a hug and a kiss on each cheek.

"We missed you terribly. I hear you had some business in Miami—what a horrible place to have to visit. Too hot and humid for me," Kristin said.

"I'll plan on tagging along next time. I'm so glad you were able to take Amanda; she was going crazy staying at home. Doesn't she look ravishing tonight?" Sergio glanced over at Bower, who was chatting Amanda up while his gaze remained locked on her cleavage.

Sergio strolled over to Amanda with his arm out. "Let's go look at the new collection." Amanda took his arm, and they made their way to the exhibit, stopped every several minutes by Amanda's friends and their husbands. Everyone seemed happy to have their Amanda back out in public, Sergio thought.

After they'd enjoyed the art and visited with various guests, Amanda nudged him. "I'm tired, Sergio. Please call your driver." She began walking toward the museum exit.

Sergio called the driver and thought about how he could raise the question of meeting Maria's family. He needed to get her home, rub her feet, and take it from there.

As they entered her penthouse, Amanda kicked off her high heels, sank into her plush sofa, and sighed. Sergio went to the bar. "May I get you some cognac, my dear?"

"Just a little would be wonderful."

Sergio rinsed each brandy snifter with hot water and then poured Frapin Cuvée 1888, enjoying its rich, delicate aroma.

He handed Amanda her snifter and sat on the carpet next to her. They gazed at the beautiful view and sipped their cognac in silence.

"It was so nice to be out with you tonight. What a lovely event. Did you have a good time?" Amanda asked.

"I had a great time watching every man there staring at you. They're all in trouble with their wives when they get home. You stole the show. Forget about the art when you show up looking like that," Sergio said.

"I did ask Harris Bower if it was okay to enjoy some bedroom time with you tonight, and he said it would be fine if I felt like it, but that we should be careful." Amanda took a sip of cognac.

"Say no more. May I escort you to your bedroom?" Sergio stood up and offered her his arm. They hadn't made love since long before her transplant.

In the bedroom, he carefully unbuttoned her dress and let it slide to the floor. She was wearing a black lace garter belt and panties. Sergio took off his suit and threw it over the chair. Amanda had already gotten between the satin sheets. As Sergio gently kissed her, he said, "I will be very careful, my love. I'm going to kiss every part of you, but you just let me know if you need me to stop." She smiled up at him as he started on her face and neck and gradually moved downward. His hands explored between her thighs, and she achieved an orgasm with only the touch of his fingers. Sergio decided to wait and pleasure himself later, as, despite her assurances, he didn't think he should make love to her so soon after her surgery.

Amanda sat up and sipped the rest of her cognac. Sergio could tell she was feeling a little tipsy.

"It's been a long time, Sergio. I miss our bedroom fun."

"Don't worry, honey. I'm going to use all my rain checks once you feel truly ready. When do you have to go back to Miami for your first checkup?" Sergio asked.

"I really don't want to go back to Miami, but Harris said

they should see me at least once before his team takes over my follow-up. I'm thinking in a couple of weeks. Oh, I forgot to tell you that I got an e-mail from the procurement agency down there. It seems the donor family—the Cuban parents whose son was the donor—contacted them and want to meet me. I don't know too many details at this point, and, frankly, I don't want to know any more."

"I really think you should visit with the donor family just once and say thank you," Sergio offered.

"I don't know about that. That nurse in Miami did say that many donor families like to meet the recipient. It's not really my thing, though." Amanda's tone was getting terse, and Sergio decided not to push.

"If you don't want to do it, don't. I'm sure it could be weird. You'll make the right decision."

Amanda stood up and went to her spacious bathroom. She took a quick shower and changed into her sleeping gown.

Sergio prepared for bed as well, then went into the kitchen to freshen up his cognac and make Amanda some hot chamomile tea. She liked to drink that before she went to bed. He poured the tea into a porcelain cup with a matching saucer and took it to her as she sat up in bed.

"Here's your tea." Sergio placed it on her nightstand, then walked around and got in bed next to her.

"Do you have plans tomorrow?" he asked her.

"Kristin and I are getting facials and massages at Nob Hill Spa, then maybe doing some shopping at Union Square if I'm up for it."

"I'm meeting Bill at the gym, and then we're going out on the bay in his sailboat. He wants you to come." Sergio clicked on the TV to watch sports updates.

Amanda turned to Sergio. "I'm not ready for any sailing." She paused, then continued, "It was kinda weird that

Harris asked me tonight how I got a directed donor. I said you had been doing business down there for some time and happened to mention to one of your restaurant managers that I was waiting for a liver. I did bring up the e-mail from the procurement agency, and he said I would be doing a service if I met the family. He said that kind of interaction can actually increase the likelihood that other people in the donor's ethnic group will donate. I'm sure he could tell by the look on my face that I wasn't wild about his suggestion."

"You don't have to have dinner or move in with them. Just meet them and thank them. Plus, it would be a great photo op for you; they could use it at the Liver Foundation gala next year."

I'm so glad I thought of this angle, he said to himself; he knew it would appeal to Amanda's ego. Even though he would have to maneuver carefully around Maria and her family, he knew he could fast-talk his way through Amanda's meeting with them. He would have to be quick, because he knew Amanda would tolerate being near them for only a few minutes maximum. Sergio had told Amanda that he had lied to Maria and her family about Amanda's being his sister, but he had left out a lot of other details, as Amanda insisted on knowing nothing about how Sergio had gone about getting her a liver.

"That's a great idea. Maybe Kristin can come with us and we can see that new designer in Miami who's been all over *Vogue*."

"Yes, let's make a fun adventure out of it. I'll try to arrange it so we can meet them at the clinic where you have your checkup, take a few photos with them and your transplant team, and then we'll go have some fun. How does that sound?" *What a relief that Amanda came to this on her own.*

"I don't want to spend any more time than I have to with those people. We must stay at the Four Seasons, and you make dinner reservations at that new restaurant you invested in. It's the only way I'll do this."

"Sounds like a plan. Consider it done." Sergio kissed Amanda on the cheek and fell asleep immediately.

Chapter 15

Sarah hugged Mo good-bye when he dropped her off at the hospital the morning after their dinner at Spruce. They promised each other that they would stay in touch and get together again when he was back in the Bay Area. As much as being with Mo reignited glimmers of hope inside Sarah that she didn't want to acknowledge, she knew better than to put any stock in them. *If it happens, it happens,* she said to herself as she took the elevator to her office, but the life of a comedian was too unpredictable for her to be able to trust Mo unconditionally.

After dealing with several crises with some of the coordinators, she went by Dr. Bower's office to discuss the living liver donor they had reviewed earlier in the week. His secretary asked her to wait outside his open office door, as he was finishing up a phone call. Sarah sat down and began answering e-mails on her phone but stopped typing when she heard Dr. Bower say the word "Amanda."

"Amanda, I think you should really go down to Miami and meet the family, especially if they want to meet you," she heard him say.

"No, they won't touch you unless you let them hug you. Really, Amanda—find some compassion."

Sarah wished she could hear what Amanda was saying.

Bower continued, "Here's how it usually works. They have a social worker from the procurement agency with them before you come, and then you'll be brought into the room. It's really moving. Oh, I forgot to tell you, I did speak with Dr. Santos, the chief of transplant down there, and he wants to do a photo op with you and the family. The consent rates in the Cuban population are relatively low, and this could help others on the waiting list."

Sarah was hanging on every word Bower said.

"Yes, come see me in clinic this week, and we'll discuss your follow-up at Miami. It's nice to know Sergio and I are on the same page about this. Maybe he's all right after all. I gotta go. See you this week in clinic." Bower hung up.

Sarah stood up and walked into Dr. Bower's office. "Good morning. How are you today?"

"Busy. I need to go to the OR in a minute. What's up?" Bower stood and started walking out of his office in his scrubs, beeper going off, as usual.

Sarah followed him. "I got a call from our almost-perfect living liver donor."

"Almost?"

"He's changed his mind. He watched the video about the operation again and decided he didn't want to have a major operation. He was very apologetic but was clear it was off. He mentioned some hippie sister who's supposed to call us. I'm disappointed. It took months to work up a donor, get all the test results back, and do the follow-up."

"It happens. Why don't you call the sister and have her see the independent donor advocate first, before we spend time or money on her work-up?" He got on the elevator, and the door closed.

Sarah walked back to her office, closed the door, and called Jackie's cell. "Hey, Jack, how's it going?"

"Usual morning chores under way, my friend. What's going on? Did Mo ask you to marry him? Sloppy seconds, but who cares?" Jackie was in a good mood.

"Ha ha ha. Mo left this morning, and we had a great time together. No promises. I called because I have to tell you about a one-way conversation I just overheard from Bower."

"Conversation with who?"

"Bower was talking to our friend Amanda. She's planning on going to Miami and meeting the donor family. I think the only reason she's doing it is because there's going to be some media coverage. She doesn't want them touching her. She's beyond gross. There is definitely more than meets the eye here, Jackie." Sarah turned her chair around and looked out her window so she wouldn't be tempted to look at her e-mail.

"I think you're onto something, considering you've said this since the beginning. What are you thinking?" Jackie asked.

"We may need to go to Miami when Amanda's down there and follow them around. Is there any chance you can take, say, four days away? I can ask for time off. Unexpected family issue—I'll make something up."

"What are we, Cagney and Lacey?" Jackie laughed.

Sarah chuckled as she remembered how many reruns of the show she and Jackie had watched when they were in nursing school. "I thought we were more like female versions of Columbo," she said. "I know this sounds crazy, but I want to figure it out. I'll find out the date she's going down there, and then let's connect. Start warming up Laura. See, this is the reason I'm glad I'm single. I want to do something, I do it. I don't have to ask anyone for permission."

"Are you done? Are you really going to start on the bandwagon? Call me when you have dates. I'm not letting you go down without me." Jackie hung up.

• • •

The next day, Sarah made a point of going to the post-transplant liver clinic. When she pulled up the list of patients scheduled for the day, she saw a VIP on Bower's schedule and knew it had to be Amanda. Sure enough, as she got near the clinic room, she heard Amanda's voice. Sarah walked in with her stethoscope around her neck and found Amanda on her cell phone. Sarah looked at her and smiled.

"I have to get off the phone, Sergio. The nurse is here to take my blood pressure. I'll call you when I'm ready. I don't want to wait, so have your driver stay close." Amanda hung up and held out her arm.

Sarah could tell that Amanda didn't recognize her. "Hi, I'm Sarah Golden, the senior coordinator here. I'm going to take your vital signs and update your record so that when Dr. Bower comes in, he'll have everything he needs."

"Dr. Bower and I are personal friends. You look vaguely familiar. Have I met you before?"

Sarah carefully concealed her disgust as she answered, "Yes, I took care of you down in Miami when you got your liver transplant."

"My goodness, you certainly did. I'm heading down to Miami soon, so I'll need to get copies of my labs before I leave." Sarah could see Amanda look at her name tag.

"When are you going?" Sarah asked.

"We're leaving next week. My boyfriend, Sergio—I think you remember him; you stole his cell phone—and I are going with Kristin, Dr. Bower's wife."

"Did I hear my name?" Dr. Bower walked in, and Amanda got up and gave him a stiff hug.

"Yes, you did. I didn't know you were in earshot. Kristin is going with Sergio and me to Miami. As you know, I've got the old corporate jet at my disposal, so we're going to have some fun after we get that donor-family thing over with." Amanda sat back down.

"First I've heard of Kristin going. Let's look at your labs." Dr. Bower reviewed the numbers on the computer screen and nodded. "Everything looks great, Amanda. Normal liver values. Negative for hepatitis C. I'm not going to change your medications. Let them do it in Miami. When are you going?"

"We're leaving next Tuesday. I've asked Sarah here for a copy of my labs. Did you know she took care of me in Miami?" Amanda said.

"I think she may have mentioned that. Lucky you. She's one of the best transplant nurses in the country, as far as I'm concerned." Bower stood up to leave. "One other thing, Amanda. We're having a press conference here this afternoon. There are some concerns about Hispanic organ donors and recipients. It's always good to have a patient on camera, thank the donor family for their generosity. Given your involvement with the Liver Foundation and all, I think you would be a great spokesperson. Can you help me out?"

"Anything for you, Harris. What time do you want me here?" Amanda asked.

"The news crew will be here at four. Why don't you come to my office around three thirty? Our media-relations folks will want you to sign some paperwork. Thanks for helping out. I appreciate it." Bower stood at the door.

"I'll get you your labs. Anything else, Dr. Bower?" Sarah asked.

"No, that's all, Sarah. I'll see you at three thirty, Amanda, and when you go to Miami, behave yourself. Be nice to the donor family, and send me the photos they take."

After Bower left to go see his next patient, Sarah asked Amanda to wait as she went to print out her labs. She returned with a white envelope and handed it to Amanda. "Here are the copies of your labs. Anything else you need?"

"I do have a question about this donor family. I believe they're a poor Cuban family. Is it appropriate for me to give them a check for their troubles? I'm sure they need the money. Is that kind of thing done?" Amanda asked.

"How do you know they're a poor Cuban family?" Sarah asked.

"I'm just guessing. It's not rocket science."

Sarah couldn't stand Amanda's condescending tone. "I don't think that would be appropriate, but you should ask the team down in Miami." Sarah excused herself before she said something she'd regret. Amanda followed her out to the reception area, already talking on her cell phone again. "Sergio, I'm going to be on TV this afternoon. Come pick me up now; I need to go get my hair and makeup done."

Sarah went back to her office, where she quickly texted Jackie the dates for their Miami trip and asked Jackie to check airfares.

Chapter 16

Sergio picked up Amanda and had his driver drop them off first at her hairdresser and then at Saks Fifth Avenue to get her makeup done. He was sticking close to her to make sure she didn't change her mind about seeing Maria's family.

"How did your appointment go with Dr. Bower?" he asked Amanda while the makeup artist worked on her eyes.

"Everything is perfect, and, for once, you and Dr. Bower agree on something—that I should see this stupid donor family—so I'll do it. Right now, I need to concentrate on today's press conference and looking fabulous."

"You will look marvelous, my dear." The makeup artist promised.

Sergio's cell phone rang. It was Maria. He excused himself, telling Amanda, "I'll be outside, waiting for you in the car. Take your time." He walked outside to Union Square, where Saks was located, and answered his cell phone.

"Hello, my love," he said to Maria.

"Hello. Why did you hang up on me the other night and call me Jim? What was that about?"

"I was talking to you and forgot I had Jim on hold. I thought I had put you on hold to tell him I would call you back. I'm so sorry. Please forgive me."

"I tried calling you back all night and left you messages. What's going on, Sergio? Is something wrong?" She started to cry.

"My phone went dead; then I had my sister to take care of. Anyway, it's all in the past now. I am so sorry. I didn't mean to upset you."

"I just got scared and worried. Then I thought you weren't going to marry me. My imagination went wild when I couldn't talk to you."

"Of course I'm going to marry you, Maria. In fact, I have some great news. My sister and I are coming down next Tuesday, and she wants to meet your family."

"My mother will be so excited to finally meet her. That's the best news ever. We'll have to have a family party at the house so she can meet everyone before the wedding."

"Slow down, honey. She is still fragile from her liver transplant. She can't really be around a lot of people right now. We're going to fly in and fly right back out this time. Meanwhile, I need you to call the procurement agency and let them know Amanda wants to meet your family but that the meeting has to be at the hospital," Sergio explained.

"My mother never wants to go back to that hospital, ever. I really don't know if she'll go. Why can't we have it at our home?" Maria asked.

"They don't allow it. It has to be at the hospital. I don't make the rules, Maria. Don't get mad at me. I'm just trying to get this arranged." Since Amanda had specifically asked him not to tell her anything about how he was going to get her liver, he had honored her request, until now. As far as she knew, Sergio had been having sex with a Cuban woman, but Amanda had no idea that her liver had come from Maria's brother. Amanda and Sergio had always had an open relationship, so Sergio's dating anyone, anywhere, had never been an issue, and the same held true in reverse. That didn't mean that they didn't fight with each other when one of them had a fling going on, but fighting was built into their relationship.

Sergio decided that he would talk to Amanda right before they met Maria and her family. He knew Amanda wouldn't lose it in front of the media; she would wait until afterward, once they were behind closed doors, to let him have it.

"Okay, my love. I didn't mean to upset you. I'll have to ask my dad to talk to my mom. Do you want to hear about the wedding plans?" Maria asked.

"I do, but there's one thing about the wedding. We can't tell Amanda about it just yet; she's too fragile, and I know she'll want to organize the whole thing herself if we tell her now. She tends to take things over, and I want this to be your wedding, Maria, not hers. Do you understand?" Sergio made his tone as stern as possible.

"Sergio, how am I going to explain that to my parents? They won't understand. They want to broadcast our wedding from the mountaintops," Maria pleaded.

"Maria, I am asking you to help me with this. We need to make all the plans by ourselves; then I'll tell Amanda in a couple of weeks. Believe me, if she finds out when we're there next week, you can consider the wedding off. You don't know my sister. Please—I'm begging you to understand this. It's very important to me." He paused dramatically, then sighed and said, "I wasn't going to tell you this, but my sister has a slight mental problem. She treats it with medications, but sometimes she goes off her meds and has to be hospitalized. That just can't happen right now."

"Oh, Sergio. I didn't know. I'm so sorry. You never said anything. Of course I will let my parents know, and we'll tell her later."

"It's not something I usually share with people; Amanda would just die if she knew I had told you, so I really appreciate your keeping this quiet. You can tell your parents, but they can't say anything to her when they meet her. I have to run now. We'll talk later. Love you," Sergio said.

"Bye, honey. Talk to you later." Maria hung up.

Amanda came out of Saks Fifth Avenue looking like a million bucks, and Sergio's driver got out and opened the car door for her. Sergio hopped in next to her.

"Hollywood, here we come," Sergio said, looking her over.

"Let's get to the hospital. I don't want to be late," she demanded.

Sergio and Amanda went to Dr. Bower's office and found him waiting. "Hi, Amanda. They called, and we'll need to get over to the clinic. The news crew is already there and set up. Oh, hi, Sergio. Nice of you to come. Be nice to have a Hispanic male in the photos. Do you mind?" Bower led the way to the elevator, and they both followed.

"That's fine. Always happy to use my ethnicity to further a cause. What *is* the exact cause here, Harris?" Sergio really didn't like Harris. He never spent any time with his wife, so it meant that most of the time Sergio and Amanda did anything social, they had to bring Kristin along. Sergio always got an earful about how Harris was married to his job and his wife and kids came second.

"We had a Hispanic patient on our liver waiting list who was passed over for a clinical reason. He went to Telemundo, the Hispanic press, and declared that we were discriminating against him. Turns out this patient is here illegally. He has medical insurance to cover his transplant but no money to pay for the medication. We put him on hold until he made financial arrangements to have the money in the bank for his medications, which run about six thousand dollars a year out of pocket."

Bower walked into the clinic, where several photographers and two major TV stations were standing by. Sergio and Amanda followed Bower and the media-relations woman into a small conference room. She had Amanda and Sergio sign release forms, then gave them some pointers on what to say and not to say. They all agreed that Sergio would stand behind Amanda but not speak. Sergio went along with the program. He knew they were using him, but he didn't really care. This was mostly about Amanda getting media attention, and it would help solidify her meeting with Maria's family.

They stood in front of the press, and Dr. Bower started to take questions.

"Dr. Bower, you were recently on CNN, claiming there is absolutely no way to game the organ-allocations system. Is that still true?" a male reporter from CBS News asked.

"I can understand that there will always be concerns about the fairness of the organ-sharing system. You should know that the transplant community has gone to great lengths to ensure that every organ is given to the appropriate patient. There are national rules, and they are monitored very closely. I'll stake my professional reputation on it." Dr. Bower called on the woman reporter from Telemundo. "Next question."

"Dr. Bower, how do you explain this recent Hispanic patient, Mr. Gomez, who went to the press, claiming that a liver that should have gone to him went to a different person? He was not aware that he had been put on hold because of some financial reason. Was it because he didn't have the money to pay for his liver?"

"Mr. Gomez's case has nothing to do with organ allocation. He was listed as a candidate pending his ability to show that he could pay for the medications he would need after his transplant. We can't in good conscience put an organ in anyone who cannot afford the medication. We need to ensure they keep the organ."

The reporter interrupted Dr. Bower: "Mr. Gomez does not speak English and is claiming that no one clearly communicated this to him in his native language. How can you call that fair, Dr. Bower? This is clearly a case of racial discrimination, and Mr. Gomez is here illegally, which begs another question: Isn't it true that you get many organs and tissues from nonresidents but turn around and give those donations to legal residents? Doesn't that seem wrong, Dr. Bower? You can use their organs, but you don't give them back to this population?"

As the Hispanic reporter waited for Dr. Bower to respond, Sergio pondered what she'd said. He hadn't been aware that nonresident organ donors were the source of organs but not the recipients of them.

Dr. Bower stepped close to the microphones. "That's simply not true. We have many patients, on both our kidney and liver transplant waiting lists, who are nonresidents, and we have also transplanted many nonresidents. When we evaluate a patient for a transplant we always have an interpreter at the evaluation who speaks the patient's native language. This was the case with Mr. Gomez. And now I would like to introduce Amanda Stein, who is the president of the Liver Foundation."

Amanda stepped up to the microphone and said, "Hello. We have worked diligently to be sure that all the materials the Liver Foundation distributes are in English, Spanish, Mandarin, and Russian. We also have a grant program for people who do not have the money to pay for their medications. Mr. Gomez has reached out to our organization, and we are currently working with him and his family to process his request. On another note, I just received a liver transplant myself and am very grateful to the donor family for this gift of life. I would encourage all of you to sign your donor cards and tell your families of your wishes. You can also sign up to be a donor by contacting our local procurement agency. We have donor cards and materials for everyone."

Before anyone could ask another question, the media-relations woman spoke. "I understand you all have many questions for Dr. Bower, but he needs to go to the operating room to perform a transplant. Please come see me with your questions. I will have Dr. Bower provide answers, which I will send to you later today. Thank you for your patience. This press conference is concluded." Sergio heard cameras snapping all over the room as the media gal led the three of them back to the conference room and closed the door.

"You did great, Dr. Bower, but we will need to confirm that Mr. Gomez did have an interpreter at his evaluation appointment. The reporter from Telemundo is not going to let this one go. This footage is going to be on national news, on both English and Spanish channels. Who can I talk to get some data on the illegal donors?"

Dr. Bower quickly jotted down a couple of names and numbers and handed them to her. "I really do have to go do a transplant. Amanda, thanks for coming on such short notice. Sergio, I appreciate you helping out, too." With that, he left the conference room. The media-relations woman looked at Amanda and asked, "Do you know where your liver came from?"

"I got my liver transplant in Miami. My liver came from a young Cuban man. I'm not sure if that would be of much help here in the Bay Area. Sergio and I really need to go as well." Amanda shook the woman's hand and walked out.

Sergio dropped Amanda off at her place and went back to his to relax for the evening. He turned on the evening news and saw the coverage from the Transplant Institute.

Bower seemed very convincing, although Sergio had no idea whether he was telling the truth. Amanda looked stunning, and he looked great as background.

His cell phone rang. It was Maria calling again.

"Hello, my love. How are things? I just got home." Sergio put his feet up on his leather ottoman.

"Sergio, we just saw you and your sister on Telemundo TV with that Dr. Bower. My parents were so glad to see your sister doing so well. She is very beautiful. But you don't look anything alike," Maria said.

"That's because she was adopted. It's another thing my family never talks about. Our parents raised us as siblings and forbade us to use the word 'adoption.'"

"My mother has arranged for our priest to be at the meeting at the hospital when you both come. She wants him to bless all of us. I thought that was so sweet of her. Would that be okay? I know you said you were both raised Catholic; I hope your sister won't mind a little blessing. How can it hurt?" Maria asked.

Sergio knew this would send Amanda right over the edge, so he was not going to tell her anything about the priest. "I think that would be fine, Maria."

"Okay, honey. I need to go now. Call me tomorrow." Maria hung up.

This meeting with Maria's family in Miami had the possibility of turning into a complete disaster. Sergio would have to figure out a way to get Amanda in and out of there as fast as possible.

Chapter 17

When Sarah walked into the operating room at 8:00 A.M., she found Dr. Bower and his cosurgeon, Dr. Daniels, three hours into a hepatectomy. "Good morning, Doctors," she said quietly. There was soft classical music playing in the back ground.

"Good morning, Sarah. What brings you to our operating room this morning?" Dr. Bower said, as they continued to operate.

"I wanted to update you on a couple things. Most important, they're going to start on the recipient. I guess it's going to take a while to remove the diseased liver—lots of adhesions from past surgeries. They wanted to be sure you were far enough along before they started." Sarah was standing near enough to the operating room table to see inside the abdominal cavity of the living liver donor.

"Let them know to go ahead and start. This donor was thin, so the surgery went faster than we expected," Dr. Bower said.

"Okay. I also wanted to let you know that it looks like we're going to have another living donor liver transplant to schedule. The donor is all cleared and wants to do it as soon as he can. It's Mr. Benjamin."

"Sarah, you're doing an amazing job. You've been here only a month, and we've done two living donor liver transplants and have three more scheduled. Keep doing what you're doing," Bower said.

"It's not just me. It's the living-donor team. They're amazing to work with. Anyway, I'll ask Jessica if she can block the operating schedule for the case next week. Will that be okay?"

Dr. Daniels looked up for a minute. "That should work with my schedule. Thanks for all your hard work, Sarah, and thank your team, too."

"Thanks, Dr. Daniels. I'll tell them. It means a great deal to them when you surgeons say thank you. Also, I'm going to be leaving early today. I'm flying to Miami for about five days."

Dr. Bower glanced over at Sarah. "What for?"

"I'm meeting my friend, Jackie—the one you met at the gala. We're taking a little vacation."

"My wife and Amanda are heading down there, too. Some big-time clothing designer is debuting his spring line. Maybe you should call the girls and have lunch." Dr. Bower started to chuckle under his mask.

"Really funny, Dr. Bower. Anyway, I'll be back next week. Do you need anything from me before I leave? The other coordinators have everything under control, as usual."

Dr. Daniels cleared her throat. "I need you both to stop talking so Dr. Bower can give the patient and me his full attention."

"I'm sorry for the interruption," Sarah said, and left the operating room. When she got back to her office, she had a voice mail from Jackie. She hit the LISTEN button. "Hey, Sarah, barely got my permission slip signed by Laura after a pretty hairy fight last night. I tried to butter her up with a homemade meal, but it didn't work. Anyway, she actually knows who Amanda Stein is and said we shouldn't mess with her. I got Wyatt taken care of, and I even got ahold of my friend Sandy who has a private investigation firm. I'm picking up a few items we can use when we're doing our undercover work in Miami. This is Detective Jackie Larsen, signing off. See you at the airport tonight."

Sarah laughed as she hung up. She would call Jackie back when she got home and firm up the rest of the details.

Chapter 18

Jackie and Sarah took the red-eye so they could arrive in Miami before Amanda and her entourage. They were both so tired that they slept the entire flight. The landing woke Jackie up. She looked over at her pal in the window seat; Sarah's head was leaning against the window, and a nice, long glob of drool hung from the corner of her mouth.

"Hey, Golden, we're here." Jackie nudged Sarah's arm. Sarah opened her eyes and glared at Jackie.

"Nice drool."

"Shut up. You're nothing to look at, either." Sarah took a tissue from her coat pocket and wiped off her mouth and chin.

Once they had picked up their rental SUV, Jackie said, "Let's get over to the terminal where the private planes arrive." She drove to the designated area and parked. She left Sarah in the SUV and went inside the waiting area, where the gate attendant told her the next private jet would arrive in an hour. She bought two coffees and took them back to the car to wait.

"So, what's the plan here?" she asked Sarah. "Do we know why we're following them and what we're going to do if we do find them doing something illegal? It's not like I'm carrying a piece."

"I think we just have to take a little at a time. I do think something's up with Amanda and Sergio and the directed Cuban donor. I'm just not sure what. I wish Bower's wife wasn't with this crew. I really don't like her, but I'd hate for this to blow back on Bower. Let's follow them to their hotel and then see where they go from there." Sarah rolled the window down and saw the plane pulling up to the terminal. "Here we go."

Sergio got out first, followed by Amanda and Kristin, all dressed up in chic clothes and high heels. A black limo was waiting for them, and they got in and drove away.

Jackie followed them at a distance to the Four Seasons. Amanda and Kristin got out, and Sergio gave Amanda a long kiss and then got back into the limo.

"Let's follow him. They probably have to get their hair fixed—it got a little messed up on the plane. Such a tough flight for them," Sarah said.

Jackie followed the limo onto the freeway. Thirty minutes later, it pulled up in front of a simple, one-story house. The neighborhood was a little rough; some of the houses had black iron bars covering their front doors.

A young, pretty Latina woman came outside and ran to the car to meet Sergio. They stood there and kissed for a while, and then two older people who looked like the girl's parents came out and hugged Sergio.

"Looks like Romeo has another girlfriend. Did you notice the fancy diamond on her hand?" Sarah was looking through the small binoculars Jackie had borrowed from her friend Sandy, who ran a private investigation firm. Sandy had also given them the names of some websites where they could find information to help with their search.

"Now we're getting somewhere. Can you read the address on their house? I want to look it up and get their name," Jackie said.

"It's twelve thirty-two. Street name is Roscoe," Sarah said, as she tried to zoom in with the binoculars to see into the front window. "Lots of hugging going on inside in the living room. They all seem friendly, and his girlfriend looks like Jennifer Lopez, but I'm not sure why Sergio would be spending time with these people. He's definitely way above their pay grade."

Jackie used her phone to search the address. "The name is Jose Chavez. Married to Luisa. States here they have two children, Maria and Marco. They're from Cuba. Maybe we should go introduce ourselves and see if they can make any recommendations for our Cuba trip."

"Wouldn't Sergio just shit if I walked up to the door right now?" Sarah said. "I'd love to see the look on his face."

Sarah and Jackie sat in the car for over an hour. Jackie kept looking up their names and soon found an obituary on Marco Chavez. She read it aloud to Sarah: "Marco Chavez died on August eighth this year. He was a victim of a gang fight and died of a gunshot wound to the head. The family donated his organs for transplant, and he was laid to rest. I think we got our Cuban liver donor, Sarah."

"Wow. I can't believe it. Now we have to figure out how and why Sergio is with this girl. Let's go back to the Four Seasons and see what the girls are up to."

"Good idea. I also want you to explain what this directed-donor thing is, exactly. I only know what a deceased donor and a living donor are," Jackie said, as she started driving back toward the hotel.

"A directed donor is when the family of the deceased donor knows someone who is on the list, waiting for an organ. The family can specify, when they make the donation, that the organ be given to that person, if it's the right blood type and fit. The transplant center where the recipient is listed has to give the organ to that patient. If for some reason it's not a good match, then it gets allocated according to the clinical rules all transplant programs are mandated to follow."

"So Jose and Luisa would have had to specify that the liver go to Amanda, then, right?"

Sarah shook her head. "Yup, which is pretty weird, since the Chavezes are not the type of people Amanda would ever associated with. It certainly explains the comments I overheard when I was taking care of her in the hospital, though. Clearly, our Sergio has himself a Cuban fiancée."

Jackie parked the car behind the hotel, and they both went inside. Jackie picked up the house phone and said, "Amanda Stein's room, please." Jackie heard the phone ringing, but she hung up when no one answered.

"They're not in their room. I bet they're at the spa. Why don't you stay here in the lobby, and I'll go look for them there? They won't recognize me," Jackie said to Sarah, and walked toward the elevators.

When she arrived on the spa floor, she strode up to the reception desk and said, "Hi, I was supposed to meet my friends Amanda Stein and Kristin Gerard here."

"They're receiving their treatments now and can't be disturbed. Would you like to wait in the lounge and have a beverage?"

"No, thanks. What time will they be done? I can come back."

"They just started their treatments and won't be finished for several hours."

"Gee, I won't recognize them by the time they finish. I'll leave a message in their room. What's their room number, again?"

"I'm sorry, we're not able to share that information."

"Thanks anyway." Jackie started to walk away.

Once Jackie got down to the lobby, she saw Sarah holding up a *Town & Country* magazine to cover her face just in case Amanda and Kristin sauntered by.

"Well, your girlfriends are having a big day at the spa, so it looks like we have some time to kill. I say we have dinner at the hotel restaurant and charge it to them. The spa lady wouldn't give me their room number, but if I had to take a wild guess, they're probably in the presidential suite. They probably don't even look at their bill."

Sarah put down the magazine and said, "I'm starving."

They walked to the restaurant and had a sumptuous meal, followed by ice-cream sundaes. As they finished, their waitress approached and Sarah said, "That was excellent."

"Let me take you to dinner tonight," Jackie said. "I'll charge it to my room." She looked up at the waitress. "We're in the presidential suite. Is it okay just to write 'Amanda Stein' and 'presidential suite'?"

The waitress nodded and said, "That would be fine, Ms. Stein."

Jackie added a nice fat tip and signed the bill. As they were entering the lobby, they saw Amanda and Kristin heading out the front door and getting into a town car.

Jackie looked at Sarah and said, "Let's hop into the car and follow them. Do you have any idea where they're going?"

"They both look like they're dressed for a night on the town. Amanda has her appointment tomorrow, so hopefully they won't stay out too late." Sarah closed the passenger door just as Jackie put the SUV in gear.

Chapter 19

Sergio woke up early in Maria's parents' guest room. He called Amanda's cell again, but there was still no answer. He had called her right before he'd gone to sleep, at three in the morning, after he and Maria had enjoyed some gentle cuddling. Where the hell could she be? Today was a big day. She was going for her clinic appointment and then to meet Maria's family for the first time. Sergio wasn't going to tell her about the party Maria's family had planned. He was simply going to say that they were going to Maria's house after Amanda's clinic visit because Maria's parents couldn't face going to the hospital so soon after Marco's death.

Sergio's car picked him up and dropped him at the Four Seasons, and he went upstairs to the presidential suite. When the three of them traveled together, they always got a suite with two separate bedrooms. That way, Amanda and Kristin could stay up late and Sergio could go to bed. He opened the door, and the common living room looked as if no one had been there. Amanda's four-inch heels were outside the bedroom door, so he knew where she was sleeping.

Sergio walked in and found Amanda naked in bed with a tall Cuban man. She heard him walk in and sat up in bed, her large, firm breasts showing. "I understand why you like your Cuban girlfriend so much. I brought home a souvenir last night." Amanda started to kiss the man gently, and he didn't even open his eyes, just kissed her back passionately, then rolled on top of her and started to rock back and forth.

Sergio picked up a lamp from the dresser and threw it at the wall. "What the fuck do you think you're doing? Get out of here, now!"

The man jolted out of bed and looked at Sergio and then Amanda. "What is going on here?" he said, in a thick Cuban accent. Sergio noted with dismay that the man was better endowed than he was.

"He's my brother," Amanda shouted, pointing at Sergio.

The Cuban went into the bathroom and closed the door. Sergio heard the shower go on inside.

"What the fuck were you thinking, Amanda? You know we have a big day today—your clinic visit, and then you're meeting Maria's parents to thank them."

"First of all, you didn't come home last night. Why is it okay for you to sleep with your Cuban whore and then come back here and act all holier than thou? Last I checked, we still have an open relationship, so you have no right to say one thing to me. And fuck seeing the parents. I bought them a gift. You give it to them. I don't want a big boo-hoo party and all the emotional shit that comes with it."

Before she could finish, the handsome Cuban came out of the bathroom, fully dressed, and walked over to Amanda. "I'm sorry we angered your brother. I will pick you up tonight at eight." He turned to Sergio and said, "You and your girlfriend are welcome to join us."

Sergio was ready to punch the guy. "Thanks, but we have other plans." He turned his back on Amanda but could see what they were doing in the reflection in the dresser mirror. The Cuban sat on the edge of the bed next to Amanda and gave her a long good-bye kiss. "See you tonight, my Amanda." Then he walked out.

Maria was looking better and better to Sergio. He was so tired of this intense, hot-and-cold relationship with Amanda.

She got up and said, "Kristin and I are going to the Julian Chang runway show. He got us front-row seats. We have to be there at four. So even if I wanted to see the parents, I can't. I will not refuse front-row seats to this fashion show." Amanda went into the bathroom, and Sergio heard her turn on the shower.

Sergio had to keep calm if he was going to pull off this family meeting. He knew how to work Amanda most of the time. He walked into the bathroom and said, over the sounds of the shower, "I'm sorry I yelled at your friend. I'm just nervous; we're almost done with Miami, and I don't want anything to happen. You got your liver, you're healthy, and we have lots of life to live together. Please forgive me." Sergio handed Amanda a towel as she stepped out of the shower.

As she started to dry off, she said, "You can be such an asshole sometimes, Sergio. Remember, we both agreed we can play the field, so you have no right to start yelling at me when you were gone all night, too."

"You're right. You know I will never love anyone the way I love you, don't you?"

"I know."

"I'll order us some room service, and then we'll head to the clinic. Would you like your usual fresh fruit and yogurt?"

"That would be great." Amanda put her robe on.

They finished their breakfast and got dressed. They were watching the morning news in the living room, when Kristin opened their bedroom door a little. "Hi, Sergio. We were naughty last night."

"I can't leave you two alone for five minutes. What am I going to do with the both of you?" he responded. "We're heading to the clinic in a little bit."

"Don't forget, we have to be at the show by four," Amanda said.

"I should be done in here by then." Kristin pointed her finger in the direction of her bedroom and then closed the door. Sergio heard a man's voice, and then Kristin's laughter.

Chapter 20

Sarah and Jackie were eating breakfast near the hospital, looking at all the photos Jackie had taken of Amanda and Kristin the night before, at a Cuban nightclub.

"Can you believe Bower's wife with that guy? They were almost doing it on the dance floor. I got some great pictures of her." Jackie showed Sarah photos on the small camera Sandy had loaned her. "I think I should e-mail them to Bower."

"No, Jackie. This isn't about him. I'm sure he and his wife have some type of agreement. He's always at the hospital. A gal has to get laid every once in a while. Anyway, Amanda and Sergio sure have some weird shit going on with their relationship. She's out grinding some big Cuban, and he's engaged to some naive girl from the suburbs," Sarah said. "Let's pay the bill and get to the hospital. I want to wait in the lobby to watch them come in. Then we'll take a different elevator up to the clinic."

They walked across the street to the new, modern clinic building. "This looks more like a hotel than a clinic. You never told me they were rolling in dough here," Jackie said.

"Oh yeah—some bigwigs donated over seven billion dollars to upgrade the entire campus. There are actually hotel rooms in this building. They discharge the patients from the hospital and have them stay here. It's cheaper, and the doctors make rounds just like they would if they were in the hospital. Great idea," Sarah explained.

As Sarah and Jackie sat in the lobby, Sergio and Amanda walked right by them and entered the elevators.

"You don't have to worry about either of them noticing us; they're too busy looking at themselves in the mirrors to notice anything," Jackie said.

Sarah directed Jackie to the elevators several hallways down, which led them into the back of the clinic. As soon as Sarah walked into the clinic, one of the nurses recognized her and said, "Hey, Sarah, good to see you. Are you back, I hope?"

"No, just visiting with my best friend from nursing school. I wanted to show her your new clinic."

"Well, make yourself at home. As you can see, we're running around like maniacs, as usual."

"Thanks. Follow me, Jackie. I'm going to look up Amanda's record real quick." A transplant fellow was just walking away from one of the computers and hadn't logged out, so Sarah opened up the clinic schedule and double-clicked on Amanda's name. It opened up her chart, and Sarah went to the donor record. She wanted to verify the donor name. Sure enough, it said "Marco Chavez." Sarah jotted a few things on a piece of paper and logged the fellow off.

Next, Sarah showed Jackie the clinic rooms and waiting area. "This is really beautiful," Jackie said. "If you have to see a doctor, better to go somewhere nice, not those old, dirty clinics back at the institute."

Sarah ducked into one of the nurse-practitioners' offices to use her phone. She dialed the organ procurement agency that had recovered Marco's organs.

"Hi, this is Sarah Golden. I'm a nurse over at the Miami

Transplant Institute transplant clinic. I need to talk to your clinical director about a donor."

"Just a minute. I'll transfer you to Van Mock."

"Hello, this is Van."

"Hi, Van. I work at the Miami Transplant Institute transplant clinic, and I need some information on a donor by the name of Marco Chavez. His UNOS donor identification number is 23929182."

"Sure thing. Let me pull up his record. Okay. What do you want to know?"

"Cause of death. Any history you have."

"Cause of death was a gunshot wound to the head. He was a member of a Cuban gang called Westside Boys. He was considered a CDC high-risk donor because he had many tattoos and was known to do drugs and drink. All his tests for HIV and hepatitis C came back negative. He was incarcerated several times for assault and battery. Mother, father, and sister alive. Family stipulated his liver be given to a patient named Amanda Stein, and it was a match. His kidneys and heart were also transplanted. I can e-mail his history," Van offered.

"I'm good, Van. Thanks a lot. You've been very helpful. If I need anything else, I'll call you back. May I have your cell number?" Sarah jotted the number down next to her other notes.

Jackie was waiting in the hall when Sarah came out. "I just saw Amanda and Sergio leaving. I thought they were supposed to meet the donor family today. Did that change?"

"I don't know. Let me ask." Sarah approached the woman behind the front desk and said, "Hi, Jane. I wanted to check on one of your patients, Amanda Stein."

"Hey, Sarah. What do you need to know?"

"She was supposed to meet her donor family today. I thought it was supposed to be here in the clinic, but I think the location may have changed. Can you see if there's a note in the clinic chart?"

Jane clicked open Amanda's clinic chart on the computer. After a few minutes, she looked up at Sarah. "Says here she was supposed to meet them here today. There's an update from the social worker. They're going to the donor family's home. The parents can't bring themselves to come to the hospital. That's odd."

"I'll say. Thanks for checking, Jane."

"Sure thing."

Jackie and Sarah headed down the elevators and stopped when they saw Amanda and Sergio in front of a black town car. They were arguing with each other and shaking their hands in the air. Sergio grabbed Amanda's arm, threw her into the front seat of the car, jumped into the drivers seat and sped away.

Chapter 21

Sergio was going to make Amanda meet Maria's family, and that was that. "Get in the car, Amanda! We're going to stop by Maria's house, and you can say a quick thank-you to them before you go to your fucking fashion show." Sergio hadn't felt this angry in a long time. He usually brushed off her spoiled, rude behavior, but not this time—not in light of all the work Maria's family had put into planning this reception especially for Amanda.

"Fuck you, Sergio. I'm not going anywhere but back to the hotel. Where's the fucking driver?" Amanda was screaming.

Sergio looked around for the driver, who was nowhere to be found. "Get in the car, Amanda. I'll take you back to the hotel." He had no plans to do that, of course; he was going to drive her straight to Maria's house.

"No! I don't trust you!"

Sergio grabbed her arm, took her to the passenger side of the car, threw her in, and slammed the door shut. He ran around to the driver's seat, started the town car, and peeled out of the driveway.

"You hurt me, you asshole. That's going to leave a bruise. Jesus Christ, Sergio."

"Shut up, Amanda." Sergio turned the car onto the side road that led toward Maria's house.

Amanda noticed they were going in the opposite direction of the hotel. "Sergio, I'm not going to Maria's, and that's final. Turn the car around and take me back to the hotel!" she screamed again.

Sergio pressed down on the gas pedal, and the car lurched forward. As they approached a stop sign, Amanda leaned over, grabbed the steering wheel, and yelled, "Stop right now!"

Sergio made a quick stop, pushed Amanda's arm away from the wheel, and started to accelerate again. He stared forward, tuning Amanda's screaming out.

Amanda leaned over and grabbed the steering wheel again, forcing the car into oncoming traffic and toward a building on the other side of the road.

Sergio barely managed to slam on the brakes to avoid a full-on collision with the brick warehouse in front of them. "Holy shit!" he yelled, as the car slowed but still hit the building. Amanda didn't have a seat belt on, and her head slammed into the windshield, causing it to crack. Sergio's airbag exploded in his face and stunned him.

He gazed out of his window and saw onlookers staring; someone was making a call on a cell phone. Then he looked over at Amanda; she was unconscious, and blood was running from her forehead where she'd hit the windshield.

"Oh my God!" Sergio screamed. He opened his door and looked at the gawkers. "Someone call 911! Amanda, can you hear me? Amanda?" She didn't respond.

Sergio heard the loud sound of sirens coming closer, then saw two red ambulances pull into the parking lot. Paramedics jumped out and approached the car; one opened Amanda's side and started to check her pulse and respirations; the other opened Sergio's car door wider and checked his vitals.

"Is she alive?" Sergio asked the paramedics, as they began to move her onto a gurney and transfer her to the back of the ambulance.

"She is alive, sir, but she's going to need immediate medical attention."

"She had a liver transplant just over a month ago at Miami Transplant Institute." Sergio blurted out, and then started to throw up uncontrollably.

Sergio could hardly think, his head hurt so much, and he got dizzy when they moved him to the stretcher. Once they had him inside the ambulance, they started an IV in his arm. Then the paramedics took his wallet and pulled out his identification.

The rest of the ride, Sergio lapsed in and out of consciousness. "Where's Amanda? Is she okay?" he mumbled to the paramedics.

"We're taking you and your friend right to the emergency room at the Miami Transplant Institute. Just relax, sir. We'll have you there in a few minutes."

They rolled Sergio into one of the emergency room stalls, and a nurse and a doctor came to assess his condition. Then the paramedics transferred him to the ER cart. Sergio could hear a paramedic telling the nurse about him but couldn't make out what the man was saying. The ER doctor examined Sergio's head, and the nurse began to take off his clothes as the doctor pushed on his abdomen.

"Ouch. That really hurts," Sergio moaned.

"I think you have a couple broken ribs, my friend. We're going to do a CT scan to see if you have any internal bleeding, as soon as we get you settled. Are you in pain?" the young ER doctor asked.

"Yes." Sergio pointed toward his head and chest. It hurt to move his arm. "My head hurts a lot."

The nurse looked at him and asked, "On a scale of one to ten, ten being the worst, where would you say you are?"

"Twelve," Sergio said softly. It hurt him even to speak.

"We'll get you something for pain as soon as we complete your CT scan, Sergio. If there's any bleeding, we'll need to take you to the operating room, so we need to hold on a little while longer."

Sergio slowly nodded his head to let them know he understood. If he was this bad, he wondered how Amanda was.

The transfer guy wheeled Sergio into the CT room and then back. The doctor came in and said, "No internal bleeding, thankfully. You have a pretty bad concussion, though, so we're going to keep you overnight to observe you. We'll get you something for pain. Are you allergic to anything?"

"No." Sergio saw the nurse come in with a syringe and push some clear fluid into his IV. He instantly felt both relieved and very spacey. "Wow, what's that?" he asked.

"That's Dilaudid. It should help you feel a little better. I'm giving you something for your upset stomach, too," the nurse said.

"Where's my friend? They brought her in at the same time. Her name is Amanda Stein."

"We're not able to disclose any information about her medical condition, but I can tell you she's being admitted up on the transplant floor."

"What floor am I going to?" Sergio asked.

"You're going to our neurology floor. It's several floors above the transplant floor. We're going to transfer you in a little bit. You should rest now and close your eyes. You were in a bad accident." The nurse pulled Sergio's covers up to his chest and positioned his pillow under his head.

"Is there anyone we can call for you?" the nurse asked, as she got ready to leave.

"Yes. My fiancée, Maria Chavez." He gave her Maria's number.

The nurse jotted down the number and said she would call Maria and tell her what floor Sergio was going to, so Maria could meet him there.

"Thanks. Tell her I'm okay, so she doesn't worry. And tell her I'm sorry about missing the party."

"I'll let you tell her when you see her. With your permission, I will let her know you are stable and are being transferred."

"Okay," Sergio mumbled, as he felt himself dozing off.

Chapter 22

Jackie and Sarah had followed Sergio's car when he'd sped out of the hospital driveway. They could tell he was heading back in the direction of Maria's house, since they had been there already. Jackie had trouble keeping up with Sergio, as he was driving extremely fast. When she saw Amanda in the front seat, grabbing the steering wheel, she knew this would not end well.

Jackie had to slow down quickly as the town car swerved, skidded across the opposite lane, and crashed into a building.

"Oh my God!" Sarah shrieked. "What the hell?"

Jackie parked the car far away enough that they could see the whole scene but not draw any attention to themselves. The ambulances came in a matter of minutes.

Jackie stared in disbelief. "I totally didn't see this coming."

"I bet they were fighting. This is bad," Sarah said.

Jackie saw them take Amanda out and put her on a stretcher and then transfer Sergio to another ambulance. Both ambulances pulled out of the parking lot, sirens blaring. The crashed town car stayed in the parking lot, where the local police were putting up yellow crime tape.

"I think we should get out of here and go over to Maria's house," Sarah said.

"What's your plan, Golden? I don't want to get into any trouble with the police down here," Jackie said.

"I'll tell them that we're from the procurement agency. I can wing it from there."

"Sounds good enough. I'm sure you'll think on your feet. You always do. Even though I don't like either one of them, I do hope those two are okay. Amanda really didn't look too good."

Jackie continued driving, and as they pulled up in front of Maria's house, they saw lots of parked cars and what looked like a party going on. Jackie found a parking place around the block, and they made their way to the house. The front door was open. Sarah rang the bell, and Maria came out.

"Yes, can I help you?" Maria said. She was all dressed up and looked even prettier up close. Laughter and Cuban music came from inside the house.

"My name is Sarah Golden. I work with the procurement agency where your brother was a donor. This is my colleague Jackie Larsen." Sarah held out her hand to Maria.

Maria shook her hand. "You just missed the social worker from your agency. She was supposed to introduce the recipient to our family. They were supposed to be here over two hours ago."

"Who was supposed to be here?" Sarah asked.

"My fiancé and his sister. His sister was the recipient of my brother's liver. Please, please, come in." Maria motioned with an outstretched arm.

Sarah and Jackie followed Maria to the living room and sat on the couch. There were lots of people in the backyard.

"It will be a little quieter in here, though not much. Now, what can I help you with?" Maria sat in a chair across from Jackie and Sarah.

"I'm sorry I missed the social worker. I wanted to get some background from you about how your brother happened to be a directed donor for your fiancé's sister. There wasn't much in his record," Sarah said.

"I'm a little worried about both of them. We planned a small party to welcome Amanda into our family. My parents really wanted to meet her. They also wanted to get some closure on the loss of my brother before the wedding," Maria said.

"Wedding?" Sarah asked.

"Yes, Sergio and I are getting married in a month, here in Miami. We are so excited. Everything is happening so fast."

Chapter 23

Sergio waited until his hospital room's door closed before he called Amanda's room. The rather rotund woman from the procurement agency had been interrogating him for over an hour about how he had come to know Maria and her brother. She'd said it was a normal line of questioning, but Sergio was concerned that somehow, someone was going to figure out he was directly involved in having had Maria's brother killed. He had taken extreme care to cover his tracks every step of the way, but the drugs were making him paranoid.

When Amanda answered, he said, "Hey, babe. I'm so sorry I got angry and you got hurt. How are you feeling?"

She sounded drugged as she mumbled, "Sergio, I'm sitting with Kristin right now and can't talk. They just gave me something for pain, and I'm waiting to see what my liver lab values are. Hopefully, everything is going to be normal. I did suffer a contusion to my liver from the accident. Can you call me later?"

"No, I can't call you back, because we're going to have to get out of this hospital, fast. The procurement agency woman asked very specific questions about how long I've known Maria and how it is that I live in San Francisco and also in Miami. She thought it was very peculiar that I was in town when Maria's brother was shot, and she was very curious about how you got his liver."

"That's concerning, but you need to stay calm. How about I call you back later? If my lab values are normal, Kristin and I are going to take a flight back home tonight."

"As long as it's not too late. Just answer yes or no: Do you agree we need to get away somewhere for a while, maybe your friend in Chicago's place?"

"I agree one hundred percent, honey. Now, take a pain pill and get some rest. Kristin sends you her love."

"Call me as soon as Kristin leaves. I'll ask for something for pain." He clicked off his cell and hit his call bell.

The nurse came and gave him a pill and informed him that if he had a quiet night, he could go home in the morning. He would need to stay nearby for a follow-up clinic appointment in a couple days.

Sergio got up to go to the bathroom and studied his bruised face in the mirror. He cringed when he saw his less-than-perfect reflection. Both of his eyes were black and blue from the explosive airbag. He gently touched both sides of his nose and was glad it wasn't broken. His chest still ached from the impact, though.

How long is this going to take to heal? he wondered. He kept running all the questions the fat lady from the procurement agency had asked; he thought she'd said her name was Jackie something. She wanted to know exactly when he'd moved to Miami, where he'd met Maria, how he knew Maria's brother, and whether he knew the name of the gang Marco had belonged to. She seemed to study his face intently when she asked each question. She was even bold enough to say that Sergio didn't seem like the marrying type when she congratulated him on his upcoming wedding. How the fuck would she know about the wedding and what type of guy he was? She had just met him.

He went back to bed and had just started to fall asleep when Maria and her parents came in.

"Oh my God! Look at your face. You poor thing. How are you feeling, honey?" Maria kissed Sergio's head and held his hand. "My parents made you a special Cuban dish and brought it for you. Are you hungry?" She kept rubbing his head.

"I just got something for pain. I'm not feeling real hungry right now." He nodded toward her parents, who were standing at the bottom of his bed, staring at him. "Thanks for coming, Jose and Luisa. And thanks for bringing food. That was very kind of you."

"You look bad, son," Jose said, studying his face intently. "Are you in a lot of pain?"

"Not so much now. The pain medication is starting to work."

"You poor man. How is your sister?" Luisa asked.

"She has a contusion on her liver and is suffering a fair amount. She's waiting to hear how her liver lab results are."

"We brought her a special Cuban soup. We'll take it down to her so you and Maria can have some private time." Luisa started to walk toward the door.

"Oh, no! Her doctor has her on strict orders to rest." Sergio realized he had raised his voice and needed to take it down a notch. "It was so thoughtful of you, really, but it's not a good time to see her. She was so disappointed not to get to meet you both. I think we should wait until she's discharged, and then we can all go out for a quiet dinner. How does that sound?"

"I understand, Sergio. This terrible car accident has been tough for everyone. We sent all the family home from the party. Thankfully, they sent two lovely ladies from the procurement agency to talk to us," Jose said.

Sergio sat up straighter in bed. "Two ladies came to your home today? Was one of them short and fat?"

"Yes, one was tall and thin, and one was short and fat. They were very nice. They started asking us about you and how you came to know our family. They congratulated us on the wedding. It was so fortunate that your sister got Marco's liver. They said there aren't many directed donors these days where everything matches. I forget—exactly where *did* you meet Maria?" Luisa said.

"We met in the café of her building. She was having lunch, and I had a business meeting that was running late, so I stopped for a cup of coffee. Once I saw her beautiful face and smile, I knew I had to meet her."

Maria bent over Sergio and kissed him on his cheek. "I love you," she whispered in his ear.

Sergio saw Maria's parents scrutinizing them as he said, "I love you, too."

The nurse came into the room to check Sergio's vital signs. She put two small ice packs on his bedside and said, "Everything looks good, and the pain medication seems to be working. You'll need to keep the ice gently over your eyes; it will help the swelling go down. The doctor wrote orders for you to go home tomorrow. Do you have somewhere to stay?" she asked.

"He will be staying at our home," Jose declared.

Sergio wasn't going to debate him, even though he planned on leaving the hospital that night and heading directly to the airport with Amanda. There were entirely too many questions floating around from those procurement agency people. If he and Amanda were gone, no one could ask anything else.

After the nurse left, Sergio decided he really needed Maria and her parents to go, too. He was feeling very anxious and needed to secure airline tickets to Chicago. He pretended to fall asleep and waited for them to notice. Shortly, he heard Luisa whisper to Jose, "We'd better let him get some rest."

Sergio opened his eyes slightly and said, "I'm so sorry. I guess I'm more tired than I thought."

Maria was rubbing Sergio's head. "My parents are going to leave. They'll see you tomorrow when I bring you home." Maria and Jose gave Sergio a little wave good-bye and left the room.

"I'm going to stay until they throw me out," Maria declared.

"I think you should go home and get some rest, too, honey. Tomorrow's going to be a long day."

"No. I'm your fiancée, and I want to be sure they take good care of my future husband."

Sergio sighed deeply and closed his eyes. He decided he'd wait a little while before he asked her to leave again. This would probably be the last time he was with her, now that he and Amanda were going to disappear in Chicago for a while. "Why don't you turn on the TV?" he said.

Maria did as he asked, then moved her chair right next to the head of his bed and started to rub his arm gently. "I am so sorry this happened, my love, but I'm relieved that you're okay. I don't want anything bad ever to happen to you again." Maria leaned over to give him a long kiss.

Sergio put his hand on her head and drew her into him, kissing her back passionately. *If only these were different times and I were a different person*, he thought. Maria had no way of knowing that once she left the hospital, she would never see or touch Sergio again.

Chapter 24

Jackie left Sergio's hospital room feeling seriously concerned about Maria and her brother. She kept playing the conversation with Sergio over and over in her head. He was clearly hiding something. The more questions Jackie had asked him about his relationship with Maria and her brother, the more agitated he'd become. And he hadn't given her any straight answers.

Sarah was waiting for her outside in the hospital parking lot. "How did it go?" she asked.

Jackie got in the driver's seat. "The guy is a major asshole. I pushed him hard on how he met Maria's brother, Marco, but he kept telling me he couldn't quite remember and brushed it off, blaming the drugs they were giving him for his pain. When I asked him about his sister, Amanda, getting Marco's liver so soon after he and Maria met, he shook his head and said what a miracle it was."

"Did he even flinch when you talked about Amanda? Did you ask him if she was really his sister?" Sarah pushed.

"Didn't even blink once. This guy is a professional liar. I have to admit, even with his bruising, he's easy on the eyes, so it's hard not to get caught up in his pretty-boy, innocent act.

I didn't want to push him too hard on Amanda. If he knows we're onto him, he may well disappear."

Sarah looked over at Jackie and said, "Let's go over to the procurement agency and get the records on Marco to see if there's anything in there that could help us understand this situation better."

"Sounds good. Just point me in the right direction." Jackie started the car while Sarah punched the address of the agency into the GPS. "I know several of the folks at the agency; we worked closely with them when I worked here. There should be no problem getting a copy of Marco's donor files."

Jackie found the office building and parked. "This doesn't look like a hospital kind of place. Do they have organs inside?"

"This is where the offices of all the staff are, but they don't bring the organs here; they take them or ship them to whatever transplant center is going to transplant them. They have to find cheap office space—helps keep the price of organs down.

"Listen, how about you relax here, and I'll go in and get whatever I can on Marco? It shouldn't take me long." Sarah opened the car door.

"Sounds like a plan."

While Sarah went inside, Jackie took some time to call home and check on Wyatt, who was staying with his best friend. No one was home, so she left a message and checked her e-mail on her iPhone. Nothing big—all things she could tend to when she got home. Within a few minutes, she looked up and saw Sarah coming toward the car, with an eight-by-eleven-inch envelope under her arm.

"Score. They were totally cool; they remembered me from before and made me a copy of Marco's chart." Sarah opened the envelope and handed some of the contents to Jackie, and they both started to read.

After ten minutes, Sarah spoke up: "Looks like he was

in a gang fight at some sketch bar. There's a police report that describes these two gangs, Latin Kings and Westside Boys, who are arch rivals. Seems there were lots of shots fired but only Marco was killed. Says here that no one else was injured, which is hard to believe. When the officers got there, all they found was Marco lying on the floor of the bar and paramedics, who had already started to resuscitate him."

"Does it say how many bullets he took or where he was shot?" Jackie asked.

"Just one bullet to the head. No other injuries. Of course, according to the bartender, he didn't see a thing—he was in the back room, doing stock. Came out when he heard the shooting and called 911."

"Typical—no one knows anything," Jackie said.

"It looks like both his kidneys, plus his liver, heart, and corneas, were transplanted, according to this, and most of the recipients were local, except for our lovely Amanda Stein," Jackie read from her paperwork.

"I think we need to go to the police department and see if the officer on this record is around and can talk to us about this case. It's worth a try," Sarah suggested.

"What do you think he can tell us that we don't know?" Jackie asked.

"I'm not really sure. I'm just curious how much of a badass this Marco was. To hear his parents paint the picture, he wasn't a hard-core gang member, so it doesn't make sense that he would have been involved in this intense of a shootout. But, you know, the parents are usually the last to know." Sarah entered the address of the station written on top of the police report into the GPS.

Jackie handed the paperwork to Sarah, and they drove toward the police station, which was clearly in a bad part of town. As they passed through the neighborhoods, they saw black metal bars on all the houses and corner stores. Some of the houses were partially burned down, and on a few corners, drug deals were under way in broad daylight.

"Good thing we're close to the police department—we can run the stop signs if any of the dealers try to stop us," Jackie said.

Jackie pulled up and parked right in front of the station. Both Jackie and Sarah went inside and asked for Officer Clark at the front desk. A short, wide policewoman, whose name tag read OFFICER TULLENS, looked up at them. "What would you like Officer Clark for?"

"We're from the organ procurement agency, and we wanted to ask him about one of his cases, which became a multiple-organ donor," Sarah said.

"He's off today. If you want to write down your name and number, I'll leave it on his desk." She picked up the phone, which had been ringing the whole time they'd stood there. "Officer Tullens, precinct twenty." There was silence, and then she transferred the call to the back room.

"Officer Tullens, when will Officer Clark be back at work?" Jackie asked, leaning toward her.

"Please step back, ma'am. No one is allowed behind the counter. I can't tell you when he'll be back. I will leave him your note. I really need to take these other calls."

She picked up another line and started to talk to the caller.

Jackie could hear parts of the one-sided conversation, and leaned over to Sarah. "Sounds like domestic violence to me."

Detective Officer Tullens looked at both of them with a mean, pissed-off expression on her small, squished face and said, "You two need to leave now. This is official police business. It's none of your affair."

Jackie nodded then backed away and started for the

door. Sarah finished writing her note and handed it to Officer Tullens. "Sorry about that—my friend is a little touched in the head. Thank you."

As they walked down the steps to the SUV, Sarah punched Jackie in the arm. "Are you crazy? We don't want to piss off the local police; we need them to like us."

"Oh, lighten up, Golden. I was just having a little fun." As they got back in the SUV and Jackie started driving back the way they had come, she said, "Let's go back to our motel and relax, maybe watch a good movie on TV. What do you say?"

"I think we should go back to the hospital and see if we can squeeze anything else out of Sergio and *then* go back to the motel," Sarah said.

Jackie nodded and typed the address into the GPS. When they arrived at the hospital, they went up to Sergio's floor. Sarah waited near the elevators while Jackie went to Sergio's room. She found his bed empty, but a nurse was there, charting on the computer.

"Excuse me. Is Mr. Torres here?" Jackie asked.

"Unfortunately, you just missed him. He signed out against medical advice; he said he had an emergency at home and needed to leave. Are you related to him?"

"No, I'm not related, thank God. I know his fiancée. He didn't leave a forwarding address, did he?"

"If he did, I couldn't give it to you. Please excuse me—I have another patient who needs to be admitted." The nurse walked past Jackie and out of the room.

Jackie found Sarah near the elevators and said, "He skipped town. Signed himself out against medical advice. I can tell you his nurse is pissed. We must have pushed some buttons."

"Shit. I'm going up to the transplant floor to see if Amanda is still here," Sarah said, as she hit the elevator button.

On the transplant floor, Sarah checked the patient board and found Amanda's name and room number. She headed down the hall, Jackie following, and entered Amanda's room.

"Hello, Ms. Stein. I don't know if you remember me, but I was your nurse right after your liver transplant."

Jackie watched as Amanda looked Sarah over with a dismissive scowl. "So? What are you doing here? Don't you work for Dr. Bower in San Francisco?"

Sarah ignored Amanda's question and said, "I came to ask you about your brother, Sergio. Are you aware that he signed himself out AMA, against medical advice?"

Jackie watched Amanda's reaction; her face dropped, and she squinted. "What my brother does is none of your fucking business. Please leave my room immediately, or I'll call the nurse and ask her to call security."

Sarah continued, "We wanted to talk with you about your brother's fiancée, Maria Chavez. It turns out her brother donated his liver to you. Were you aware of that?" Sarah walked to the head of Amanda's bed.

"I have no idea what you're talking about! Please leave now. I will get you fired in two seconds when I get back to San Francisco." Amanda hit her call bell to summon the nurse.

Sarah persisted: "I just think it's so special that your brother's in-laws were able to save your life. What a gift. I gather you and your brother are really close."

Jackie silently applauded Sarah for what a good job she was doing trying to provoke Amanda.

The on-duty nurse walked in and said, "Yes, Ms. Stein. Is there a problem?"

"Yes, these women are harassing me, and I want them escorted out by security, now," Amanda demanded.

The nurse looked at Sarah and must have recognized her immediately, because she winked at Sarah without Amanda's seeing, then said, "I don't think I need to call security. I can escort them out myself. Please follow me, ladies."

Sarah and Jackie trailed the nurse out into the hall, where the nurse asked Sarah, "What was that all about?"

"It was nothing. I asked her about her brother, and she lost it big-time. Turns out he signed out AMA a couple hours ago."

"She is beyond high maintenance, and I'll be glad when she gets discharged—hopefully tomorrow. Listen, stay away from that insane woman. Now, I have to go give a patient some meds. Good to see you, Sarah. Are you coming back to work with us? We miss you."

"Thanks, but I'm not coming back anytime soon. Take care, and say hi to everyone for me," Sarah responded, as she and Jackie headed for the elevator.

Chapter 25

As soon as Sergio settled back into his first-class seat on his direct flight from Miami to Chicago, he waved the flight attendant over. "Bring me a vodka rocks, and keep 'em coming." He eyeballed the cute young blonde up and down and winked at her as she nodded. When she returned with his cocktail, he gently placed his hand on hers and said, "Thanks. Will Chicago be your last leg?"

"How did you know?" She blinked naively.

Sergio drank down the vodka. "Just a wild guess."

"Looks like you have a nasty bump on your head. Are you feeling all right?" She picked up his empty glass.

"Just a little car accident. Not my fault some dumb-ass ran a stop sign. I'm okay, though; thanks for asking." Sergio touched the bandage on his forehead. *Nothing like a sympathetic flight attendant to spoil me. Maybe I can convince her to join my mile-high club. The count is at about fifty, if I recall correctly.*

"If there's anything I can do to make your flight more comfortable, just let me know, Mr. Torres." She went to refill his glass, and Sergio touched her arm. "You can call me Sergio.

Why don't you make the next one a double so you don't have to come back so often?"

"You can call me Dawn." She returned promptly with his refreshed drink and a dinner menu. "I'll be back to take your order after we've leveled off." She winked at him.

This flight is going to be a lot more fun than I anticipated, he thought.

Sergio replayed the fat woman's questions from when he'd been in the hospital. *There's no way she could figure out what I did, but why was she even there in the first place?* He would call Amanda after he arrived in Chicago and see if she knew any more than he did. Poor Maria would need to find another husband, but at least she had a decent ring. She was unlikely to meet a man of her socioeconomic class who could afford a diamond that size. After she got over losing Sergio, she would move on. She was a beautiful gal, a little on the dumb side, but nice, and shouldn't have any problem finding a man.

"Sergio, Sergio. We're getting ready to land. I need you to put your seat in the upright position." Dawn was tapping him on the shoulder and handing him a warm towel to wipe his hands.

"Are you kidding me? I feel like I closed my eyes only a minute ago. We're landing?" He had taken a pain pill before boarding; the combination of the drugs and alcohol must have knocked him out.

"I'm not kidding. You were resting so comfortably, I let you sleep through dinner. I did leave you some fresh nuts to snack on during our descent." Dawn waited while Sergio wiped his hands.

"It was very kind of you to take such good care of me. Thanks for putting this warm blanket over me. Any chance I can repay you and take you out to dinner when we arrive in Chicago? I have a good friend who owns the Goosefoot."

"I've wanted to go to that restaurant for years but have heard it's impossible to get into. I would love to join you for dinner. I'll need to finish work and then head into the city and change."

"Tell you what: I'll arrange a town car to take us to the city. We can drop by your place and then enjoy some fine dining. How does that sound?" Sergio smiled, thinking about how he already knew how his evening was going to start and end.

"Sounds wonderful. I could really use a night out on the town. I live in the Gold Coast." Dawn took a piece of paper out of her pocket, wrote her address and cell number on it, and handed it to Sergio. "Why don't you call my cell when the town car arrives, and I'll meet you after I close out my shift and finish my paperwork? It should take me about thirty minutes after everyone is off the plane."

"Wonderful. I look forward to spending the evening with you, Dawn. I'm glad I fell asleep after all." Sergio put his hand on her arm and gave her the killer smile that he knew melted all the ladies' hearts.

After he deplaned, Sergio went to the private United Airlines club in the terminal and had the concierge arrange a town car for him while he called Maria and had a quick cocktail.

Maria picked up on the first ring. "Sergio. Where in the world are you? I've been worried sick. They said you signed yourself out against medical advice. Are you okay?"

"I'm fine, dear. I just got an emergency business call that I had to deal with, and they were going to discharge me in the morning anyway, so I decided to hop the last direct flight to San Francisco. Listen, I can't talk long, but I'll call you tomorrow. Don't worry—everything is good. We can finish making our wedding plans and get back on track."

"My family is so upset they didn't get to meet Amanda

and had to cancel the party because of your car accident. Those two ladies from the procurement agency came to our house, asking questions about you and Amanda. It's too much. They won't like it that now you're gone all of a sudden, Sergio. When are you coming back? I have to tell them something. They want to go visit Amanda in the hospital tomorrow and take her some flowers."

Sergio tried to ignore the frantic tone in Maria's voice. "Calm down, Maria. Listen to me. First of all, do not talk to those ladies from the procurement agency anymore. If they contact you or your family, tell them to call me directly. And do not, under any circumstances, go see Amanda. She is in isolation and can't have visitors until they stabilize her liver; plus, she's in no mood for guests right now. Let's arrange something after she gets discharged and I'm back. Maybe send her flowers then."

"Sergio, I'm starting to think we'll never get married. I'm scared, I'm pregnant, and now you're gone. I don't know if I can take all this stress."

What a pain in the ass women are, he thought. *I'm so glad this wedding isn't going to happen. Now I just need to figure out what those other two women are up to and disappear for a while.*

"Maria, I'll call you tomorrow. Everything's going to be fine. Believe in me, honey. Have I let you down yet?"

"No. It's just that I'm a little fragile right now. All those questions about my brother's death brought up more sad feelings for me and my parents." She was starting to cry.

"Come on, baby. All of this craziness will be over before you know it. I really have to go now. I promise I'll call you tomorrow after my big business meeting. I love you. Take care." He hung up and dialed Amanda's number.

After a few rings, Amanda picked up her cell. "Hello, Sergio." Her voice was groggy.

"I'm sorry. Did I wake you up, honey?"

"Yeah, it's late here, and they gave me something for pain. The biopsy was painful. Where are you?"

"I just landed in Chicago. I'm going to have dinner and then head to bed myself. I wanted to check in with you to let you know that some fat, short woman from the procurement agency came to my hospital room before I left and was asking me all these questions about Maria's brother and how it was that my sister got his liver. Very persistent." Sergio took a sip of his vodka.

"Not good, Sergio. Her friend stopped by my room and asked me similar questions. Her friend was my nurse after I received my liver transplant and then went to work for Bower at the Transplant Institute in San Francisco. I don't know what the two of them are up to, sticking their noses in our business, but you're going to have to do something."

"What do you mean, 'do something'? There is no way these two bitches could know anything. *No way*," Sergio insisted.

"Well, they know *something*. I had to have that bitch thrown out of my hospital room. She was very pushy, and I threatened to have Bower fire her, but I don't want Bower to know anything about this. You'd better take care of this!" Amanda demanded.

"Okay, I hear you, Amanda. I'll see if I can find someone to scare them enough to mind their own business. I'll hire someone to rough them up if I have to. I'll take care of it." Sergio started tapping his finger on the bar, signaling to the bartender to pour him another drink.

"I don't think we should be in touch for a while—maybe take two weeks, to let things calm down. Why don't you stay with my friend who lives in Chicago?" Amanda offered.

"I'll be okay. I know several people here, so don't worry about that. I think you're right, though—things do need to cool down. I'm going off the grid. I'll contact you in a couple weeks, and hopefully by then all this will be history. In the meantime, feel better and get out of that hospital. I'll be back sleeping next to you before you know it." Sergio stood up and finished his drink.

"That sounds good to me. Take it easy and enjoy Chicago." Amanda hung up.

Sergio's mind was reeling. The concierge handed him a piece of paper with the name of the car service waiting for him outside the airport. "I arranged a chilled bottle of Dom Pérignon for you and your guest, Mr. Torres. It will be in the back of the town car with the crystal glasses you specified."

Sergio took a $50 bill out of his pocket and handed it to her. "Nice work. Thanks."

He walked toward the exit, called Dawn, and left her a brief message about where to meet him. Then he scrolled through his phone and dialed another number.

"Hello. This is Sergio Torres. I need you to take care of something for me immediately." He gave the man all the details and then hung up as Dawn approached.

The driver opened the back door of the limo, and Sergio and Dawn slid inside.

Chapter 26

Sarah woke early and took a long, hot shower while she ran through all the conversations she and Jackie had had with Amanda, Sergio, and the organ procurement agency folks. She hoped Amanda wouldn't call Bower and ask him to fire her. Sarah got the impression from Dr. Bower that if Amanda weren't his wife's best friend, he wouldn't have anything to do with her.

Sarah heard her cell phone ringing. She threw a towel around herself and went to her bedside table to grab it before it woke up Jackie.

"Hello."

"This is Officer Clark. May I please speak with Sarah Golden?"

"This is Sarah Golden."

"I believe you and your friend came by yesterday and wanted to speak with me about a case. You should know that all cases are confidential, so I really can't share any information with you."

Sarah already knew this but needed to figure out how to get him to talk to her anyway. "I work at the transplant program, and I had some questions about one of the gang victims, Marco Chavez. He donated some organs, and our OPO asked me to do some follow-up."

"Ms. Golden, I don't have a lot of time. I'll be here, doing some paperwork, for about another hour, and then I have to leave. If you get here soon, I may be able to give you a few minutes."

"Thank you, Officer Clark. I really appreciate your time. I'll be there in about fifteen minutes."

Sarah hung up and shook Jackie, who was snoring and mumbling in her sleep.

"Jackie, get up. We need to go to the police station now. Come on, get up. Officer Clark just called and said he'd give us a few minutes."

Jackie opened up one eye and squinted at Sarah. "I was having the best dream: we were dancing and drinking rum in Cuba."

"You can tell me in the car. Come on—we'll get coffee after we see the cop."

Jackie sluggishly got out of bed and went into the bathroom. She came out as Sarah was opening the motel door. "Are you going to wait for me or what? You know I don't like hurrying in the morning, and no coffee? This is just wrong."

Sarah threw Jackie's coat at her. "Come *on*, sleepyhead. We have to make tracks."

Jackie followed Sarah to the SUV, and Sarah started up the engine and drove straight to the police station. They walked into the precinct, and Sarah approached the desk; thankfully, Officer Tullens was not on duty.

"Hi, I'm here to see Officer Clark. I have an appointment with him. My name is Sarah Golden."

The gray-haired officer slowly glanced up at Sarah. "Take a seat, and I'll let him know you're here." While Sarah sat, he picked up the desk phone and said, "Clark, you have some guests out here. Do you want me to send them back?"

The officer hung up the phone and said nothing to Sarah or Jackie. Sarah had just gotten up to ask what was going on, when an extremely handsome officer came out from behind the door. Sarah checked him out from head to toe quickly and took a deep breath. "Wow, we need to meet more police officers in Miami if they all look like this," she said to Jackie out of the corner of her mouth.

The officer walked right up to Sarah and said, "I'm Officer Clark. How may I help you?" He held out his hand to shake Sarah's.

Sarah took a gulp and extended her hand. "Nice to meet you, Officer Clark. I'm Sarah Golden, and this is my friend Jackie Larsen. Is there somewhere we can have a few words in private?" Sarah looked into his big brown eyes and thought, *After we talk, maybe you can come back to my motel, handcuff me to my bed, and make me confess.*

"Like I told you on the phone, I don't have much time. Follow me." Officer Clark turned toward the desk cop and said, "I'm going to use room twenty-four for about ten minutes. Kick me out if you need it."

The desk cop nodded, and Officer Clark led Sarah and Jackie to a small, barren room with three chairs and a gray metal table inside. He sat across from both of them and asked, "What can I do for you?"

It was all Sarah could do to concentrate; Officer Clark's bulging biceps stretched his police uniform sleeves, and she could almost see his abdominal six-pack through his clothes. His dark skin tone made her think he either was Latino or spent all his downtime in the sun. But she had to get serious, so she forced herself to concentrate.

She began, "We have a man named Marco Chavez who

was a liver donor about five weeks ago. I understand from the paperwork at the procurement agency that he was a gang member and was involved in some kind of fight in a bar and was shot in the head, which rendered him brain-dead. His family subsequently agreed for him to be an organ donor. Both his kidneys and his liver were used locally, at the Miami Transplant Institute, and his heart was transplanted in New York. I was wondering if you could tell us anything about this gang he was a member of. We've already spoken to his family, and they've been most cooperative." Sarah saw Clark's shoulders relax, and he leaned back a little in his chair. She gave him one of her best flirtatious looks and felt Jackie kick her under the table.

"Well, Ms. Golden, I reviewed his case before you came. I'm wondering why you need any more information on the circumstances surrounding his death. I always thought once you folks got your organs, you didn't care what happened. Don't get me wrong, my brother's wife got a kidney transplant, so I'm a believer in organ donation and all, but. . ." As he waited for her to respond, he took off his police hat, and his thick, curly black hair made Sarah smile.

"You have a beautiful head of hair," she said, before she could stop herself.

Jackie kicked her again under table. "Office Clark, what we'd like to know is whether this case was suspicious at all—anything out of the ordinary. My friend Sarah here seems to have regressed into a teenage girl. Sorry about that."

He smiled, showing dimples on both sides of a perfect set of pearly whites that sealed the deal for Sarah. "To answer your questions . . . Jackie, is it? This was a very routine, cut-and-dried case. The gang that Marco belonged to averages at least five to ten murders a year, and rival gangs always seek revenge. I believe Marco was just in the wrong place at the wrong time. This case was closed a week after it happened.

Like I said, unfortunately, we see this activity on a regular basis. Take my card, though, and if you need to call me about anything else, please feel free to contact me." Officer Clark handed each of them a card and stood up.

Sarah and Jackie stood, too, and Sarah extended her hand to shake his again. "And if you ever find yourself coming to San Francisco, please feel free to contact me. I would love to show you around." She took one of her business cards out of her purse and handed it to him.

"I thought you said you worked here, Ms. Golden. You mean I have to fly across the country to take you out on a date?" He winked at her.

"I did work here at the Miami Transplant Institute but just joined the team at the Transplant Institute in San Francisco. So, yes, you'll need to come there." She winked back.

Jackie let out a loud sigh and opened the door of the room. "If you two are done, I think I'll go throw up before I leave." Jackie walked out, and Sarah and Officer Clark followed, laughing. Officer Clark walked them outside to the SUV and asked, "When are you two going back?"

"We're leaving today. I'm really glad we got a chance to talk to you before we left. Looks like there's nothing to worry about here." Sarah hopped into the driver's seat.

"Nope. Like I said, these are typical gang-warfare cases. Safe travels, ladies."

As Sarah drove out of the parking lot, Jackie said, "Are you kidding me or what? I thought you were going to jump that guy. You are something else, sister. You're nothing but a big slut. But good for you that you can nail any guy you want. Now, let's go back and pack up."

"Gee, Jack, thanks for the compliment."

When Sarah parked outside their motel room, she saw a housekeeping cart by their door. "I can see they're in hurry to turn our room around," Jackie said, as she pulled out the room key and went inside, Sarah right behind her.

"Let's throw our stuff in our bags and drive to the airport. We can figure out what we want to do next, if anything," Sarah said.

Before they could close the door, two large men with ski masks over their heads, walked into their room, pulling guns out of their pockets. One of them turned on the TV at top volume, while the other one locked the door from inside and pulled the curtains closed.

"What the fuck!" Jackie yelled out.

"Sit down and shut up, you nosy bitches," one man said, then hit Jackie in the face with the butt of his gun. Blood started to leak from her mouth.

"Stop it right now!" Sarah screamed, and started to get up.

The guy in front of her slapped her hard on the cheek and took the lock off his gun, pointing it at her face. "Shut the fuck up!" he yelled.

The guy in front of Jackie said, "You two stupid bitches have been talking to people you have no business talking to, and you need to stop *now*. Get the fuck out of Miami, and don't ever come back. Do you understand?" When Jackie didn't speak, he repeated, "*Do you understand?*"

"Yes. We do. Please don't hurt us anymore. We'll leave now." Jackie's right eye had swollen shut, and blood was still trickling out of her mouth. Sarah tasted salt from the blood in her own mouth.

The guy in front of Sarah slapped her hard again, this time on her other cheek, and she cried out in pain.

"Please stop. We're leaving for the airport now. Please!" Jackie said.

"You're lucky we don't fuck you both, shoot you in the head, and leave you in a ditch," the man in front of Sarah said.

"And don't get any ideas of going to the cops, or you'll never make it to the airport. We're real good at making people disappear."

They walked out, leaving Jackie and Sarah stunned.

Sarah immediately went over to Jackie. "Oh my God, your poor eye. Are you okay?"

"It hurts like fuck. Let's get the hell out of here and get some ice on the way. I did *not* see that coming." Jackie stood up and looked in the bathroom mirror. "That's nasty—how am I going to explain this one to Laura?"

They quickly grabbed all their stuff and shoved it in their bags. Sarah peeked out to see if the thugs were in the parking lot. "No sign of those motherfuckers. Let's get out of here."

Sarah sped out of the driveway and got on the expressway heading toward the airport. She put her hand to her face, which stung like a million bee stings. "I'm so sorry I got you into this, Jack. I am so sorry."

"This does push the limits, Golden. If you weren't my best friend, I'd be really pissed right now. Clearly, we hit a nerve, big-time."

"I think we should just drop this whole thing, Jackie. No one's life is worth getting in danger for this. You have a wife and a family. I think we call it a day. Fuck Amanda and Sergio. I don't care about this whole insane thing. Game over."

Jackie gently patted Sarah's hand. "It's not your fault, Sarah. I think this must be bigger than we think, and I for one am not going to let those fucking rich people get away with whatever they did."

"We have over four hours before our flight leaves. Let's call Clark and tell him what happened." Sarah pulled off the expressway and into a local coffee shop parking lot.

"Good idea," Jackie said.

When Sarah got off the phone with Clark, she told Jackie,

"He wants to talk to us in person. He said to meet him at some cop bar near the airport. He said no smart crook would go near this bar. Sound good?"

"Sounds great. Let's go meet with him and take it from there. I know someone wants to either kill us or mess us up," Jackie responded.

The bar's parking lot was full of cop cars and motorcycles. When Sarah and Jackie walked in, they saw Clark sitting at a booth, still sporting his uniform.

They walked over and sat across from him.

"Jesus Christ, what the hell happened to you two? Looks like you got hit in the face with the butt of a gun," he said to Jackie. "You need some ice." He got up and went to the bar and came back with a bag of ice. "Put this over your eye."

He reached over and gently touched Sarah's face. "That must sting."

An older waitress approached the booth. "Can I get you girls something?"

"We need a drink," Jackie said. "A big shot of rum for me, and some gin on the rocks for my friend Sarah here."

"Be right back."

When she left, Clark leaned in and said, "Okay, tell me what happened."

Sarah recounted the story. Clark sat back quietly after she was done. Their drinks had come, and Jackie had already downed hers and ordered two more.

"If you had to guess who ordered those guys to rough you up, who would pick?" Clark asked.

Without hesitation, Sarah blurted out, "Sergio Torres." She gave Clark some background on him and Maria.

"Do you have a picture of the guy?"

Jackie took out her phone. "I took some pictures of him at some point. Here he is." She showed Clark the pictures.

"Why don't you send me those photos, and I'll ask around the bar where Marco got shot to see if anyone recognizes him. No promises on this—like I told you, the case is closed. And the chief doesn't reopen cases, so I'm not going there."

Sarah gently touched his hand. "Thanks, Officer Clark. We really appreciate your finding out what you can. Listen, we need to get going to the airport, or we're going to miss our fight."

Jackie turned to Sarah. "I'm not flying home. Laura isn't expecting me for a couple more days. I'm going to stay and go make Maria my best friend and see what I can dig up on Sergio. You go back to work and see what you can get on Amanda."

"There is no way I can leave you down here after what just happened. Did you hear those guys? They threatened to kill us. It's too dangerous, Jackie." Sarah looked to Clark for support.

"She may have a good idea, Sarah," he said. "I can keep an eye on her here, and she can spend more time on this than I can."

Sarah looked at Jackie. "You really think this is a good idea?"

"I do. I will be careful and stay in close contact with you. Plus, I have Officer Handsome here to protect me. What else do I need?"

Sarah looked back at Jackie. "Okay, but if one more thing, even a tiny thing, happens, promise me you'll get your ass on a plane. Promise!"

"I promise, I promise. You can drop me off at the car rental place when we get to the airport, and then I'll book a room near Maria's house. That way, we can put this to rest. I'm a big girl, and I can't go home with my eye looking like this anyway."

Sarah sighed and said, "Okay. I don't like it, but okay."

Jackie reached over and gave her friend a hug. "It's going to be all right, Golden. Clark, do you know any good bars in Maria's neighborhood? I think they call the area Little Havana. Once I get settled, I'm going out and getting drunk. Better yet, I'll buy a bottle and stay in my room, where I'm safe and sound."

"Better idea, Jackie." Clark's police radio was going off, asking officers to respond to a call nearby. "I have to go. You both have my number. Sarah, you have a safe trip home. Jackie, text me once you know where you're staying."

Chapter 27

After Jackie said good-bye to Sarah at the airport, she returned the big SUV and got a smaller, less expensive car. She checked in to a Motel 6 several blocks from Maria's parents' house, threw her bags in the room, and hit the bathroom. When she saw her reflection in the mirror, she let out a gasp. "Holy shit! I look like I was in a the ring with Muhammad Ali."

She turned the TV on for some background noise, to make people think there was someone in her room, grabbed her coat, and left. Jackie noticed a dive bar, its neon sign flashing TONY's, a couple blocks away and decided she would walk there and make herself at home.

She stepped inside and took in the atmosphere. To the left was a pool table, where two heavyset men were playing and drinking bottled beer. The odor of cigarettes and Lysol washed over her as she approached the bar, where a husky, black-haired woman was washing glasses. She looked up at Jackie. "What can I do you out of today?"

She kept washing the glasses as Jackie stood there, deciding what her poison would be. Finally, Jackie said, "I'll have a double shot of your best rum and a Diet Coke on the side." She settled onto a stool and checked out the three other men sitting there, drinking and staring at the TV hanging in the corner of the bar, playing some basketball game.

The bartender laid out two empty shot glasses and poured Bacardi dark rum up to the top of each one. She scooped ice into a glass, filled it with Diet Coke from the soda gun, and slid all three glasses in front of Jackie. "Here you go. You want some ice for your eye? It's pretty swollen. Doesn't look so good, if you don't mind me saying." Her voice was raspy.

"I just looked at it in the mirror. Not good. I'll take some ice, or a cold steak if you got one." Jackie picked up one shot glass, downed the rum, and chased it with a swig of Diet Coke.

"I'd have to charge for the steak, but the ice is free. If you're hungry, our menu is on the chalkboard over by the pool table."

Jackie slugged down the second shot with another Diet Coke chaser. "I'll take the ice, thanks. I'll check out the menu later. Can you line me up with two more of those shots?"

The bartender grabbed the rum bottle and refilled the shot glasses. Several Latino men came into the bar and sat at the end opposite from where Jackie was. The rum was starting to kick in, and she was feeling better and better with each shot she took; she wanted to be sure to get a nice buzz going before she talked to anyone or ate anything. She sipped her Diet Coke and stared up at the TV, not really caring who was playing.

After about half an hour had passed, she decided to hit the bathroom and check out the menu. When she stood up, she got a little dizzy and had to center herself. "I think I've arrived at my destination—I'm feeling good and relaxed," she told the bartender, as she started to walk toward the back of the bar.

The menu had four things on it: hamburgers, cheeseburgers, french fries, and chili. Jackie decided she'd have a cheeseburger and fries when she got back from the john.

The pool players didn't even look up when she walked by them. *Seems like the type of place where everyone minds their own business,* she thought. *I like that.* When she returned to the bar, she discovered an older Latino man sitting on the stool next to hers. She looked over at him and noticed, to her surprise, that it was Jose, Maria's dad. He seemed deep in thought when she tapped his shoulder. "Why, hello, Mr. Chavez. Nice to see you again."

Mr. Chavez looked at Jackie with furrowed eyebrows, clearly not remembering her. "I'm sorry, I don't think I know you." His voice sounded sad.

"My coworker and I were at your home a couple days ago, meeting with you and your daughter. We're from the procurement agency where your son was a donor."

He gazed down at the floor and then back up at her. "Yes, I remember you. Sorry I didn't recognize you. Looks like you had a bit of an accident. Are you all right?" He sipped his bottle of Budweiser.

"I'm fine, just had a run-in with the corner of the kitchen cabinet. Looks worse than it feels, especially because I'm having my favorite medicine: rum. Can I get you a shot?" She finished off her fourth one.

"You know, I think I will join you. It's been a crazy couple days, and I could use a little pick-me-up. Thank you."

Jackie motioned to the bartender to come over and pour each of them a shot. Mr. Chavez picked his up. "*Salud.*" They clinked their glasses together and swallowed the contents.

Jackie took a sip of her Diet Coke, then said, "I'm sorry you've had a tough time. Anything you'd like to talk about? I hope your wife and Maria are okay."

"They're both fine. It's just that we had planned a nice party for Maria's fiancé's sister, but then they got in an accident. Sergio and Maria are engaged to be married, and the family is most anxious to meet him and Amanda. As you know, she got our Marco's liver. It's all very emotional. Can I get you a shot now?"

"Why, sure. Would you like to join me for dinner? I'm planning to have a cheeseburger."

"I can't stay for dinner, but I'm happy to keep you company for a while. What brings you to this neighborhood?" Mr. Chavez motioned for another pour from the bartender, who obliged.

"I'm staying around the corner at the Motel 6. I have some work I need to do for the procurement agency. I'll only be here for a couple of days." Jackie lifted her shot glass. "Cheers to you, Mr. Chavez. May you see better days soon."

He nodded and said, "Please, call me Jose," before they drank up.

"I'd like a cheeseburger and fries," Jackie said to the bartender. "We're going to move over to that table by the window."

The bartender yelled back to the kitchen, "Cheeseburger and fries."

Once they had settled across from each other at the table, Jose said, "This is my home away from home some days. After Marco died, I spent a little too much time here. It was a very sad day for my family."

"I'm sure it was, Jose. I am so sorry for your loss. How is Maria's fiancé?"

"Sergio. Got a bad bump on his head and a few cuts on his face. He's okay, but he had to leave on an emergency business trip, in the middle of the night, no less. Frightened poor Maria to death. His sister is still in the hospital, but I think she's going home tomorrow, from what Maria told us.

We still haven't met her, and I know it would help my wife to see that Marco's death was not in vain."

"It must be hard for your wife. I hope you can all meet his sister soon. How about another beer?" Jackie was already motioning to the bartender, who was about to bring over her dinner.

The cheeseburger was in a red plastic basket lined with parchment paper, with fries piled high on top of it. Jackie put some ketchup and mayonnaise on the patty and took a big bite.

"Did your son come to this bar with you, Jose?" she asked, as the bartender put their drinks down.

"Oh, no. He hung out at a bar in East Miami, bad part of town, and he ran with a tough crowd. Called themselves the Westside Boys. Once he got mixed up with that group, everything went downhill." Jose took a long sip of his beer and added, "He dropped out of junior college, said it was for losers and he could make more money working for a friend of a friend. He even stopped coming home to sleep."

"That had to be hard. Do you remember the name of that bar?" Jackie asked casually, as she continued to eat her fries.

"It was called the Lost Weekend. It's where he got shot and killed."

They were silent for a bit. Many more patrons were coming in by now, and the bar was becoming loud and crowded.

Jose finally said, "It was a blessing Sergio met Maria when he did. He tried to get Marco away from the bad crowd, but Marco wouldn't listen to him, either. Sergio promised him a job at one of his companies. Marco wouldn't give Sergio the time of day."

"That was nice of Sergio." *At least the asshole did one good thing*, Jackie thought.

"Sergio and Maria were inseparable from the time they met. Thank God she had him when her brother died."

"How long had they known each other?" Jackie asked.

She watched Jose as he calculated the answer. "I think about three months before we lost Marco. If it wasn't for Sergio, we would never even have thought to donate Marco's organs. He had been telling us all about his sister on the liver wait list, and then, thankfully, she was a match with Marco's blood type." Jose picked up his beer glass and clinked it against Jackie's.

"At least something good came out of this sadness. Oh, look who's here." Jose stood up. Jackie's back was facing the bar's door. As she turned around, she saw Maria walking toward them. She was smiling at first, but the expression on Maria's face changed dramatically when she saw that her dad was sitting with Jackie.

Jose went to hug Maria, but she walked past her dad and up to Jackie. "What are you doing here?" she demanded.

"Maria! Don't be so rude. You remember this is one of the women from the procurement agency. What's wrong?" Jose asked. He put his hand on his daughter's shoulder. "Sit down, Mija. Have a glass of wine with us."

"No, Father. We're leaving now. Pay the bill. Sergio said to have nothing to do with this woman or her friend. They are not to be trusted, Dad. Let's go, now. I mean it. If Sergio doesn't trust them, then neither do I."

Jackie stood up. "Please, Maria. We've done nothing wrong. Sit down, and let's talk this out. I don't understand."

"I don't care if you don't understand. My fiancé said not to trust you, and that's enough for me. Now leave me and my family alone."

Maria took her father's arm and walked out of the bar. Jackie was shocked at Maria's reaction to her. Sergio must have told her some big lie. *At least I got the name of the bar where Marco hung out*, she thought. *I'll go there tomorrow.* For now, she would have one last shot of rum and call it a night.

Chapter 28

Sarah was at her desk in the transplant unit when Jackie called her on her cell. "Hey, Jack. How are things at the Motel 6? You having a spa day?"

"Right. I'll be having lunch at the vending machine in the lobby. You can have a lovely meal if you like those peanut butter crackers and Monster energy drinks. I had an interesting evening last night at the dive bar down the street. Excellent burgers and fries, and they have my favorite rum. The bartender and I are best friends already. How about you—did you have any time to do a little background work on our buddy Amanda?"

"I did. Seems like we have ourselves a really wealthy, spoiled brat with no end to her connections. I e-mailed your friend Sandy before my flight took off, and this morning she sent me a whole background document on Amanda Stein. She's been married twice; seems she liked Jewish men up until now. Got a sweet divorce settlement from both of them for the remainder of her life. In addition to that, she made over two million a year when she worked with Cisco and got a really nice severance package when she had to leave because of her liver failure. She also has access to the company's Learjet, which is what she used when she came down for her liver transplant." Sarah realized her office door was open and got up to close it.

"Well, I had an interesting evening talking to Jose, Maria's dad—that is, until Maria walked in and made a scene. That connection is dead now."

"What happened?" Sarah asked.

"I got myself nice and settled in at the bar, had several shots of rum, and then glanced over and saw Jose. He was very kind and rehashed some of the same things he told us about Marco's death. I did get the name of the gang Marco was a member of and the bar where he was shot. I'm planning on going tonight."

"What pissed off Maria? She seemed pretty nice last time we met with her." Sarah took a long sip of her coffee.

"When she saw her dad and me sitting together at a table, she marched up to him and demanded he leave with her immediately. When he asked why, she almost screamed that Sergio told her to stay away from us—that we were nothing but trouble. Jose felt so bad, but he got up and followed her out. He was embarrassed because all these people were staring at us. Maria was practically yelling. You would have thought I was a murderer."

"Wow, that sucks. Good thing you had enough rum on board that you didn't get too humiliated."

"You know me all too well. I'm going to head to the gang bar tonight and see if I can find out anything about Marco and what happened. I called your boyfriend, Officer Handsome, and asked him if he'd meet me there. Said it was no place for any woman to be alone, straight or gay, and he'll meet me there after work."

"Lucky you. I wish I was going with you. This place is

jumping, as usual. We're doing two living-liver transplants this week. Two of the coordinators are at a transplant meeting in Las Vegas, so I'm covering call. I did find out that Sergio and Amanda have been together off and on for over six years. I looked through some more society-page pictures of the two of them with Bower and his wife."

"Speaking of Bower, have you seen him yet?"

Sarah finished her coffee and threw the empty cup in her tiny garbage can. "I haven't seen him since I got back; he's been in surgery. I can't imagine he would let Amanda tell him to do anything. Speaking of Amanda, I think it might be a good idea for you to give her one more visit today before you head off to the bar. See if you can rattle her cage and make her tell you where Sergio went. You up for that?"

"Sure. I can go back to the hospital, as long as she doesn't have me thrown out. It would be a pleasure to piss her off again."

"Just do your best to ruffle her feathers and put her on edge."

"Sounds doable. What are you thinking about this whole Marco thing?"

Sarah took a deep breath. "I think Sergio had something to do with him being a donor, not sure how much or how little. It's too much of a coincidence for him to be down in Miami several months before Amanda gets her liver and falls in love with Maria. Then—voilà—her brother dies and he's the same blood type as Amanda."

Jackie chimed in, "I agree. But these guys are really slick, so I'm not sure if we're going to find anything. But I know we're onto something; otherwise, they wouldn't have sent those asshole thugs. You should see my eye; it's all blue and red. I slept with an ice bag on my face last night—courtesy of the bartender."

Sarah let out a chuckle. "Always making friends—that's

my gal. I'm going to call Maria's mom next and see if I can get her to talk to me. We have to warn them away from Sergio, if that's possible."

"Good luck with that. He's already brainwashed Maria, so hopefully you can get ahold of her mother when Maria's not home."

Sarah's beeper started going off, "Keep me posted, Jackie, and be careful today and tonight. Those gangs are nothing to play with. Give Officer Handsome a big hug and kiss from me."

"I'm not into Officer Handsome, but I'll give him your regards. I'm going for a burrito after we hang up. Got a little bit of a hangover. Let's plan to talk tomorrow."

"You be careful."

"I will. I'm a big girl. Later."

During the next hour, while Sarah met with a couple of surgeons about the kidney-pancreas programs and then answered e-mails, Jackie called her back and left her a voice mail. "Hey, it's me. Went to the hospital and walked into our friend Amanda's room. I asked her where her brother—I mean boyfriend—was, and she immediately turned on her call light. Before I bolted, I looked at her skinny blond ass and told her we knew what they had done and that she'd better watch her back. I did ask her if she was going to be a bridesmaid when Maria and Sergio got married. She threw her water glass at me and told me to get the fuck out of her room or I would be really sorry. That's all I could do before I hightailed it out of there. I walked right past the nurse who was heading to her room. Amanda looked good and pissed. Mission accomplished. I'm meeting Handsome in a couple minutes for an early dinner; he's working the night shift. Call me tomorrow."

Sarah ended the call and looked up Maria's parents' home number. She dialed it, and Maria's mom picked up on the first ring.

"Hi, Luisa. This is Sarah from the procurement agency. We met last week at your home. Do you have a few minutes to talk?"

"I don't mean to be rude, Sarah, but Maria asked that my husband and I have nothing more to do with you. Sergio has forbidden it, and with their marriage and their new baby coming, I think it best we listen to Sergio. I'm so sorry."

"Wait, wait, Luisa. I don't want to take too much of your time. Please just hear me out; then if you still want to hang up, I promise I will never call you again. Please."

Sarah heard a long silence; then Luisa said, "I will listen, but then I really must go. Maria will be home from work, and she has already scolded Jose for meeting with your friend at the bar last night. We don't want any more trouble."

"I understand completely, Luisa. I really do. I'll be quick: Sergio is not Amanda's brother, Luisa. He's Amanda's boy-friend. He only befriended you and your family to somehow get Marco's liver. I know this sounds crazy, but I will send you and Maria some strong evidence to support this. I am so sorry to have to tell you this bad news on the phone. We don't know what Sergio has done, but we know that he's not who he says he is, and you and your family need to know the truth."

"This is crazy talk. How could this be true?" Luisa asked.

"I wish more than anything it wasn't true, Luisa. I really do. I can't even imagine how this news is going to affect your family. I will e-mail you some information; once you see it, please share it with Maria. If either of you wants to call me, we can talk. If not, I will not attempt to contact you again. Does that sound fair?"

"This is sad news if it's true. I will give you the benefit of the doubt. You seemed like a nice girl when we met, and Jose said your friend was very kind to him as well. I think there is just a big misunderstanding here, but I will look at

Amy S. Peele · 191

your e-mail and talk to Maria. I hope for Maria's sake and her baby's sake you are wrong." Luisa gave Sarah her e-mail address and hung up.

Sarah pulled photographs from the information Jackie's friend Sandy had sent her that featured Sergio and Amanda together, along with captions under them. She wrote a simple note that included her cell number and sent everything to Luisa.

Chapter 29

Sergio made love to Dawn all night long before sending her off on a weeklong tour to England. Sergio was excited to stay in her condominium in Chicago's Gold Coast neighborhood while she was away. It was a perfect location for him to walk to any upscale bar, drink, and bring his woman *du jour* home for a fling.

As soon as Dawn left, he called Maria's cell. "Hello, my love. How are you?" he asked when she picked up.

"How am I? I'm scared, very scared. Where are you, Sergio?"

The desperation in her voice was palpable. He needed to keep her calm until Amanda was discharged from the hospital and was safely back in San Francisco. "What's wrong? I'm in a business meeting but was thinking of you and wanted to call you to tell you how much I love you and am looking forward to seeing you again."

"That large woman from the procurement agency found my dad at our local bar and was asking him all these questions about Marco and how he died. Why do they keep asking my family about Marco, when it's still such a painful memory? I was able to get my dad away from her, but he was confused and so am I. We just buried Marco six weeks ago." Sergio could tell Maria was on a roll and there was no way to stop her from ranting this time.

"Why did you have to leave so quickly? I don't understand what's happening with you and your sister. Why can't she just meet my parents? She's got their son's liver inside her; it's the least she could do. We need to get on with our wedding plans, and I can't until you meet my entire family so they can give you their blessings. It's our way." Maria was sobbing by now.

Sergio took a long, exasperated breath. "I know it's your way, Maria, but I need you to calm down and trust me. We will be together the rest of our lives. I have to take care of this business problem; then I'll fly back down to make amends with your family." He could feel his face getting red.

"Maybe we should just call this off if you don't trust me enough to be patient."

Maria sniffled, and her voice cracked as she spoke. "You know I love you, Sergio. I'm pregnant with your child. If these women weren't bothering my family, I wouldn't be as upset. It's just that you left so fast and all the plans got canceled and you won't even let my parents go to the hospital to see your sister. We want to take care of her; she's family now, especially since you're gone. Where are you right now?"

"I'm staying in Chicago with a friend, and I'm not sure how long it will take me to clean up this mess. So, for now, I'm asking you to relax. Can you do that for me, my love? I would hate for anything bad to happen to the baby because you're so upset."

"Why don't I just fly to Chicago? We can elope and then come back here after you settle all your business. It would make me feel so much better, and safer, too. Please, honey, we can have the big celebration later." Maria was still weepy.

"That sounds like a great idea, as long as you're sure your parents won't be too angry. Why don't you let me look into where we can get married here in Chicago and find out how soon I can make it happen? You're a legal citizen, right?"

"Yes. My parents aren't, but I was born here."

"Can you get your birth certificate ready? Then I'll call you back once I've researched all the details. It will take me a couple of days to finish my business, and then we'll make arrangements for you to fly out here. How does that sound?" He could hear Maria's breath slowing down.

"Thank you, my love. I'll need some time to let my parents know and give my boss time to find someone to replace me at the shop. Mr. Rico, the owner, doesn't like last-minute things."

"I wouldn't tell your parents just yet; we don't want them to prevent you from coming. Just tell them that I need you to come stay with me. Don't tell them we're going to elope. I don't want them any more angry at me than they already are. Sound okay?"

"I never lie to them, but maybe this once. I'll find all my paperwork. When do you think you'll make the plane arrangements?"

"I may need you to make your own plane arrangements. I really hate to hang up on you, but the folks in the meeting room are waiting for me, so I need to go. Thank you for understanding this crazy life I lead, Maria. I'll call you tonight. Love you."

"I love you, too."

Sergio hung up and immediately called Amanda's cell, combing his thick black hair back from his forehead with his manicured fingers.

"Hello." Amanda sounded tired and groggy.

"Amanda, we have problems. I need you to sit up in bed and listen very carefully to me. Are you on drugs?" He was tapping his pen on the dining room table of Dawn's condo.

"Wait a minute—slow down. They just gave me something for pain, so I probably won't remember a word you're saying. Call back tonight." Amanda hung up.

Sergio stood up and went into the bathroom. As he washed his hands, he studied his face in the mirror. Not bad overall; the bruising from the accident was almost gone, but he still looked a little stressed. "I know what you need, he said to himself in the mirror. "You need to go to Gibson's steakhouse tonight and find yourself a young blonde. Bring her back here and fuck her brains out. That'll get this Maria thing off your mind." Sergio nodded in the affirmative at his reflection. Then he dialed Amanda again.

"Amanda, don't hang up. Please. I need to disappear for a while, and I need you to get back to San Francisco as soon as possible."

"What the fuck are you talking about, Sergio? Are you snorting coke again? I told you to lay off that shit; you never know when to stop unless you're with me."

Sergio began pacing around Dawn's plush condo as they talked. The cream-colored drapes framed a wall-to-wall window that revealed a beautiful view of Lake Michigan and Lakeshore Drive. A line of cars at a standstill confirmed that it was rush hour. "No, I'm not on coke. I need you to sit up and listen."

"I don't know what the emergency is; everything is fine here. I'm going home tomorrow or the next day. My liver biopsy was normal, in case you care."

"I'm glad to hear everything is fine with your liver. I think Maria and her family suspect something. I need you gone from Miami by tomorrow. Do you understand?" Sergio opened the mahogany bar and poured himself a glass of scotch.

"I don't know how they can know anything. There's no traceable evidence. They can think all they want. Boy, they sure have you on pins and needles. I can't believe you told Maria you'd marry her. What were you thinking? You need to chill. Too bad you're not here; I could slip you some of these pain pills. They're awesome." Amanda started to giggle, which pissed Sergio off. He took a sip of his scotch and sat down in the well-appointed living room.

"I *am* relaxed, Amanda. I'm telling you, they know something and I'm going to disappear for a while. Maria's parents want to come to the hospital to take care of you tomorrow. Do you want them to visit?"

"Fuck no!" Her voice sounded clearer now. "I hate those motherfucking Cubans. They're dirty people and should all go back to Cuba, where they belong. We can't support everyone."

Sergio started to chuckle. "Easy there, tiger—you have a Cuban liver inside you. Settle down. Can you go home tomorrow?"

"I'll make it happen. I'll ring the nurse when I hang up and tell her I need to get back. I think they were just keeping me an extra day to be sure everything was perfect. The chair of the department of surgery has been by twice a day, so I think they're eyeballing me for a big donation to their transplant program. Serious kiss-up action going on. Bower must have told them how rich I am."

Sergio said, "First thing tomorrow morning, or you're going to have at least twenty Cubans in your room. They're so excited to meet you, isn't that nice?" He knew he needed to light a fire under Amanda's ass to get her going.

"You're just full of jokes today. What makes you think they know so much? They don't sound like very smart people. No college, here illegally—I'm surprised they can put two and two together."

Sergio stood up and looked at the lake again. "They're smarter than they appear, and those two bitches won't leave them alone. I thought having them knocked around would shut them up, but then the fat one finds Maria's dad and buddies up to him at the neighborhood bar."

"Maybe you should make them donors, too. Where's the know-it-all nurse—back in San Francisco?" Amanda asked.

"I'm not sure. Don't worry—I'm going to make sure they shut up for good one way or another. I won't be in contact with you for a while. This time I mean it. We need to create some distance between us, at least temporarily."

Sergio ventured into Dawn's walk-in closet, eyeballing all the designer clothes. *This one has great taste. How can she afford all this on a flight attendant's salary?* he wondered. Then he vaguely remembered her mentioning something about having gotten a nice inheritance when her parents died.

Just then, Sergio heard noise in the background and realized it was Amanda yelling at someone. "You need to leave my room right now! I'm calling the nurse."

"What's wrong, Amanda? Who's there? Are you all right?"

"Looks like you hired the wrong guys for the job, because Fatty is standing in my hospital doorway right now." Amanda hung up.

Chapter 30

Jackie charged Amanda and said, "Go ahead, Amanda— push your call light. When your nurse gets here, we'll have her call the Miami Police Department. We know exactly how you got your liver." Jackie wanted to take Amanda's skinny neck and choke her.

She watched as Amanda sat straight up in bed and casually flipped her blond hair behind her ears. "You don't know anything, you fat bitch. Get out of here, now! You're the one who's going to jail for harassment. You need to stop bothering the donor family and go back to whatever hole you climbed out of."

Jackie felt her cheeks heating up; she knew she had to scare the shit out of Amanda before Amanda summoned anyone. She yanked the call bell from Amanda's hand and threw it behind the bed. Amanda started swinging her legs over the side, and Jackie pushed them back onto the mattress and got right up in Amanda's face.

"Listen here, you fucking waste of space. You and your Spanish gigolo are heading to prison. We have all the proof we need to put you away. We know what you did to Maria's brother, and we know that's how you got your liver. I suggest you get the hell out of here and go turn yourself in right now. Who knows? Maybe they'll put you in a prison where you can learn how to cook Cuban food, so you can get a job in a kitchen when you're released—*if* you ever get released."

Amanda pushed Jackie away. "Quit spitting while you talk, you pig. You and your stupid friend have no idea what's going on, and I'm not going anywhere." Amanda stood up and started to walk toward the door.

Jackie headed her off, slammed the door shut, and stood in front of it. "You're not going anywhere. We know that Sergio was down in Miami months before you got your liver. We know that he weaseled his way into that poor Maria's heart, got her pregnant, and promised to marry her. We know that her brother was killed in a gang fight and became a donor who had the same blood type as you. What a coincidence." Jackie could tell that Amanda was trying desperately not to react, but she was glaring and clenching her jaw.

Jackie went on, "Right now, Sarah is telling your pal Dr. Bower everything, so don't even think about calling his cheating wife. By the time you get back to San Francisco, if you ever do, your name is going to be all over the headlines, and it won't be on the social pages. Now you get your bony ass back in that bed!"

Amanda walked back to her bed and sat on the side. Before Jackie realized it, Amanda had grabbed the call light and begun pressing it repeatedly. Jackie could hear the dinging of the bell outside the room. Just then, she noticed Amanda's cell phone on the bedside table and quickly moved toward it, but the door opened and the nurse entered. Immediately, Amanda yelled, "Help me! This person is threatening to hurt me. Please call the police. Please!"

Jackie grabbed Amanda's cell phone, put it in her pocket, and quickly walked past the nurse, toward the open door.

The nurse followed her and said, "You need to leave now."

"Oh, I'm leaving, all right. Good luck in prison, Amanda. You're gonna be there a long time."

Amanda grabbed the water glass sitting next to her bed and threw it at Jackie's back.

As Jackie was leaving, she heard the nurse ask Amanda if she wanted her to call the police.

"No, don't bother," Amanda answered. "I think that person is mentally unstable. I just need something to settle my nerves. Then I think it's time I go back to San Francisco."

Chapter 31

Sergio was pissed. He had paid those thugs in Miami to really scare the shit out of those two women, but the meddlers obviously hadn't gotten the message. And after his conversation with Amanda, he realized they weren't going to go away, so he was going to have to make some arrangements using a different contact. He also knew he had to disappear, and he decided that if this was going to be his last night in Chicago, he was going to do it up right.

He dialed the number of one of his favorite restaurants, and a woman with a sexy voice answered the phone. "Thank you for calling the Pump Room. How may I be of service?"

"I'd like to make a reservation for two in the private booth around nine tonight."

"I'm sorry, sir," she said breathily, "but we're completely booked tonight. May I suggest another restaurant?"

"I'm so disappointed," he said. "I was going to propose to my girlfriend tonight, and I was so hoping to do it in your fine establishment. I just found out she has to go out of the country for a month, and I can't bear to let her go overseas without a diamond on her finger. I'm sure you understand." Sergio let out a long, slow sigh.

After a few moments, she responded, "Well, we can't let that happen. Can you hold?"

"Absolutely. I was hoping to suggest to her tonight that we have our wedding at the Ambassador East. You still host weddings there, don't you?"

"Yes, we do, sir. But the hotel was remodeled in 2011, and the new name is the Public Chicago Hotel. It's even more lovely. Please hold, and I'll see what I can do. What is your name?"

"Sergio Torres. Thanks. I do appreciate anything you can do."

As classical hold music played, Sergio put the phone on speaker so he could pour himself another scotch, sat down on the leather couch, put his feet up on the ottoman, and enjoyed the view of Lake Michigan.

"Hello, Mr. Torres. I think we can accommodate you at nine thirty tonight. Will that work?"

Sergio took a sip of his cocktail and let out another long sigh. "Well, if that's the best you can do . . . I guess I could take her to the Drake for a few appetizers."

"You're welcome to sit at our bar and order some right here; if your table opens up early, we can seat you."

Man, did she sound sexy. "That sounds wonderful. What did you say your name was?"

"My name is Carla, and I'll be here all evening. Be sure to come introduce yourself when you arrive."

"I will do that, Carla. You have been most kind. I'll need your staff to take the ring and put it under a silver dome when you bring us our entrée. I'd also like a bottle of Dom Pérignon chilled and ready when we sit down at our table. Could you do that for me?"

"We would be delighted. You'd be surprised how many people get engaged here. I'll just need to get your credit card number, and then we'll see you both at nine tonight, Mr. Torres."

After he gave her his information and hung up, Sergio looked through his iPhone for Gretchen's contact information and called her cell number. While it was ringing, he tried to remember the last time they had been together—maybe three years earlier.

She answered, "Sergio, you wild man, please tell me you're in town. I was just fantasizing about you the other day."

"You're in luck, my love. Not only am I here, but I just made a dinner reservation at the Pump Room for nine thirty tonight. When can you meet me there?"

"As soon as I cancel my date with my boring stockbroker. How did you get reservations there? The place books up months in advance."

"I used our go-to: told him I was proposing tonight. Wear something really sexy and no underwear."

"When was the last time I wore underwear out with you?"

"Forgive me. What time can you meet me in the lobby? Say, nine?"

"Nine would be perfect. I can't wait to see you and catch up on all your monkey business. Are you still dating Amanda?"

"That I am, but you know we have an open relationship."

"Thankfully! See you at nine. Public Chicago Hotel lobby."

"One more thing: bring that big diamond engagement ring you have from your second husband. I'll need to borrow it temporarily."

"No problem, Sergio. See you soon. I hope you got plenty of rest last night."

"I guess you'll just have to wait and see, won't you, Gretchen? Bye-bye."

Sergio went into the massive bathroom. The white marble floors were exquisite. Thick, dark green rugs were placed in front of the shower, sinks, and Jacuzzi tub. He took off his clothes and sized himself up in the full-length mirror. *Not bad. Not bad at all*, he thought. His ribs weren't nearly as tender as they had been. His thick black beard had grown in nicely, and his six-pack was as tight as his ass. His daily workout routine had done what he wanted it to do; plus, he knew he'd need all his stamina tonight to please Gretchen. The last time they'd been together, they hadn't stopped making love for over two hours.

Sergio took a long shower, shaved the upper part of his cheeks, and made sure his neckline was cleaned up. He brushed back his hair and then let some casually fall to the right side of his forehead. He put on his favorite cologne, Clive Christian No. 1, and donned his dark black Armani suit with a crisp white collared shirt. It looked to be getting chilly outside, so he pulled out his light blue cashmere scarf to take with him. Black Ferragamo loafers finished off the look.

Sergio took one more look at himself in the mirror. "Look out, ladies, here I come," he said to his reflection. He stepped outside and had the doorman summon a cab for him. Ten minutes later, he emerged from the car to some sighs from a group of women leaving the Public Chicago Hotel.

"Oh my. I think he must be a movie star," he overheard one of them say.

Sergio shot her a smile and winked as he went through the swinging doors.

He immediately saw Gretchen. Sitting in a chair in the lobby, with her long, model-quality legs crossed, thumbing through a *Vogue* magazine, she was stunning. Her long black hair was draped over her bare shoulders. Her short, tight-fitting, black Debbie Wingham dress exposed a healthy amount of cleavage. Gretchen looked up as Sergio approached and smiled widely to acknowledge him. She placed the magazine on a table, and when she stood up, her dress hugged her slim hips, stopping several inches from her ass. She strolled elegantly toward him, wearing four-inch Christian Louboutin heels.

"Hello, my love." Gretchen kissed Sergio on both of his cheeks.

"Hello yourself, you beautiful bombshell. Are you getting younger? You look ravishing." Sergio placed his arm around her and guided her toward the Pump Room.

Gretchen stopped for a moment and retrieved something from her clutch. "Here's my engagement ring. I had an extra Tiffany box, so I thought, why not do it up big?" She handed Sergio the box, and he put it in his suit pocket.

When they got to the restaurant's hostess stand, a tall redhead was there to greet them. "Good evening. How may I assist you?"

"My name is Sergio. I called earlier. You must be Carla." He smiled and nodded at her.

"Welcome to the Pump Room. We're delighted to have you join us. May I escort you to the bar? I believe we'll have a table ready a little earlier that we expected." Carla led them to a tall table with two chairs near the bar. "I'll have a waiter over here right away." Carla started to walk away, but Gretchen interrupted her.

"Excuse me. Could you point me toward the powder room?"

"Absolutely. It's right out the entrance and downstairs," Carla responded. When Gretchen walked away, Sergio put his hand on Carla's arm.

"I have her ring right here. May I give it to you?" Sergio took the Tiffany box out of his pocket and placed in Carla's hand.

"This is so romantic. May I take a quick peek? I wish my boyfriend had half the class you have."

"Absolutely."

Carla opened the box and let out a gasp. "It's magnificent! It must be over three carats."

"Great eye. It's exactly three carats. After I order the champagne at our table, would you tell our waiter to put it under a silver dome and serve it after he pours?"

"No problem, Mr. Torres. Very romantic evening you have planned. Our staff knows all about this, and we're honored to be part of this important event."

"You can call me Sergio. I so appreciate your fitting us in on such short notice."

Carla walked away as Gretchen returned to the table.

After Pastis, Gretchen's favorite French aperitif, they were escorted to a booth tucked away in the corner. Their waiter approached, introduced himself, and took Sergio's order of caviar and champagne. On cue, he poured their champagne and then returned with caviar, chopped egg and onion, and capers, as well as the silver dome containing the ring. Sergio nodded at him, and the waiter lifted the dome.

Sergio got on his knee right next to Gretchen. "Gretchen, I love you. Will you marry me?" Sergio knew that everyone's eyes were on Gretchen and the ring as he slipped his hand beneath her dress and up her leg. *No underwear, as promised*, he thought.

As nearby diners let out audible "awws," Gretchen played her part perfectly. She looked genuinely surprised, then said, "Of course I will, my darling."

With that, Sergio took the ring out of the Tiffany box and slipped it on her finger. He stood up and leaned down to give her a long passionate kiss, to a round of applause.

Once things settled down, they placed the rest of their order and gazed into each other's eyes. "Well played, well played," Sergio said, as he took Gretchen's hand.

"I love doing this with you. I wouldn't marry you if you

were the last man on Earth, but the foreplay leading up to it? Anytime. So, tell me: Where have you been, and what have you been up to? I haven't heard from you in over a year." Gretchen sipped her champagne and prepared herself a piece of toast with caviar and all the trimmings.

Sergio leaned forward. "You wouldn't believe me if I told you, so let's just say I've been spending time in Miami with Amanda and all is well. What have *you* been up to?"

"I've been modeling for Ralph Lauren in Italy. He has a new line, and it's been so much fun. He seems to like my style and pays me very well. You were lucky to catch me home. I leave in two days for Milan. Big show." Gretchen paused as the waiter appeared to serve their first course: salad for her, escargots for Sergio.

"I consider myself extremely lucky to have caught you, because I have a trip scheduled tomorrow, so I won't likely be seeing you for quite a long time," Sergio said. Before Gretchen could ask why, his cell phone rang. It was Amanda.

"I need to take this. I'll be right back." Sergio walked past reception and out into the lobby, which was crowded with people waiting for a table.

"Hello, Amanda. I told you we couldn't talk. I can hardly hear you, it's so noisy." Sergio pressed the phone as close as he could to his ear. If he went outside, the traffic and cabs would be just as loud. He could hear a female voice; it didn't really sound like Amanda, but it was hard to hear.

"Where are you, Sergio? I need to talk to you. Your big, fat friend was back in my hospital room and caused a scene. She and her friend know something. I'm telling you."

"I'm at the Pump Room. I'm leaving tomorrow."

"Don't leave. We need to talk. Text me tonight."

"I can hardly hear you, Amanda. And you don't sound like yourself. I'll text you tomorrow morning. Then we need to stop all contact. If they've figured things out, I need to leave the country." Sergio hung up and walked outside to settle his nerves. *There's no way they could have figured out what I did*, he reminded himself. He took a deep breath, composed himself, and walked back into the Pump Room.

After he sat down and started to eat his escargots, Gretchen looked over at him.

"Who was that? Don't tell me it was Amanda. I swear, that woman has radar for whenever we are together. What does she want, to ruin our engagement party?"

"She just wanted to check in. We haven't spoken since I left her in Miami. I'll call her tomorrow."

"Perfect. Let's enjoy our time together." Gretchen held up her ring finger. "You have such good taste."

For the rest of the evening, Sergio was careful to avoid speaking further about Amanda. A neighboring table sent over a celebratory dessert, which Gretchen moved around the plate but didn't eat. As they were walking out to catch a cab, she looked over at Sergio and said, "Let's go back to my place, honey. I have a few play toys I want to share with you."

"If you insist."

"I insist." Gretchen told their taxi driver to take them to Water Tower Place.

Gretchen unlocked the double doors to her penthouse, revealing an amazing view of the Chicago skyline.

"Wow, you must be doing well." He walked over to her and started to unzip her dress slowly. "Where would you like to start: in the living room, kitchen, or bedroom?"

"I'd like you to relax and pour us some cognac while I go change into something I think you'll like." She leaned in and kissed him slowly.

Sergio turned on the light that illuminated the thick glass cupboard in the dining room. He opened up the doors and took out a fifty-year-old bottle of Courvoisier and two crystal snifters. As he picked up the full snifters, Gretchen walked into the adjoining living room, wearing a red lace garter belt and nothing else.

He couldn't take his eyes off her perfect body. "Oh my. I can see we're going to have quite an evening."

Gretchen motioned with her index finger for Sergio to follow her into the bedroom.

Chapter 32

Jackie knew that Sergio was in Chicago at the Pump Room and was planning to leave the country. It was so loud when they spoke, she was sure Sergio couldn't tell it was her, not Amanda on the phone. Jackie had a little more time, but not much if she was going to catch him.

She quickly called the Pump Room, and when the hostess answered, she said, "Hi, I have a funny question. My brother, a tall, handsome man, is eating there tonight. His name is Sergio Torres—"

Before Jackie could ask if he was there with anyone, Carla interrupted, "I met him. He is *so* handsome. He just proposed to a very famous Ralph Lauren model, Gretchen Regal. It was so romantic."

Jackie hung up and called her friend Sandy, who picked up right away, "Hey, Jackie, what's up?"

"I need a quick favor. Can you run a name for me and get a Chicago address for a Gretchen Regal?"

"Sure thing. I'll text it to you. Sounds like you're in a hurry. You okay?"

"Yeah, I'm great. I just need the address 'cause I'm going to Chicago to catch this motherfucker. Thanks, Sandy. I'll call when I'm home and give you all the gory details. I couldn't have done this without you, my friend."

Jackie hung up, hopped in her car, and drove to the police station, where she asked to talk to Officer Clark. The clerk shook her head and sluggishly picked up the phone. "Hey, that lady is here again. She says she has an emergency and needs to see you now."

After the clerk hung up, she looked at Jackie. "He'll be out in a couple of minutes. You need to go over there and sit down." The clerk pointed to a row of ugly black plastic chairs bolted to the floor.

Jackie couldn't sit still, so she started pacing back and forth. Her best guess was that Sergio had knocked off Maria's brother but had done a great job of covering his tracks. *Those assholes are going to get away with it because there's no evidence.* Right now, it was Jackie and Sarah against the rich people.

"Shit!" she said out loud.

"Hey, watch your language out there," the clerk yelled.

Just then, Officer Clark came through the back-room door.

"Hey, Officer, sorry to be such a pest, but I really need your help." Jackie looked at him intensely. "Can we go somewhere and talk?"

"Sure. Follow me." He led Jackie through the door he'd just walked through and into a small room, then closed the door. "I thought we were going to meet after I got off work tonight."

"Things are starting to happen fast. We're almost positive that Sergio had Maria's brother killed and set him up to be Amanda's liver donor. The guy is the biggest slime pig on the planet, and he's about to leave the country because he knows we're onto him—"

Officer Clark interrupted her: "Remember, this case is closed. It was another gang shooting. I told you and Sarah that before. Who really cares if this loser was shot for his liver anyway? One less gang member to deal with."

"*We* care, that's who. It's horrible. We can't let these motherfuckers get away with this. Would you please take one more look at the file?"

"Simmer down now. I'll see if the paperwork is even here anymore. We usually get that stuff closed out and sent to Records. Take a breath, will ya? How's Sarah doing? Have you talked to her?"

Jackie was ready to scream, but Officer Clark was the only other person she knew who could possibly help her. "I'll tell you, Sarah is a little sweet on you, and if you can help us at all, there's a good chance you'll get lucky when you go visit her in San Francisco."

"Enough said. Let me go back there and see what I can find. Why don't you go get a drink somewhere, and I'll meet you after I get off? We'll go to that gang bar and see what we can dig up. There's a cop bar called Lucky's one block from here, on Lincoln. I'll come as soon as I can, probably forty-five minutes to an hour."

Jackie gave Officer Clark a light slug on his arm and headed out of the precinct.

When she walked into Lucky's, the customers were indeed mostly cops, with a few locals sprinkled around. She was feeling both nervous and pissed off—not a good combination for her. The bartender put a coaster down in front of her and asked, "What'll it be?"

Jackie quickly surveyed the bar. "I'll take a shot of that Bacardi rum, and Diet Coke on the side."

The bartender set the drinks down and asked, "You want me to start a tab?"

Jackie downed the shot. "Sounds like a good idea. I'll have another."

"You know this is a cop bar and no one will let you drive when you're bombed." The bartender refilled her shot glass.

"I'm waiting for Officer Clark. He's my driver tonight." Jackie downed the second round.

The bartender nodded. "You're in good hands. Another?"

"No, I'd better slow down. We're heading over to a gang bar called the Lost Weekend once Clark gets here."

"That's not a good idea, but he knows what he's getting himself into. Yell if you want another." As the bartender walked away to serve some rookies at the end of the bar, Jackie realized she was already feeling buzzed.

The cell in her pocket started to ring. It wasn't her cell; it was Amanda's. The caller ID said it was Kristin Gerard. Jackie put the phone on mute and ignored it. It buzzed three more times. *Kristin "Mrs. Cheater" Gerard*, she thought. *I wonder if Sarah told Dr. Bower what she thought was going on, and that's why Mrs. Cheater was calling Amanda.* She took a long swig of her Diet Coke and tried to calm herself down. When she got like this, she tended to drink too much and it didn't usually turn out well. *Take a breath. Let the rum work*, she said to herself.

She felt a tap on her shoulder and turned to see Officer Clark. He sat down next to her. "How you doing there? You seem a little better than you did at the precinct."

The bartender put a coaster down in front of Officer Clark and said, "She *should* feel a little better with two shots of rum under her belt. What'll you have?"

"I'll have Miller draft, hold the rum." Handsome started to chuckle.

Jackie shook her head. Handsome had changed into his street clothes. "So, were you able to find anything? Any eyewitnesses? Any names?"

The bartender returned with Handsome's beer, and

he took a slug, then said, "I hate to tell you this, but there are no names. Nobody saw anything. Not the bartender, no one. They questioned everyone, even brought some of the hard-ass lifers down to the station. But no one spilled. Maria's brother was shot in the head at the bar. Bartender heard the shot and called 911."

Jackie studied Handsome's face. "Very disappointing. I guess you can get away with murder down here—pure and simple. Well, I'm going to that gang bar anyway, with or without you."

Jackie finished her drink and stood up. Handsome gulped down the rest of his beer and walked out behind her leaving a twenty on the bar.

"Come on, I'll drive you there, but don't get your hopes up." He opened the passenger door of his Toyota Tacoma pickup truck.

"I would never have pegged you as a pickup-truck kind of guy. Do you need it for your farm or something?" She was still pissed off about the lack of evidence.

"I don't have a farm, but my mother still lives out in the boondocks, so I help her move stuff and take care of her acreage." He pulled out of the driveway and hopped on the highway.

"I do appreciate you helping Sarah and me. It's just that we know this dick arranged this murder, even had the nerve to knock up the sister and promised to marry her. It's really sad and disgusting. This family couldn't be nicer." Jackie put the window down.

"It just doesn't sound like we have any hard evidence, and if these people are as rich as you say they are, they'll just lawyer up, big-time."

"You're probably right, but we have to give it a try. If we could find one person who could place Sergio at the gang bar, saw him hanging around. There are so many people waiting for a liver who play by the rules and sometimes die waiting. It's just wrong."

Handsome didn't respond, but Jackie could tell she was getting to him. He just shook his head. He got off at the next exit and drove through a bad neighborhood, full of burned-down buildings and featuring a choice collection of hookers on the corners.

"You sure you want to walk into this place? Once we're in there, we'll need to stay for a while and do our best to blend in. That might not work, but we can go for it." He put the truck in park.

"Let's do it. Nothing to lose at this point, hopefully." Handsome came around and opened Jackie's door. "What a gentleman," she said. "Sarah will be impressed when I tell her." Handsome smiled.

As they walked into the packed bar, a heavy cloud of cigarette smoke encompassed them. They found a couple of chairs in the far back, near the jukebox, and sat down. Jackie could tell that they were getting some looks, but it was late enough that people were on their way to being good and drunk.

"I'll go up and get us a round. Rum and Coke?"

Jackie shook her head and tried to give Handsome some money, but he ignored her and made his way to the bar. Jackie saw three guys leave a booth right nearby and head for the door, so she grabbed it. When Handsome came back with her drinks, she waved him over.

"Thanks. The next round is on me."

"Fair enough. I'm not sure, but I think the bartender who's on tonight is the same one who was here the night Maria's brother got shot. Fits the description from the files. They certainly don't wear name tags in a joint like this."

Jackie raised her drink to toast with Handsome. "Here's to finding someone tonight who will talk, even if it's a little." They both clinked their glasses and drank in silence for a while. Jimi Hendrix was blasting, and Jackie looked around casually to get the lay of the land. Lots of tattoos, big pool game going on in the far right of the bar, lots of "motherfucker this and that"–type conversations going on. Nobody blinked at any of it.

Handsome finished his beer and slipped out from behind the booth. "I'm going to the head, and then I'll get us another round. I think it's best if I muscle up there right now."

Jackie shoved $40 into his hand. "Okay, but I'm buying."

As soon as Handsome walked away, three intense biker dudes came through the door and the crowd cleared so the men could get right to the bar. They looked pretty badass: chain wallets; skintight jeans; bulging biceps showing off their cutoff-sleeved jean jackets; serious leather boots that looked like they could really hurt someone. Jackie turned her gaze away from them, but one of the bikers sidled up right next to her. "Anyone sitting here?" He didn't wait for an answer; he just slid in across from her.

"Not now. Nope. Just you." She slugged down the rest of her rum.

"You like rum?" he barked at her.

"I love rum. I make it my business to drink it wherever I go—I like to try all the different types." Jackie nodded at the huge, black-haired biker with hands the size of the Incredible Hulk's. He had tattoos on each of his fingers and covering both of his arms. *I won't be messing with this one*, she thought.

He looked Jackie square in the eye and asked, "You want to taste the best rum in all of Miami, Ms. Rum Drinker?"

Jackie was feeling drunker by the minute after three shots. One little voice in her head was telling her, *Say no. Get out. Say no*, while another voice was saying, *Sure, why the hell not? When are you ever going to be in Miami again? What the fuck*. She quickly realized that she had said that out loud. "I mean, I can't leave. I'm here with a friend, and he's in the john right now. He likes rum, too, he'll want to come with us."

Biker Bob smiled at Jackie. "I'm not as mean as I look. I won't hurt you, anyway, you look like you can take care of yourself. I rarely meet a woman who likes rum as much as I do. How about we call your friend when we get where we're going? Sound fair?"

Jackie took a deep breath. "You're not carrying a piece, are you?"

Biker Bob let out a hearty laugh. "Never saw the need to carry."

Jackie looked at Biker Bob and added, "I have to tell you, you're not my type. I don't bat for your team. Just sayin'."

Biker Bob laughed. "I could tell the minute I laid eyes on you. Now, come on—let's go." He took her hand and started to escort her toward the door. Jackie took a quick look around the bar and didn't see Handsome anywhere. Then she looked back at Biker Bob. *I don't think this guy would go to jail for killing the likes of me. I'm going for it.* And with that, she followed her new friend outside. As they were flying out of the parking lot, Jackie went to double-check that her phone and Amanda's phone were still in her back pocket and realized they must have fallen out on her seat at the booth. *Holy shit, what have I gotten myself into now? At least Handsome has Sarah's cell number.*

Chapter 33

When Sarah had spoken to Jackie late the night before, she had sensed how nervous Jackie was about contacting Officer Handsome for help, but they had both decided she had no other choice. Now that Jackie had stolen Amanda's phone and called Sergio, they knew he was about to leave the country, unless they could get to Chicago to stop him. Sarah decided she would go find Dr. Bower and tell him everything she knew about Amanda and Sergio, test him out to see how loyal he was to his wife's best friend.

It was late in the evening when Sarah walked into Bower's office. His door was open, and he was dressed in a tie, which meant he was probably on his way to some dinner event.

"Well, hello, Sarah. To what do I owe this visit? Please sit down." He took his reading glasses off and looked directly at her. "I hope you're not here to tell me you need to go traveling again. We really need you on deck."

Sarah sat down and returned Bower's stare. "I'm very uncomfortable about pursuing this topic, but I have to ask you a few questions about Amanda Stein."

"Amanda Stein? I'm not sure why you'd need to know

anything about her." Bower leaned forward and gave Sarah his undivided attention.

"How long have you known Amanda?" Jackie watched his face carefully.

"As long as I've known my wife. They were in the same sorority together at Vassar. About twenty years. Didn't I tell you this before?"

Sarah could see his eyebrows furrowing. *Man, is he handsome*, she thought. But she forced herself to focus. "I guess you did. Do you trust her?"

"Sarah, I'm not sure where all this is heading, but you need to know that Amanda has done amazing work for both the Liver Foundation and the San Francisco Transplant Institute. She generated over three million dollars to create an endowed chair for the head of our hepatology department. Major accomplishment."

"I understand the importance of that effort, Dr. Bower. Do you have any idea how she received her liver?" Sarah started to second-guess herself about having come to Bower. Her stomach was churning.

"Amanda received her liver from a directed donor, as many folks do these days. You know that." Bower cocked his head.

"How did she get a directed donor all the way in Miami? She doesn't know anyone down there, does she?"

"I can't pretend to know what or who Amanda knows. All I know is that she and my wife still spend a great deal of time together, and if my wife thought there was some type of foul play going on, she would tell me directly. I really am confused about your line of questioning."

Sarah leaned in toward Bower. "I was a traveling transplant nurse when Amanda was transplanted down in Miami. I overheard a very disturbing conversation between Amanda and Sergio when she was recovering on the transplant unit. Did you discuss directed donation with Amanda or Sergio?"

Bower let out a long sigh. "I'm sure she knew all about them, since she sat on the local board of the liver foundation. That topic was something we discussed when we reviewed the lack of deceased donors. Listen, we need to talk about the transplant coordinators. There a few who have to go, and I need you to take care of that in between your important investigations on Amanda and Sergio. Really, Sarah, we have a transplant program to run here."

Bower put his glasses back on and started to look at one of the journals on his desk. Sarah knew that signal all too well—it was Bower-ese for *I'm done with you.* She decided that she couldn't trust Bower with any more information about Amanda's liver, so she followed his not-so-subtle lead and changed the subject.

"Which coordinators do you want me to get rid of? Wait, let me guess: Becky and Peggy."

"Bingo." He didn't even look up at her. "I don't care what you have to do—just send them on their way. Talk to Human Resources about it." His pager started to beep at the same time as Sarah's cell phone started to buzz. Sarah looked down and saw Jackie's name on her caller ID.

"I'll talk to HR and let you know what we can do with Becky and Peggy. I need to take this call. Sorry about the Amanda thing." Sarah stood up and walked out of Bower's office while he was answering his pager. Once she was out of Bower's office, she answered her cell. "Hey, Jackie. I sure hope you got some good news for me. I hit a brick wall with Bower. Don't plan on him backing us on anything. Are you with my boyfriend, Officer Handsome?"

There was a long pause on the other end of the phone; then a man's voice started to speak. "Is this Sarah Golden?"

"Yes, it is. Who is this?" Sarah's heart sped up.

"It's Officer Clark, from Miami."

Sarah's face grew warm, and she said, "Oh my goodness. Why are you calling me from Jackie's phone? Is she okay?"

"I wish I knew, Sarah. Jackie came by the precinct early this evening and asked me to help her find Marco's killer. She said you both believe you know who it is, a guy by the name of Sergio Torres. I'll tell you what I told her: I don't think there's any hard evidence, so I think you should both give up this goose chase."

Sarah really didn't care what he thought. Bower had been of no help, and now Handsome was throwing up a white flag.

"Office Clark, I really appreciate your thoughts, but you still haven't told me where Jackie is and why you have her phone."

"Jackie was insistent on going to the gang bar where Marco was shot, and I took her there. We were having drinks, and I went to the bathroom, and when I got back, she was gone. All that was left was two cell phones on the seat where she was sitting. I think your friend could be in some serious danger. This is not a neighborhood where you can just go out for a walk. Do you have any idea where she might have gone? Have you heard from her? I do need to tell you she was on her way to being pretty drunk before we got to the bar, which is why I drove."

Sarah said, "If she had lots of rum, it's a good bet she was drunk. When she drinks, she throws caution to the wind and will do almost anything. I have no idea where she is, and I haven't spoken to her since last night. This is not good."

Sarah could hear Handsome breathing into the phone. "I already asked some of the seedy clientele here, and of course no one saw anything, which is the standard response. I'll see if I can find someone who will talk to me. I'm really sorry I lost your friend. I had no idea."

Sarah wasn't sure what she was going to do; she might have to go back down to Miami herself to see if she could find Jackie. "Let me give you my office, pager, and cell numbers in case Jackie's cell goes dead."

She heard Handsome writing down the information; then he said, "One more thing, Sarah: this other cell phone is ringing off the hook. I finally turned it off. Do you think whoever is calling might be able to help us find Jackie?"

Sarah knew it was Amanda's phone. "I don't think so; probably best to keep it turned off for now. Call me if you hear anything, or I'll call you in a couple of hours to see if she's surfaced. She usually comes to her senses once she sobers up."

"I'll let you know if I hear anything. Hopefully, she'll be back in the picture soon."

Sarah hung up and made her way back to her office, her mind racing. When she got to her desk, she checked airfares to both Miami and Chicago.

Chapter 34

The name of the bar Biker Bob took Jackie to was Rum Wreck Dive Bar. It was a private, by-invitation-only speakeasy inside someone's home. The owner gave Biker Bob a warm, manly embrace when they walked in and told Jackie that they had over three hundred types of her favorite liquor. Jackie was in heaven as Biker Bob ordered the best rum she had ever drunk in her life. It went down nice and smooth. Some of the bottles weren't even labeled. Jackie asked if she could buy a couple of bottles, but got the stink-eye from the owner in return. "This stuff never leaves our place," he barked at her.

During the next two hours, she and Biker Bob had a heart-to-heart talk, stopping for sips and shots of rum along the way. The more Jackie drank, the more she believed that anyone, including Biker Bob, was her best friend—after Sarah, of course. She had a passing thought of Officer Handsome and wondered for a second if she should call him, but then she patted her pants pockets and remembered that she'd left both cell phones at the bar. *Not surprising*, she thought; logic usually never made its way into her thought process when she was liquored up.

Jackie told Biker Bob all about Sergio and what she and Sarah thought he had done to Maria's brother. She painted a clear picture of what huge assholes Sergio and Amanda were and included all the details about Sergio's pretending to be engaged to Maria and messing with Maria's parents. Jackie could tell, even in her compromised mental state, that Biker Bob was getting pissed off about Sergio and Amanda.

"These assholes think that just because they're rich, they can fuck with other people's lives. I fucking hate those motherfuckers." Biker Bob took another shot and slammed the empty glass down on the table. Jackie was wondering just how many times he could use "fuck" in the same sentence. Biker Bob stood up. "I'm going to the john." His six-four-foot, muscular body towered over Jackie. She really had to stretch her neck to look up. His biceps were each the size of Jackie's head.

"I'll be right here," she slurred.

When Biker Bob returned, he sat across from Jackie, looking very serious. "Listen. I'll see what I can do for you, but I will not have anything to do with the motherfucking pigs. No gang member deals with them. Minute I see any sign of cops, we're done. Got it?" Biker Bob slammed down the last shot and stood back up. "Let's get you back to the bar while I can still drive."

Jackie wasn't sure he could drive, but she was certain she couldn't, so she put on his motorcycle helmet, which covered her eyes. She slid it back up and swayed toward the bar doors, calling out, "See ya" to the bartender, who was serving another biker and raised his eyebrows.

The ride back was a blast. Biker Bob gave it all he had, and Jackie felt as if she were on a roller coaster ride. "Whee!" she yelled, holding on to the part of his waist that she could grip with her short arms. She really had to get one of these motorcycles when she got home.

Once Biker Bob parked in front of the gang bar, Jackie threw her leg over to get off and landed on her ass. She started to laugh uncontrollably, and Biker Bob put his hand out and helped her up with one pull. The bar was packed to the rafters with bikers and their chicks. Jackie looked way up at Biker Bob and said, "I'm hitting the head. I'll meet you at the bar." She made her way through the mass of people and waited in line with an assortment of bandannas, tattoos, and nose and eyebrow rings. The tall girl in front of her turned around and looked at Jackie. "If that broad doesn't get her ass out here, I'm going to break down the door and piss right on top of her." Thick black eyeliner framed her half-mast eyes.

Just then, a large black woman emerged and pushed Eyeliner Lady aside. Then she stopped and glared at Jackie. "You here with anyone?"

Jackie looked at her. "Yeah. Maybe next time." It had been a long time since she had been picked up in a bar; it felt kind of good, in a weird way.

Once Jackie got her turn, she found Biker Bob at the bar with two shots of rum. "Hey, it was my turn to buy," she slurred.

"You'll buy the next round." They clinked glasses and tossed back the alcohol. "You know, you're not half bad. I had a good time with you tonight. I'll ask around about Marco, but I'm telling you, he was known as a real big asshole, so it's no wonder someone offed him. I'll see if anyone knows anything about this Sergio guy, but I'll need a photo. I'm not making any promises."

Jackie waved for the bartender to pour another shot. "That's all I can ask. If I were batting for your team, I'd be taking you home right now, you hunka-hunk of burning love."

The grin on Biker Bob's mouth was cute. "Remember, it's our creed to never, ever have anything to do with the cops."

"I got it, buddy."

Biker Bob turned and walked toward the john without a word.

Jackie looked over at the door and saw Handsome walking toward her. She gave him a quick, intense nod and then used her index finder to mimic cutting across her throat, meaning *stay away*. She could tell he got it—he turned around and walked back out of the bar. Just then, Biker Bob was walking back from the bathrooms with a tattooed, drunk blonde on his arm. She quickly grabbed a pen from the bar, wrote her phone number on a napkin, and put it in his leather vest pocket. Jackie gave him a quick hug and looked over at the blonde. "He's very sensitive, so be gentle with him." The blonde didn't catch it, but Biker Bob laughed. Jackie headed out the door and glanced over her shoulder to see them locking lips. *At least someone's going to get lucky tonight*, she thought.

Jackie looked over to the right of the parking lot and saw Handsome's truck parked way down the road. She walked over to it and opened the door. "Hi, Handsome. Long time no see. I have lots to share; let's go to your place and have some rum."

She saw Handsome's head shake back and forth, and that was the last thing she remembered.

Chapter 35

At eight o'clock in the morning, Dr. Bower summoned Sarah into his office. "Hey, what's up?" she asked, closing the door behind her.

"I just got off the phone with Dr. Javier Santos at the Miami Transplant Institute. Seems Amanda has been down there, creating all kinds of chaos. I asked him about her directed donor, and it was a Cuban gang member, which was odd. Amanda happened to be in Miami already, so there was almost no cold ischemia time with the liver because they didn't have to wait for her to fly cross-country. She and the donor were the same blood type, and the liver worked immediately." Dr. Bower sat back in his chair and rubbed his temples. "I didn't know Amanda was running with gangs. Pretty bizarre." He chuckled. "But it seems you and your friend may be onto something after all, I'm sad to say."

Sarah leaned forward in her chair. "Can I trust you to keep what I'm about to tell you confidential and not tell anyone, not even your wife?"

"You have my word."

Sarah spelled out what she and Jackie knew so far about Sergio's being engaged to Maria, who was now pregnant with his child. She briefed him on Maria's parents and how lovely they were and shared that Jackie was down in Miami at that moment, working with Miami police to connect Sergio to the death of Maria's brother.

"This is really bad. All the way around." Bower closed his eyes.

"You can't tell your wife any of this. I know she'll tip off Amanda," Sarah insisted.

"I won't say a word. I promise. If what you say is true, this is going to cause a national scandal for organ donation. Every time this type of thing happens, you know the donor numbers go down." Bower shook his head.

"I know. It's a shame that because people like Amanda and Sergio couldn't wait their turn, they'll cause more people on the wait list to die—unless there's a way you and I can contain the media while this all goes down."

"I'm heading to Germany tomorrow for a meeting of the International Transplant Society. I will be forcing my wife to join me, which will not go well. She was supposed to go to Los Angeles for a photo shoot with Tiffany. I need to distance her and myself from Amanda and Sergio immediately."

"You do what you need to do, Dr. Bower. Jackie and I aren't going to give up on nailing both of these assholes. I'll keep you posted." Sarah stood up.

Bower rose, too, and put on his lab coat over his operating-room scrubs. "I have to go to the OR. Let me know as soon as you find out anything. Hopefully, I can call in a few favors with my friends in the media. Once you know this is happening, give me as much notice as you can. The one thing we have going for us is that it was a gang member and most people don't have any sympathy for them."

Sarah followed Dr. Bower out of his office. "That's exactly what Sergio and Amanda are banking on, too."

Chapter 36

Jackie slowly opened her eyes and tried to sit up, but her head felt like it had an ax planted through it. She had no idea where she was. She closed her eyes and tried to remember anything. There was a lot of rum, mass quantities of it, and she was on the back of a Harley with a large man. She tried to remember his name, but it wasn't coming to her. Was she at his house?

"Oh, shit, what have I done?" she mumbled out loud. She ran her hands over her clothes and could feel that everything was still in place. She pushed herself up to a seated position and ever so slowly opened her right eye and then her left. There was a white paper on the coffee table in front of the couch she was lying on. She picked it up and brought it close to her face so she could read it: *Here's 3 Advil, a chocolate donut, and a glass of water. Call me once you're able to talk. I'm at the precinct. My cell is 305-517-7939. Officer Handsome.*

Officer Handsome—good man. She'd been in his truck; that was the last thing she remembered. Jackie took a bite of the donut, waited until she knew it wouldn't come back up, downed the Advil and chased it with water, then lay back down. She hadn't had a hangover like this in years.

She fell asleep again and awoke to a wet pillow; she thought she might have thrown up, until she realized she'd just been drooling. "Nice, Jackie. Really nice, you're as bad as Sarah." She slowly stood up and then found the bathroom in Handsome's condominium. Surveying the furniture and the tidy kitchen, she was impressed with his place.

Jackie picked up her cell phone, which was lying next to the note, and dialed his number, but her call went right to voice mail. She lay back down, moaning.

Her cell phone rang. "Hello."

"Hi, Jackie. I hope you're feeling a little better. Did you take the Advil?"

"Yup. I think I might need brain surgery. My head is not in a good place at all."

"I think it's safe to say that you were overserved last night. You passed out in my truck and gave me a hard time when I took you up to my place. Made me promise I wouldn't try anything. You kept telling me you didn't bat for my team, over and over again."

Jackie felt redness creeping up her neck and onto her face. "Well, I can see I made a great impression. I am so sorry. Really."

"No need to apologize. I've been there before, once or twice. I'm just glad I found you and you were safe. I went back to the bar after I was sure you were okay and was able to find two drunken bikers who knew Maria's brother. As long as I was buying, they were talking."

Jackie's head was starting to clear a little. "That's great news. Were they able to tell you anything about him? Did they know Sergio?"

"Turns out Marco was a real loser and most everyone in the gang he hung with didn't like him. They didn't think it was any loss at all that he got killed. I did describe Sergio to them, and one of them seemed to remember him hanging out at their bar for a couple of months before Marco died."

Jackie started to pace around the living room as she listened to Handsome. "Nice work, Detective. Wait till Sarah hears about this." Jackie picked up one of the photographs on his mantel. It was a picture of him and two young boys. "I didn't know you had kids. These are some good-looking boys."

Handsome sighed. "I don't have any kids. Those are my nephews. Anyway, I put a call in to my friend who works the beat where the shooting took place. He's going to go there tonight and see what he can find out about Sergio. Will you send me Sergio's picture so I can send it off to him?"

"Sure thing. As soon as I hang up, I'll send it. Hey, did you find another cell phone at the bar?" Jackie had just realized she might have lost Amanda's phone.

"I found it, along with your phone, in the booth where we were before you disappeared with—what did you call him?"

Jackie said sheepishly, "Biker Bob. I called him Biker Bob."

"That's right. Biker Bob. And I'm Officer Handsome. Did you find these names in some children's book?"

Jackie let out a laugh. "Good one, Handsome. Sure sounds like they could have been in the *Dick and Jane* books, though. I make up a lot of nicknames, and so does Sarah. It makes it easier to talk about all these new people. We don't do well with long last names and funny-sounding first names, so why bother learning them if we're not really going to be seeing them for the holidays? Keeping it simple, Officer."

"I did find both phones, and one of them was ringing off the hook. Whose phone is it?"

"It belongs to Sergio's girlfriend, Amanda Stein. I stole it from her at the hospital yesterday and called Sergio with it."

"I did want you to know that, based on what you and Sarah have discovered and my conversation with the bikers at the bar last night, I was able to convince the chief to reopen the case on Marco Chavez. Once the detective gets intel from the bar tonight, we will likely be working this case again. I don't think there's really any need for you to stay in Miami any longer. I'm not sure if there's any rum left, anyway." He chuckled.

"I don't think I'll be drinking rum or anything for a while," she said.

"I also called a detective I know in Chicago, and he's going to see if he can find Sergio once I send a photo. It would be helpful if I could keep Amanda's cell phone, as we can have our IT people see what other valuable information we can get out of it that may help the case."

Jackie said, "That's a great idea. I need to call Sarah and give her an update."

"I did speak with Sarah, several times, last night." Handsome mentioned.

"Oh boy. Did she know I left with Biker Bob?" Jackie knew Sarah would give her all kinds of shit once she knew Jackie had been on the drunko rum train with Hells Angels.

"I called her when you disappeared into thin air at the bar and promised I would let her know as soon as I found you. She was worried but didn't seem surprised."

Jackie smiled. "Well, we *have* been on some creative capers together, but I don't usually fly solo."

"I called her at three this morning to let her know you were safe and passed out on my couch. How about I pick us up some food on my way home?"

"That sounds perfect. I'll make my plane reservations after I call my wife. See you when you get here. When will you be home?"

"I've got some case work to complete, so plan on seeing me in about an hour."

After Handsome hung up, Jackie called Laura and got her voice mail. She left a long message about how important this trip was, along with all the details. Wyatt would be fine with his best friend for a couple more days. Jackie knew that Laura would understand. She might not be thrilled about it, but Jackie would iron things out when she got home.

After she took a shower, she booked a red-eye flight to Chicago. Then she called Sarah, who had called her several times the previous night.

Sarah picked up immediately. "I was worried sick about you. I can't leave you anywhere, Larsen. Anytime the words 'you' and 'rum' appear in the same sentence, it never turns out well. How the hell are you?"

"My head's better, thanks to your boyfriend. He knows how to cure a hangover, so he's got that clearance. I have to give you the rundown. Lots happening—"

Sarah interrupted, "Listen I'm in clinic, and it's crazy. I'll call you back in a couple hours."

"I'm taking the red-eye to Chicago tonight. I'll call you when I get to the airport. Everything is good. Handsome is bringing me dinner. This guy just might be a keeper, Golden."

"Just because he feeds you and saves your ass from Easy Rider doesn't mean I want to keep him. Have sex with him, absolutely. Keep him, too early to call that. I had a serious talk with Bower that I need to tell you about. He believes us. I have to run."

Just as Jackie hung up, Handsome walked in with two white bags of cheeseburgers and french fries. After they had finished every morsel, Handsome said, "I can drop you off at the airport. What time to do you want to leave?"

"I need to get my bag from the motel, so let's leave at eight. Sound good?"

Handsome checked his watch. "That will give us about

an hour. I have some paperwork I need to finish, so that sounds good."

While Handsome was in his home office, Jackie called Laura back. After a long conversation, during which Laura expressed all her concerns about Jackie's safety, she finally agreed that Jackie should go to Chicago. The only stipulation was that Jackie work with the Chicago detective and not try to solve the case by herself. Jackie agreed. After she hung up, she took a much-needed moment of gratitude for a wife who trusted her and supported her no matter what, and who had done such a good job as the mother of their son.

Handsome dropped Jackie in front of her room and waited for her to come back out. When ten minutes had passed, he went to find her. He tapped on the slightly open door and walked in. Jackie was picking up her clothes and toiletries, which were strewn all over the room. She looked up at him. "Someone broke into my room and went through all my stuff. Go into the bathroom and look at what they wrote on the mirror."

She followed behind him. Written on the mirror in black marker was STOP OR YOU AND YOUR FRIEND WILL DIE!

Handsome looked at the mirror and immediately stepped outside. As Jackie shoved her things into her carry-on with shaking hands, she could hear him calling the precinct to come out and investigate.

Once the officer got to the motel and took down Jackie's information, he let Handsome take her to the airport. They drove in silence most of the way. Finally, Handsome said, "Jackie, these people are not amateurs. Once they're hired to kill someone, they will follow them anywhere until the job is done. I've seen it many times. You have to be extremely careful. Do not talk to anyone except Sarah, your wife, and me about anything. I gave my friend Officer Mars all the information he'll need to find Sergio in Chicago. He's a very seasoned detective and knows Chicago inside and out. He said to thank you for the intel on Sergio's girlfriend's address. You're starting to act a little like a detective, Jackie Larsen."

Handsome pulled up to the airport departures curb and got out and helped Jackie with her suitcase. "Call when you get home."

Jackie gave him a hug. "I promise. Thanks for everything. I'll be in touch." She walked toward the airport doors, thinking all the while that if Handsome knew she was going to Chicago, he'd try to stop her.

"No more rum until you're back home, Larsen," he called out.

Jackie turned around, smiled at Handsome, and gave him a thumbs-up. Once she cleared security, she called Sarah. She updated her friend on what Handsome had said and about his friend Mars in Chicago. When Jackie told her about the motel room, Sarah let out a gasp. "Shit. It's probably the same guys who roughed us up before."

"Dunno, but they're going to see if anyone at the motel saw anyone or anything. We have to be careful; this shit is getting serious, Golden." Jackie was walking toward her gate. Loud announcements on the overhead speakers made it hard to hear Sarah.

"Talk louder, Sarah. Everyone and their brother seems to be here tonight."

"Bower is leaving for Germany tonight and making his wife miss her fancy Tiffany photo shoot. He wants them to be out of town when this goes down. He's taking the whole family."

"Did you tell him everything? I never trusted that bastard."

"I didn't tell him where Sergio was, and I did leave out a few other details. He's mostly concerned about how this whole thing is going to affect organ donations nationally when it hits the media. It's not going to be good."

As Jackie approached her gate, the plane was already boarding. "I hope those assholes get locked up for life. They may be calling my row soon." She put her finger in her other ear so she could hear Sarah.

"Bower and I think we have a plan that may keep this away from the press for at least a little bit. That way, innocent people who are waiting for organs won't die. I still can't believe you were on the back of a Harley and got bombed with a biker. I want all the details."

Jackie looked at her ticket to double-check her row number. "I'll give you all the details I remember when we talk, but right now I'm boarding. I'll call you when I land in Chicago."

"Be careful, Jackie—really. I couldn't take it if anything happened to you."

"Don't go soft on me, Golden. I'm going to our old stomping grounds. Love Chicago, love the Chicago police. I'll be in good hands. I'll talk to you later."

Chapter 37

Sergio and Gretchen had an amazing, sex-filled evening that lasted into the early-morning hours. Exhausted, they fell asleep naked in each other's arms on the plush living room carpet. The sun coming in through the floor-to-ceiling windows awoke Sergio. He sat up on his elbow, careful not to awaken Gretchen. She was sprawled out completely naked, with her head resting on the satin pillow he had placed under it before they had passed out from exhaustion. He checked his watch; it was nearly ten. Lying back down next to Gretchen, he whispered in her ear, "Good morning, you goddess. What can I get you for breakfast?"

Her long black lashes fluttered, and she gradually opened her eyes and said, "I would like an Americano and a side of Sergio."

Sergio leaned over and kissed her. They decided to have the side of Sergio first. When they had finished making love, Gretchen sat up. "You've learned lots of new tricks since I saw you three years ago. I don't know who's coaching you, but you need to keep seeing whoever it is. You were amazing."

Sergio smiled and stood up, still aroused. "I'm honored

you enjoyed yourself. It's my mission to please. Just tell me where you get your coffee, and I'll make a run."

"I just call down and have the doorman send someone. I'll order us a light breakfast, too. What would you like?" Gretchen stood up and walked to the phone.

"I'll take a tall black coffee and some scrambled eggs."

After Gretchen called in their order, Sergio approached her from behind. "Shower time." He picked her up and carried her into the spacious marble bathroom. The custom shower had large showerheads on both sides. Gretchen pulled out two lush white towels, and Sergio set the water temperature. They lathered each other front and back with luxurious French bath gel.

The doorbell rang just as Gretchen was stepping out of the shower. She threw on her bathrobe while Sergio finished rinsing off. He got out, wiped the steam off the mirror, and took a look at himself. *You don't look half bad for someone who was up all night*, he thought.

Gretchen yelled from the front room, "Breakfast is served, your highness."

Sergio grabbed another robe and walked toward the kitchen. The table was set with linen placemats and napkins, and Gretchen had already transferred the food onto china and poured their coffee into mugs. Sergio picked up his cup and took a big sip. "This is just what I needed. Mmm." He sat across from Gretchen, who looked as beautiful as she had when he'd first seen her the night before at the Pump Room. They ate in silence, smiling at each other with sexy grins.

"You're leaving for Milan tomorrow, then?" Sergio asked.

"Yes. Early. We're sharing a Learjet with one of the designers. It really is the only way to fly. He has two flight attendants who make us fabulous meals, and we sleep in real beds. They wake us up just an hour before we land so we can shower and be fresh for the paparazzi when we get off the plane. You're welcome to stay at my place as long as you like." Gretchen finished her eggs and put the dish in the sink.

"I agree with you, we only take Learjets now, too. We know enough people who share them that there's always one available. We pitch in for the gas and tip the flight crew. I don't know how people stand that cattle call and security at the airport. Poor souls." Sergio handed Gretchen his empty plate and started to read the *Tribune*, which Gretchen had laid next to his place.

"I appreciate the offer to stay here, but I really need to hit the road, too," he added. "I'm going to go to Cancún for a while. This Amanda liver thing has been one royal pain in my ass, and I just need to sit by a pool, read a good book, and relax."

"Relax? You never relax. Cancún sounds fun, though. They have amazing spas there. Remind me to give you the name of my massage therapist there. Best one I ever had."

"Just a massage?" Sergio looked over at Gretchen.

"Maybe, maybe not. I need to go start packing for my trip. I'll be gone over two months. After the fashion show and parties, a bunch of us are invited to spend two weeks on Ralph Lauren's yacht. I can't wait."

"Gretchen, you know how to live. I love it. I need to make some calls and confirm my reservations. I'll check on you to be sure you're packing all the important things. You never know—I may fly to Milan to surprise you." Sergio winked.

"The girls would be so jealous if they got a look at you. If you come, no sharing," Gretchen said, as she walked out of the kitchen.

"No sharing both ways. I'll see what I can do. You just never know. I haven't been to Italy in over a year." Sergio followed Gretchen into the living room, where he had left his cell phone. He noticed he had missed a call, no caller ID. He hit the CALL BACK button, and a gruff-sounding man answered, "Yeah. What do you want?"

"This is Sergio Torres. Did you call me?" Sergio walked into the kitchen so Gretchen couldn't hear him.

"Yeah, I called you. You asked me to rough up the two bimbos in Miami. I'm not going there anymore. You must have done something big. There are cops all over them."

Sergio cleared his throat. He was starting to get pissed. "Look, all you had to do was do what you and your pals do. It's not like you're dealing with CIA agents here. What's the problem?"

"The problem is that one of them left town and the other is best friends with some Miami detective. We followed the fat one. Turns out she's also into biker dudes, big ones. Not smart to mess with them or their chicks. This is gonna cost you extra."

"Were you able to do *anything*, you fucking loser? You guys are supposed to be the high end of thugs in Miami. Jesus Christ. Isn't that why you demand the big bucks?" Sergio could feel his face getting redder by the minute.

"Listen, asshole. We messed up the fat one's motel room and left a death threat on her mirror, but she had that cop with her, so we bailed. Both of those bitches may be able to identify us from the last time we roughed them up. That fat one has a mouth on her. Believe me, I would love nothing more than to beat the living shit out of her, then kill her, but now we have to disappear for a few weeks, in case they try to hunt us down. Thanks a lot. You said this was going to be a slam dunk. Which reminds me: you need to send us money for the last gig, and we need it today."

"I'm not sending you shit. You didn't complete the job, and your rough-up certainly didn't stop them. I don't owe you a fucking dime." Sergio was thinking about hiring someone to kill these thugs *and* the nosy bitches.

"You don't get that money to us today, an anonymous phone call with your name and details goes to the Miami police. You want to start trouble, you dick, we can make big trouble for you. I'll text you where to send the money. If it's not there by five tonight, your new best friends from the Miami PD will be giving you a call." The man hung up, and seconds later the name and number of a currency exchange in Miami showed up on Sergio's phone.

He stared at the text; he wasn't going to send them anything. He would be on a plane to Mexico by five o'clock that day, he didn't care what those assholes told the Miami PD.

"Fuck and fuck," he said out loud.

He heard Gretchen yell from across the penthouse, "What's wrong?"

Sergio walked into the bedroom. Clothes were strewn all over the bed, and two large Louis Vuitton suitcases were sitting on luggage stands, waiting to be fed. Gretchen looked up at him. "You all right? You look like you're going to kill someone."

Even Gretchen's vibrant beauty wasn't enough to distract him from his fears just then. He managed to say, "I'm fine." Then he walked back into the dining room, called Aeroméxico, and booked a first-class seat on a seven o'clock flight to Cancún. He wrote a few notes in the small black datebook that he always kept in his jacket pocket and went back in to say good-bye to Gretchen.

"I know you'll have an amazing time in Italy, you have fun no matter where you go." He put his strong arms around her and gave her a long embrace.

Gretchen hugged him back. "I don't have to tell you to have fun. Be careful, and don't break too many Mexican girls hearts. When will I see you again?"

Sergio looked at her and gave her his signature smile. "You never know where I'll turn up. I really need to get packed myself and get a car to the airport."

"Bon voyage, Sergio." Gretchen returned to her packing as Sergio blew her a kiss.

Sergio left the penthouse, took the elevator downstairs, and put his sunglasses on. The doorman nodded at him as he opened the building's tall, gold-framed door. Sergio started walking toward Dawn's condo so he could pick up his clothes. He noticed a black sedan parked across the street from Gretchen's place but couldn't see who was inside, through the heavily tinted windows. He casually glanced in the direction opposite where he was going and noticed a short person, dressed in all black, with a hoodie covering their face. "Chicago," he said out loud, then made tracks toward Dawn's condo.

Chapter 38

Sarah had just finished teaching a newly transplanted liver patient about all the new drugs she'd be taking, when she ran into Dr. Bower, who was clearly on his way out of the Transplant Institute, with his briefcase in hand.

"Sarah, I'm so glad I ran into you. Saved me a call." Dr. Bower gestured for her to follow him into a private consultation room.

"What's going on? You didn't tell your wife anything, did you?"

"Nope, not a thing. Unfortunately, I do have some disturbing news on my end. My wife has refused to go to Germany with me tonight. Actually, she's not going to go at all. I'll save you the marital-fight part of this whole conversation, but she left for Los Angeles this morning and is meeting Amanda there for the Tiffany shoot. Then they're heading for Cabo San Lucas for a private party with one of Amanda's friends." Bower was checking his watch. He was visibly upset. "You have to keep my wife out of this when the police start arresting people. She's an innocent bystander, and we have a family and a reputation to protect."

Sarah remembered having seen his wife locking lips with some Cuban dancer when she and Jackie were tracking them in Miami. *I wouldn't be too concerned about her reputation if I were you*, she thought.

"I'll do my best to keep her out of it, but it's not really my call. I can ask the detective to do what he can. I have no idea if they bring everyone in for questioning, which is why I really hope you didn't tell your wife anything." Sarah studied Bower's face; she could tell he was starting to get angry.

"I told you I didn't tell her anything. How many ways do you want me to say it, Sarah? We wouldn't even be here if you and your friend had just minded your own business. Seriously, what's one liver in the grand scheme of things? I have to go."

Before Bower left, Sarah stood up and looked into his eyes. "You of all people know how wrong this is. If Amanda and Sergio did this, how many other people are doing it? They need to be stopped. We're talking about murder here. I thought we were in the business of saving lives."

He looked down. "I know you're right. It's just that I wish my family wasn't being dragged down with the likes of them." He looked back up at Sarah.

For a moment, she felt the familiar chemistry tugging at her, and she quickly lowered her head. "I'm sorry, Dr. Bower. You know I didn't want to hurt you or your family. Maybe there's still a way for us to avoid that. I'll do everything in my power to keep the law as far away from your wife as I can. I promise."

"Tiffany is putting them both up at the Beverly Wilshire, under my wife's name. I really have to go now." Bower walked out and closed the door behind him.

Sarah's cell phone rang. She didn't recognize the number but could tell it was a Florida area code. "Hello, this is Sarah Golden."

"Hi, Sarah. This is Officer Handsome from the Miami PD. I need to talk to you."

"I see you haven't forgotten our code name for you. That's embarrassing."

"Wait until Jackie tells you all about her new friend Biker Bob. I really think you should both quit your day jobs and write children's books." Sarah could hear him chuckling on the other end of the phone.

"Everything okay in San Francisco? You're well, I hope."

Good—he still seems interested, she thought, then answered, "It's a shit storm here, as usual. Really busy at work, and Dr. Bower is heading out of the country to Germany. What's up?"

"I need you to get Jackie out of Chicago right now. She shouldn't have gone there to find Sergio. She never mentioned where she was going when I dropped her off at the Miami airport; I just assumed she was heading home. She needs to fly back to San Francisco immediately."

"How do you know she's in Chicago?"

"Based on what you've both told me about the case and what I got from one our local Miami detectives, we have probable cause to arrest Sergio for the murder of Marco Chavez. I'm working with a Chicago detective who's trailing Jackie and Sergio. He needs her to stop trailing Sergio now. She has no idea what she's doing, and we don't want to lose him when we're this close."

Sarah's heart pounded as she said, "This is really going to happen. Holy shit! What did the Miami detective find?"

"I'm not at liberty to share any more information on the case, just know we will be working with the San Francisco, Chicago, and Los Angeles homicide departments. I need you to call Jackie off and get her out of Chicago. Can you do that?"

"Three homicide departments? Is Jackie in immediate danger?" Sarah was starting to freak out.

"Yes, real danger. Sergio would not hesitate to have her killed. We believe he's the one who hired the two thugs who beat you and Jackie up when you were down here. I need you to go to San Francisco Homicide and ask for Officer Florence O'Shea. She's going to be the lead on this case, since it will be prosecuted in San Francisco, where Sergio and Amanda live. She's waiting for a call from you; I gave her your name and number. We need you to give her a description of the thugs so we be on the look out for them. They likely have something to share about Sergio."

Sarah sat back down. This was far bigger and scarier than she had thought it would turn out to be. "I'll call Jackie as soon as I hang up. I do have a favor to ask of you and your detective teams. If there is any way to keep Dr. Bower and his wife out of this, would you do your best to make that happen? Please. Dr. Bower's wife is best friends with Amanda. Also, when this type of thing happens, it causes the nationwide organ donation rates to drop. That means some of the innocent people who are on the waiting list for transplants will die. Can you do that?"

"That shouldn't be a problem for now. We don't have any evidence on Amanda, but once we have Sergio in the interrogation room, we think we'll be able to convince him to implicate her."

Sarah took a deep breath. "I should go and call Jackie. Will you keep me posted on the case? Should I be concerned for my safety?"

"I don't think you're in any danger, Sarah. When you meet with Officer O'Shea, let her know what's going on, in case they need to keep an eye on you until we get more information. I'll let you know when we arrest Sergio, and I'll tell you everything I can as this unfolds. Maybe after all the dust settles and we get these assholes behind bars, I'll come out to see you and we can go to wine country and taste all those fancy Sonoma wines everyone brags about. How's that sound?"

"Let's get Jackie home and those pigs put away for life, then we'll plan a big party in wine country. I have a good friend who works at Cline, one of the best wineries. My treat."

"Sounds fair. Let me know when you get ahold of Jackie and when she's flying home, so I can let Detective Mars know. You have my cell number."

"I do. Keep me posted. Thanks so much."

Sarah hung up and dialed Jackie, who answered on the first ring. "Sarah, I'm trailing Sergio. I can't really talk right now. He walks really fast. I have to work on my hiking skills when I get home. I'm barely able to keep up." Jackie was whispering.

"Jackie, you have to leave Chicago and come home today. You don't need to trail Sergio. There's a Chicago detective already trailing him—and you, by the way. Just hop a cab to the airport and get on the next plane home. Call me when you get to the airport, and I'll give you all the details. This thing has blown up. We both have to step back. Jackie, are you listening?"

Sarah could hear her friend huffing and puffing, and then what sounded like a phone hitting pavement. After that, the only audible noises were Jackie's screams and crashing cars.

Chapter 39

S ergio finished his espresso at the quaint coffee shop on the corner of Rush and Division streets. He planned to run upstairs to Dawn's condo and then catch a cab to O'Hare International Airport. He was anxious to get to Mexico and kick back for a while. Just as he was about to cross the street, a medium-size man wearing a suit and tie approached him. "Are you Sergio Torres?"

"Who wants to know?" Sergio eyeballed this loser wearing low-class clothes.

"I'm Detective Mars with Chicago Homicide. I'm going to need you to come with me down to the precinct for questioning." Mars moved closer to Sergio, and he saw a uniformed policeman walk up behind Mars.

"Questioning for what? I don't even live here, and I need to catch a plane. You and your friend need to get out of my way." Sergio tried to walk around both men.

"I would rather not make a scene, Mr. Torres. I think you know why I'm here. It will be easier for all of us if you come with me peacefully." Mars looked at the policeman. "Cuff him."

The tall, muscular officer stepped right in front of Sergio and said, "Put your hands behind your back."

Sergio's heart was beating too fast. He had to keep it together. He knew there was no way they could hold him. He put his hands behind his back, and the cop handcuffed him. "Sergio Torres, you are under arrest for the murder of Marco Chavez. You have the right to remain silent." The officer opened the car door, and Sergio got inside. As he looked out the squad car window, he saw small groups of people pointing and gawking at him.

"I have the right to call my attorney," he yelled.

Mars responded from the front seat, "You'll get your call after we book you at the precinct. You have some new friends from the Miami and San Francisco homicide departments waiting to meet you personally once you're processed."

When they arrived at the precinct, Sergio was fingerprinted and had his mug shot taken. Then he was escorted into a small, gray-painted room with a table and chairs. The officer handcuffed one of Sergio's wrists to the table leg. He shouted at the officer as he was leaving, "I demand my fucking lawyer now!"

He sat in the room working out in his mind how he could possibly get himself out of this. *Those fucking broads did this. I am going to have them fucking killed when I get out of this shithole*, he thought.

Detective Mars walked in with a tall, thin man. "Sergio, I'd like you to meet Detective Clark from Miami and Officer O'Shea from San Francisco. Officer O'Shea will be conducting the interview with assistance from Detective Clark."

"I'm not talking to any of you assholes until my lawyer is present. I have done nothing wrong, and I will not be bullied. When is my lawyer coming?" Sergio had to force himself not to yell more profanities.

Mars and Clark leaned against the wall where the two-way mirror was. Officer O'Shea sat down in front of Sergio and said, "Your lawyer has been notified, and I believe they are sending someone from their Chicago office. He should be here shortly. I can assure you that he will not be able to help you. We have hard evidence that links you directly to the murder of Marco Chavez in Miami. The only option you have is to confess exactly what your part in this murder was and provide us with the names of anyone else who is connected with this premeditated crime."

O'Shea folded her hands, placed them on the table, and looked directly into Sergio's eyes.

"I have absolutely no idea what you're talking about. I haven't killed anyone. I want some water!" *A blond woman detective*, Sergio thought. *She's probably stupid and will fuck up this case.*

Mars walked toward the door. "Have it your way, Torres. By the time you do decide to talk, your friend Amanda Stein will be out of the country and untouchable without lots of federal paperwork. If she's smart, she'll never come back to the States, which means you'll have to take the blame for everything. I'll get you some water." Mars closed the door. O'Shea sat quietly across from Sergio. The silence consumed the room. Sergio's mind would not stop. *I'm not taking all the blame for this. Amanda's the reason for this whole fucking mess*, he thought.

Mars came back with a bottle of water for Sergio and coffee for O'Shea. As O'Shea drank her coffee, Clark looked directly at Sergio and said, "I believe Sergio's Cuban fiancée is Maria Chavez—is that right? Her parents have agreed to go on record about their relationship with Sergio and their son."

Mars left the room again, and a young man who looked like he had just graduated from high school walked through the door. "Hello, I'm Dan Getter. I'm here to represent Sergio Torres. May I please have a moment with my client?"

O'Shea got up and offered him her chair, "Absolutely, Dan. We'll need to start our questioning in ten minutes so would ask that you be quick. We are under serious time constraints, as another individual related to this case may be a flight risk."

"I understand, Detective. I will be as quick as I can." Dan sat down.

As soon as the door shut, Sergio started, "Who the fuck are you? I asked them to send a seasoned attorney. Why the fuck do I keep them on retainer if they send me some kid?"

"I can assure you that I am competent in handling these types of cases, Mr. Torres. Are you aware of what you are being charged with?" Dan opened his briefcase and took out a yellow legal pad.

"They told me it's for murder. I did not commit any murder. I have no idea where they're getting this information. I need you to get me out of here on bail. They're looking for the wrong man."

Dan looked right at Sergio. "They have evidence that you were directly linked to hiring someone to kill Marco Chavez, for the purpose of using his liver for your longtime girlfriend, Amanda Stein. Marco's parents and sister have given complete statements to the Miami police. They also received an anonymous call regarding the gang member you hired to kill Marco. It's only a matter of time before they find that guy and interrogate him. Your time is running out." Dan started to write some things down.

"What is the charge?" Sergio asked.

"First-degree murder. You're looking at twenty to thirty years in a state prison in California. Not the place you want to serve even a day. If we show them you're willing to cooperate, we may be able to get you less time."

Sergio finished his water and asked, "Are you suggesting I confess here, or what?"

"I'm not suggesting you confess anything. I can tell them you're willing to name names and cooperate without incriminating yourself. If we can prove that Amanda was a co-conspirator in the crime, maybe we can get you a lesser sentence. I will be here when they question you. Do not answer anything unless I give you the nod. Chances are, they will disclose more details as they are questioning you, and that may help me in pitching your case for a much lesser sentence."

Sergio took a deep breath. "I cannot stay in this shitty place much longer. I'm willing to hear what they want, but I'm not agreeing to anything right now."

Dan stood up. "I'll go get the detectives. I suggest you be as respectful as possible. These are the guys who can recommend you get out on bail."

As Sergio sat alone, he decided that he would incriminate Amanda. His part was minimal. He was relieved this whole thing had gone down after he'd fucked Gretchen and left her penthouse. There was no way they could directly link him to hiring the gang member who killed Marco. He had been careful never to call the man from his cell; he had always used a pay phone. He'd paid the killer in cash, so that wasn't traceable, either. There was no direct evidence to put him on the spot.

Detectives O'Shea, Clark, and Mars came in with Dan, bringing a couple of chairs so all five could sit around the table. After everyone sat down, Detective O'Shea confirmed that Sergio had been read his rights and his attorney now represented him. Sergio nodded in the affirmative.

"Mr. Torres, you are being charged with the murder of Marco Chavez. Your attorney informs us that you are willing to cooperate with the stipulation that your case be heard in

California and that we recommend that you be released on bail." O'Shea had a tablet of paper she was making notes on as well.

Sergio replied, "That's correct. I may be able to shed some light on this case in a way that enables you to arrest the right person. It's not me. I did not kill anyone. I've never owned a gun. I don't even know how to use one."

O'Shea started the questioning: "You are stating that you are innocent and had nothing to do with the murder of Marco Chavez. Is that correct?"

Sergio looked at his attorney, who nodded. "I did not kill Marco Chavez."

O'Shea continued, "We understand that you have been in a relationship with Amanda Stein for over six years. Did she have anything to do with the death of Marco?"

Sergio really didn't want to turn in Amanda, but he was not going to take the fall for her, either. "Amanda and I are close friends. I think you will need to ask her if she was involved. I don't want to speak for her."

"Were you aware that Amanda received Marco's liver? That she just happened to be in Miami the same day Marco was shot in the head? That Marco's sister, Maria, your fiancée, said you were also in Miami with her when her brother was murdered? Maria and her parents are all on the record as stating that you were the one who suggested Marco be a directed donor specifically for Amanda. Maria and her parents stated they have never met Amanda Stein, the person you told them was your sister. Is any of this ringing a bell, Mr. Torres?" O'Shea took off her suit coat and placed it on the back on her chair.

Sergio looked for a nod from Dan, who was writing quickly. Dan looked up. "My client is clearly trying to protect his friend Amanda here. I would suggest that you take her into custody and ask her directly."

Mars spoke up. "The Los Angeles police are on their way to bring her in for questioning as we speak. Maybe she'll be able to share exactly what Sergio's role in this case was."

Chapter 40

S arah was frantically trying to reach Jackie, with no luck. She kept dialing Officer Handsome's cell number, but it went to voice mail each time. Why wasn't he calling her back? Finally, just as she started to call his precinct to see if they knew where he was, she saw his cell number pop up on her screen.

"Hello. What the hell is going on?" she demanded.

Officer Handsome tried to talk, but she cut him off. "Something bad has happened to Jackie. She was trailing Sergio and was talking to me, and the last thing I heard was screeching tires, and then her phone went dead. I've been trying to get in touch with you; I'm going crazy here. Please say you know something." Sarah's heart was beating out of her chest. "If anything bad happened to Jackie, I would never forgive myself."

Officer Handsome said, "I'm in Chicago now to assist the local homicide detective after they arrested Sergio. I know where Jackie is. Take a breath."

"Oh my God, please tell me she's not dead or hurt badly," Sarah begged.

"She was hit by an unmarked car on Rush Street. We think it may have been one of the men Sergio hired to kill both of you in Miami. Jackie is in surgery at Northwestern right now. She's got a bad concussion, a broken leg, and several broken ribs."

"Holy shit!" Sarah screamed. "Did you call her wife?"

"Jackie called her wife before they took her to surgery to set her leg; she's going to need several pins. She has a compound fracture. You know what that is?"

"Of course I know what the fuck it is. I'm a nurse. How bad was it?"

"Bad. It'll be a while before she walks. Laura wants you to call her immediately."

Sarah's heart sank. "My poor friend. It's my fault. I got her into this mess. Laura will never let her be with me again. How do you know all this, anyway?"

"Once I found out Sergio was in Chicago, I called my friend Detective Mars. He was arresting Sergio at the same time the car hit Jackie, who was nearby. Then he asked me to come to Chicago, since I have the evidence on the case. The detective from San Francisco was flying in at the same time I was, so we shared a cab to the city. Mars is at the hospital now. I plan to meet him there after I hand over all our paperwork on Sergio. They have an officer watching her in case the assholes try to come and finish her off. They're running the plates, but with this type of thing, they're probably fake plates and the car's probably sitting in a garage already."

Sarah had been standing the whole time she'd been talking to Handsome. Now she sat down and started to sob. "Why the fuck didn't I just leave this alone? It wasn't worth risking my best friend's life, she's married and has a kid." Sarah blew her nose and wiped her eyes. "I'm flying to Chicago right away. Can you give me Officer Mars's phone number?"

"Now, Sarah, don't blame yourself. I'll give you Mars number—I told him you'd be in touch. I do have some good news in all of this, Sergio and Amanda are both in custody and being questioned. Sergio gave the Chicago PD everything, his slimy lawyer is negotiating a deal. Our local Miami detective was able to find the guy Sergio hired to kill Marco, and he's willing to testify against Sergio, so, no matter what, Sergio is looking at some serious prison time. A pretty boy like him won't fare well at all once he's behind bars."

"Good. I hope he gets killed. If I knew any gang members on the inside, I'd pay them to do it!" Sarah shrieked.

"Don't stoop to his level. The LAPD picked up Amanda on Rodeo Drive, she was in Gucci, buying out the place. They cuffed her right in the store."

Sarah said, "Do you know if Dr. Bower's wife was with her?"

"The LA detective I talked to said she was alone. Hopefully, Sergio and Amanda will never be out in public again. You just need to be patient."

"Fuck being patient. I'm going to call Laura and then Detective Mars. Will you promise me you'll call me if you hear anything more?" Sarah was about to hang up.

"Yes, I promise I'll stay in touch. I plan on stopping by the hospital on my way to the airport to look in on Jackie."

Sarah said a quick good-bye; she was too frantic to be polite to anyone. She placed a call to Laura and, thankfully, got her voice mail. She left a brief message saying that she was flying to Chicago and that she would call back as soon as she laid eyes on Jackie. Sarah apologized profusely on the phone, hoping Laura would forgive her.

Then she called Detective Mars, but he didn't know any more than what Handsome had already shared. He told Sarah to call his cell when she landed. Sarah told her assistant at work she had a family emergency in Chicago and didn't know when she'd be back. After she called and reserved a one-way ticket to Chicago, she made sure that her on-call was covered and created an out-of-office reply on her e-mail and her work phone. She stopped by her apartment, threw some things in a bag, and took a cab to San Francisco International Airport.

Sarah had over an hour before her flight left, so she decided to call Handsome back. He picked up immediately. "Sorry I was such a bitch earlier. I just feel so guilty about what's happened to Jackie."

"I understand—no need to apologize. I spent some time with Jackie, and it's clear she's loyal to the core when it comes to you. I have to tell you, I think she was really enjoying her undercover work in Miami. She had me laughing my ass off in the biker bar. I wish I'd taken a picture of the guy she left with. Did she tell you that she and Biker Bob made up a new drink? It's called the Jackie Larsen."

Sarah took a deep breath and smiled. "Jackie told me a little about Biker Bob but didn't mention the drink. Only Jackie would do something like that. What's in it?"

Handsome laughed. "She told me that if Arnold Palmer could have a drink named after him, there was no reason she couldn't have a drink named after her. It's two shots of rum, coconut water, and fresh lime. Her thinking was that if she was going to get drunk, why not head off the hangover with some coconut water, since it helps with rehydration."

Sarah chuckled. "She does have a point there. No one likes a hangover. She's got quite an imagination. I just didn't think it would be this dangerous. She won't be disco dancing for a while. My poor friend."

"I do need to tell you that after Amanda was booked at the LA station, she denied any connection to Sergio and anything to do with her donor family. Thankfully, they found enough evidence that her story didn't hold any water."

At least they won't both get away with what they did, Sarah thought. "Has the press been involved?"

"I don't think so. Nobody really knows them in Chicago or LA. Amanda seems to be famous only in the Bay Area. My friend in LA did say some reporter was sniffing around, but he doesn't know anything about Sergio. No formal charges have been pressed yet, so there's not really any news on that front. I do think this will hit the media at some point. I'm not sure how you can stop it."

Officer Handsome's tone relaxed Sarah. "There might be a way to spin this horrible story in a way that we could actually increase organ donation. Could you get the reporter's name? I need to send Dr. Bower an update, he has some connection with the higher-ups in the media."

Officer Handsome said, "Sarah, I don't think it would be wise to tell him anything. We don't know for sure that he and his wife weren't involved with this somehow. I won't be able to disclose any more information if I know you're talking to him. As it is, I shouldn't be giving you any of these updates."

"I promise I won't tell him any details. I just need him to know that we may have a media shit storm on our hands unless we can spin this somehow. I would hate to have more innocent people dying on the wait list because of this."

When the agent announced that her flight was boarding, she said, "I have to go. I promise I won't compromise the case. I'll call you when I get to Chicago, after I see Jackie. Will I see you when I'm there?"

"No. I fly out tonight. They need me back home to work a few other cases. These are usually short-turnaround trips. I'll send you the name of the reporter in LA when I get it. Take care and travel safe, Sarah Golden."

Sarah's heart melted a little when he said her name; it had been a while since a man had been this sweet to her. "I will, Handsome. Don't forget, when this nightmare is over, you're coming to see me in San Francisco and we're going wine tasting."

"It's a date. Be careful," Handsome said.

Sarah hung up and quickly fell asleep as her plane took off. She didn't wake up at all until the flight attendant announced their landing in Chicago.

Chapter 41

Jackie felt someone shaking her arm and calling her name. She tried to open her eyes, but her lids felt too heavy to lift.

"Jackie, can you squeeze my hand?"

She had no idea who was talking to her, but she squeezed the hand that was squeezing hers.

"That's great. Now can you try to open your eyes?"

With her eyes closed, Jackie mumbled, "Do I have to? I feel like I'm floating in the clouds here. Did someone give me drugs? 'Cause they're really good."

"You're in a hospital room at Northwestern Hospital in Chicago. Do you remember why you're here?"

"Not really. But I'm feeling mighty fine right now. Whatever it was, you must have fixed it." Jackie tried to blink. Slowly, she managed to open one eye, then the other. A tall, thin nurse wearing blue hospital scrubs was by her side.

"Hi, Jackie. I'm Helen. You just got back from surgery. Can you tell me your full name?"

"Jackie Larsen. Surgery? I don't need surgery. Did you take out my gallbladder?"

Jackie could see the nurse smile. "No your gallbladder is still where it should be. You had a broken leg, and the doctor needed to put some pins in it. Do you remember how your leg was broken?"

Jackie furrowed her eyebrows. She could see some guy in a suit behind the nurse. "Did that guy behind you break my leg? What's he doing here?"

The nurse chuckled. "No, that man is Detective Mars, from the Chicago Police Department. Do you remember meeting him before your surgery?"

"Uh-oh, did I commit a crime? Chicago? I live in San Francisco, not Chicago." Jackie closed her eyes again. She just wanted to sleep.

"Jackie, I need you to keep your eyes open. You had surgery, and I need to ask you some questions. Can you open your eyes and look at me?"

"How about I answer the questions with my eyes closed?" Jackie could feel herself dozing off.

"No, I need to see your pupils. I hear you're a nurse. Do you remember that you were hit by a car?"

Jackie opened her eyes slowly. "I remember some crashing, and I think I talked to my wife. Oh boy, is she here? She's going to be mad at me. How do you know I'm a nurse?"

Jackie watched as the nurse wrote some things down and then pulled a penlight out of her pocket. "I'm going to check your pupils. You have a concussion. Your wife, Laura, told us you were a nurse and gave us your history on the phone before surgery. She's not mad at you, just very concerned. I'm going to open your eyes a little wider and use this penlight to see if your pupils respond to it. That way, we can see if your concussion is getting any better." With that, the nurse flashed the light in each of Jackie's eyes and then wrote something down on her paper.

"My right leg is really heavy. How long was I in surgery?" Jackie started to look slowly around her room.

"You were in surgery for over four hours. The doctor

said you should heal just fine. You'll just set off the alarm at the airport when you go through security from now on. You have some fancy hardware in that leg. Are you in pain?" The nurse was fixing Jackie's IV tubing.

Jackie was looking at the man again. "Why is the detective here? Did I do something illegal? I'm not feeling much of anything right now, except a pretty good buzz." Jackie grinned.

"I'll let Detective Mars talk to you in a little bit. First, I need to check your vital signs and your mental status. Can you wiggle the toes of your right foot?"

Jackie thought about her right foot and wiggled her toes. "I still feel something heavy on my leg. Can you see me wiggle my toes?"

The nurse moved to the head of the bed. "I sure can. Good job. Squeeze my hand. Good. Now squeeze my hand with your left hand. Good. I'm going to put the head of your bed up to help you wake up." Jackie heard the hum of the bed as it elevated her into an upright position.

"Not too far up—my chest hurts." She put her right hand under the hospital gown and felt the left side of her chest. There was some sort of dressing wrapped all the way around it. She glanced at her nurse. "Broken ribs?"

"Sorry to say, yes. When the car hit you, it broke your leg and four ribs. You have a binder on your chest to support your ribs from moving too much. Thankfully, your lungs are fine. Do you remember anything about the accident?"

Jackie winced as she tried to move. "I feel like someone beat me up. I'm starting to remember now—some black car drove onto the curb, right at me. Oh, shit! What happened to that asshole Sergio? Did he get away?" Jackie looked past the nurse to the detective.

The nurse said, "Let's get you all settled, and then I'll let the detective talk to you. Are you in pain?"

The more awake Jackie felt, the more her pain began to announce itself throughout her body. "Yes, I'm in pain—mostly my chest, but my head is starting to hurt, too."

The nurse put her hand gently on the back of Jackie's head. "You have quite a big bump here. You're lucky you have such a thick skull. Your CT scan showed some bruising but no active bleeding, thankfully. Would you like something for pain?"

Jackie slowly lifted her arm and touched the back of her head. It was the size of softball, "Ouch. Feels like an alien could be in there, fighting her way out. Yes, I would like something for pain."

"On a scale of one to ten, ten being the worst, what number is your pain?"

"I'm about a six and climbing, now that I've lost my postsurgery buzz."

The nurse jotted down a few more notes, then looked at Jackie. "I'm going to get you some IV morphine and make sure you're comfortable; then we'll let you and Detective Mars talk, if you're up for it."

She left the room and asked the detective to follow her. Jackie could hear them talking unintelligibly in the hall. She looked around her room and saw a basket with flowers in it by her bedside. She reached over, took the card, and read it: *Mom: Get better and come home soon. We love you. Wyatt & Laura.* Jackie tried to hold back her tears but couldn't. She started to sob just as the nurse walked in with her pain medication.

The nurse handed Jackie some tissues; her nose was running. She put her hands over her face and kept sobbing. The nurse waited patiently.

"I'm sorry. I just feel awful. I miss my wife and my son. My body is killing me. I sure hope my friend Sarah is okay. *Is she okay?* They didn't try to kill her, did they?"

The nurse handed Jackie some more tissues and took

the used ones away. "Sarah will be here first thing tomorrow morning. She's worried sick about you. Now, let's get you some pain medication." The nurse asked Jackie to say her full name and birth date. Jackie responded without a pause. She felt the medication almost immediately after the nurse pushed it through her IV.

The nurse checked Jackie's pupils again and made some more notes. "I asked Detective Mars to come back tomorrow, when you're more stable and alert. You should know that they placed a uniformed policewoman outside your door for your safety. I'm going to get you some ice chips. Do you need anything else?"

"No, thanks."

Jackie dozed off and awoke early the next morning when she felt a hand on her arm. She opened her eyes, and there was Sarah, right next to her bed.

"Oh my God!" Sarah was staring at Jackie's face, and tears were running down her cheeks. "I'm so sorry, Jackie. This is all my fault. I'm so sorry, my friend. I love you so much."

Sarah went in to give her friend a hug, and Jackie grimaced. "Easy does it, Golden, every part of me hurts. But it's not your fault."

Sarah kept looking her over and shaking her head, sobbing, "Those fucking assholes. I hope they fucking die."

"It's *not* your fault, Sarah. You didn't make me do anything. Do you know if they got Sergio, speaking of fucking assholes?" Jackie was still feeling pretty high from the pain medication.

Sarah pulled up a chair next to Jackie's bedside. "Good news, girlfriend. They arrested Sergio and Amanda. They're fucked big-time."

"Well, then it was worth it, wasn't it?"

"I don't think it was worth you almost getting killed, but

yes, I'm so relieved that after everything we've been through, they're going to prison."

Jackie smiled and closed her eyes, then opened them and asked, "Did you talk to Laura?"

Sarah shook her head. "Not yet. I did leave her a message and promised I'd call as soon as I set eyes on you. She'll never let us go to Cuba now, probably won't even let you be my friend ever again. I can't say I blame her. What kind of person lets her best friend be run down by a car?"

Jackie started to laugh. "No one will ever keep us apart, Golden, we've been through too much together. But you're right—the Cuba outing may have to be put on hold. Maybe she'll let us go somewhere stateside."

Sarah took out her cell phone. "How about I call her and we go from there?" Sarah dialed Laura's number and put the cell phone on speaker. Jackie heard Laura pick up and say, "Hi, Sarah. How's my wife?"

Sarah said tentatively, "She just got something for pain, so she's feeling pretty good right now. Let me give her the phone."

Jackie took the phone. "Hi, honey. I'm so sorry I put you and Wyatt through this—"

Laura interrupted, "We love you so much. I was so worried when I spoke to you before surgery. You were out of it. You didn't even remember who I was at first. Do you remember talking to me?"

Jackie held the phone closer to her ear. "I don't remember talking to you, but the nurse told me we spoke. I have a huge lump on the back of my head, and my leg has pins in it, some cracked ribs. I'm in bad shape, you may have to trade me in for a younger model."

Laura chuckled. "I spoke with the surgeon after he was done putting that leg back together. Sounds like you've got some healing to do. I'm not trading you in for anyone, they broke the mold after they made you. We're married for better or for worse, which includes Sarah. Let me talk to her. You feel better. I'll call you from home tonight so Wyatt can talk to you."

Jackie started to tear up. "You tell him I love him and that I'll be home soon and he can play with my crutches. I love you, honey."

"I love you, too, you crazy woman."

Jackie handed the phone to Sarah. Sarah listened for a minute, then said, "She's seen better days, that's for sure. I wanted to bring her to my grandmother's house in Berwyn for a couple days before we fly home. I'm so sorry for all of this. It's my fault."

Several minutes passed, while Sarah listened to whatever Laura was saying and gave her brief responses. When she hung up, Jackie studied her face. "So, what's the bad news?"

Sarah put the cell phone back in her pocket. "Well, she doesn't hate me. Your mother-in-law is staying at your house. I did get permission to take you to my Nana's house for a couple days after you get discharged."

Jackie let out a sigh. "My mother-in-law? That woman is relentless. She never thinks I do the right thing for Wyatt. I think I'll stay at Nana's for a couple of *months*. How did Laura sound?"

"She's concerned but okay."

Sarah turned around as Detective Mars walked into the room and approached Jackie's bedside. "Are you both ready to have a little talk?"

"Ready as we'll ever be. No Officer Handsome—I mean, Clark?" Sarah said.

"No. Handsome had to fly home late last night. He sends Jackie his best wishes and told me to tell you that he does plan on taking you up on that offer to go wine tasting." Mars smiled.

Jackie used the spoon to put a few ice chips in her mouth. "Ready, Detective Mars Bar." She started to laugh, then put her hand on her ribs and stopped.

Detective Mars updated both of them on Sergio and Amanda. It was exactly what Officer Handsome had told Sarah earlier. Jackie smiled when she heard that the gang member Sergio had hired to kill Marco had confessed. "That Sergio has to be the world's biggest dick!"

Mars smiled and said, "We haven't found the driver of the car that tried to run you over, Jackie, but now that we have Sergio and the gang member in custody, it will only be a matter of time before we get the person's name. Meanwhile, we're going to keep an officer outside your hospital room around the clock."

Then Detective Mars looked directly at Sarah. "I need you to keep me abreast of your whereabouts until you are both safely back in San Francisco." Then Mars's cell phone rang, and he jumped up—"Mars here"—and left the room.

The nurse came in, changed Jackie's IV bag, and checked her vitals and pupils. "Everything is looking good, Jackie. The doctor wrote orders for you to get some physical therapy today, and if that goes well, we may be able to get you discharged in a couple days." She glanced at Sarah. "Sounds like I'd better order a cot for you."

Sarah sat back down next to the bed. "I'm not leaving her side until we're back in San Francisco and she's safe in her wife's arms."

• • •

Jackie was discharged several days later to Nana's house. Nana was ready to spoil both of them, just as she had done throughout their nursing-school years. Detective Mars had called Sarah before Jackie was discharged to let her know that they had in fact found the guy who had tried to run down Jackie, and he was in custody, so there would be no more police watching over them.

Once they were settled at Nana's, they placed a call to Maria and had a long conversation with her about Sergio and Amanda. They thanked her and her family for all they had done to bring the pair to justice. Maria was heartbroken, as she had fallen in love with Sergio and now, in addition to not being his wife, would be a single mother. She told them that Sergio had done one kind thing, however: he had set up a bank account for her that was supposed to pay for the wedding and reception. She planned to use the $30,000 to help support her and the baby.

Maria also shared that her parents had received a letter from the procurement agency saying that the recipients of Marco's heart and kidney wanted to meet them. The meeting was to occur in a month, and her mother was thrilled.

After they hung up, Jackie looked at Sarah and said, "At least her family can see the positive outcomes from Marco's death after all."

"No kidding. What Sergio did to Marco was horrible, but at least some good came of it. I'm glad you asked her about how Sergio knew Marco's blood type. I've been wondering about that, but there never was a good time to ask." Sarah poured Jackie a glass of water and added, "Drink up—you don't want to get constipated from all those pain drugs."

"My bowels are just fine. Have you seen the bowl of prunes Nana makes me eat every morning?"

Sarah changed the subject: "That Sergio, what a slimeball, offering to drive Maria to pick Marco up at the ER after Marco had stitches from a knife fight. Of course the ER paperwork would have had all the lab information in it, including his blood type. Maria said she had just met Sergio the day before that happened. Sergio was probably just trying to get into her pants but then struck gold when he noticed that Marco's blood type was the same as Amanda's."

"Talk about bad luck. But she's so beautiful, I bet some nice fella will come along soon. And she has such a loving family. I just know her luck will turn around," Jackie said.

• • •

After a week at Nana's, Jackie and Sarah flew home to San Francisco. Jackie used her crutches to get off the plane. A wheelchair awaited her at the gate, and Wyatt and Laura were waiting right outside security with flowers and balloons. When Wyatt saw her, he yelled, "Mama!" He ran to Jackie and threw his arms around her neck, and all the balloons he was holding flew up into the air. Laura waited until they had finished embracing, then bent down and kissed her wife. "Welcome home, Jack. We sure did miss you."

Laura took the wheelchair from the attendant and began to wheel Jackie toward the elevator down to baggage claim. Once they had retrieved the bags, they headed for the parking-garage elevators.

Sarah walked them as far as the elevator doors, then said, "I'm going to leave you with your family and hop a cab home." With that, Sarah took Jackie's face in her hands and gave her a kiss on the forehead. "I'm going to miss seeing you hobbling around on those crutches every day, but you call me when you get all settled. I can never repay you for all that you did, my friend. I love you!"

As Jackie saw Sarah tear up, she felt her own eyes stinging. "Bye, buddy. I'll talk to you once I get settled." Jackie gave her friend a wave and returned to her family.

Chapter 42

It had been over a month since Sarah had seen Jackie, but they had spoken on the phone every day. Jackie was in a walking cast and was barely tolerating her mother-in-law.

Sarah was watching CNN one evening, when a reporter declared, "A huge win for the Cuban population in Miami, a donation of twenty million dollars to build a community center and library in the city's Little Havana neighborhood."

Sarah turned up the volume as CNN showed where the center was to be located. She recognized it as the same neighborhood where Maria and her family lived. The news continued: "On another note, the international marketing firm Saatchi & Saatchi was selected to execute a national transplant education campaign. The two-pronged campaign will focus on an education program that will teach non-English-speaking people how to access all types of transplant care and will implement an organ- and tissue-awareness program in every Latino community in the United States. This multimillion-dollar grant was a generous gift from an anonymous donor."

Sarah's jaw dropped. She immediately called Jackie and asked, "Did you see the news?"

Jackie said, "Nope. Watching *SpongeBob SquarePants*

with Wyatt while my favorite mother-in-law makes pancakes that will constipate the hell out of me, but who cares?"

Sarah laughed. "Thanks for the update on your bowels. You're not going to believe this." She recited what she had just heard the reporter say on TV.

"No shit!" Jackie replied. "I guess our buddies must have tried to buy their way out of prison, or at least cut down on their time."

Sarah smiled. "They're both serving time for sure. I got the details from a friend who's here visiting from Miami. I can't tell you much, but just know that justice has been served and our friends won't be enjoying the lives of the rich and famous anymore."

"Officer Handsome is here, and you didn't even tell me?" Jackie yelled.

"We were going to drive up and surprise you today. Rescue you from the tyrant and take you wine tasting in Sonoma. I already cleared it with Laura. So, surprise! Don't eat the pancakes. We'll go to the Swiss Hotel in downtown Sonoma for some classic Italian food afterward," Sarah said.

She walked into her bedroom, where Handsome was sipping a cup of coffee, and handed him the phone, mouthing that she was talking to Jackie. "Well, hello, my friend. How are you feeling?" he asked.

Jackie let out a loud laugh that Sarah could hear through the speaker. "Welcome to San Francisco, Handsome. How the hell are ya?"

"I'm better than you—that's for sure. You ready to go out and have a Jackie Larsen today?"

Jackie replied, "Haven't touched the rum since I was with you, but you do have to admit it's a good idea."

Sarah watched as Handsome smiled. "You mean, you and Biker Bob haven't had a date since you returned?"

"Real funny, Handsome. I'd like to say some special things to you, but my son is in earshot, so I'll save them for when we go out. What time are you two coming to spring me?"

Handsome handed the phone back to Sarah. "Your friend needs details." He stood up and put his arms around her from behind as she tried to talk to Jackie.

"We should be there around eleven. We'll hit a few wineries and then have a nice, long lunch. We can give you all the gory details Handsome is willing to share about Amanda and Sergio's new vacation spots. Three square meals and a cot. See you soon."

"I'll be outside at the curb, so don't be late. No last-minute sex. You got it, Golden?" Jackie said.

"Got it, Larsen. See you soon. Can't wait." Sarah hung up, and Handsome began to nibble on her neck.

"We are under orders not to have any last-minute sex, mister, so let's wash up and head over the Golden Gate Bridge to pick up Jackie." Sarah directed him to the bathroom.

They showered together, with a few make-out sessions sprinkled in between. Sure enough, when they got to San Rafael, Jackie was outside with her walking cane.

Handsome got out of Sarah's car, opened the front passenger door for Jackie, and helped her inside after a hug. "Damn good to see you, Handsome." Jackie slid onto the seat and handed him her cane.

"You don't look too much the worse for wear," Handsome said. "I bought you the fixings for a Jackie Larsen—a bottle of rum, coconut water, and a lime—just in case you couldn't wait until we get to the winery." He laughed as he placed the bag on her lap and closed the car door.

Jackie leaned toward Sarah and gave her a quick hug and kiss on the cheek. "It's so good to see you. I've been on house arrest too long. Let's get the hell out of here."

Sarah steered the car toward Sonoma. It was the end of October. All the grapes had been harvested, and the hilly vineyards were shifting to their yellow and red fall colors.

"I called my friend at Cline Cellars, and we're getting a VIP tour and tasting when we get there," Sarah said.

"I'll skip the tour—let's get a bottle and get this party started. I can't wait to sit outside, relax, and hear the whole story. Don't leave out any details, Handsome." Jackie peered over her shoulder at him in the backseat.

Sarah dropped Jackie and Handsome off in front of the winery and parked the car. The sky was bright blue, and a gentle breeze wove through the vineyards and around the picnic tables. A tall, dark-haired man with glasses, sporting a Cline Cellars shirt and cap, brought out three glasses and a dried fruit–and–cheese plate.

"Welcome to Cline. My name's Mark, and I'm going to be serving you today. How about we start with our rosé? It's selling off the shelf."

Jackie sat down and looked up at the server. "Hey, Mark, how about we start with a bottle of the rosé, and could you please bring me a chair to put my leg on?"

"No problem. I'll be right back." Mark returned quickly with a chair and the wine. As he opened the bottle, he explained that the rosé was like a white wine made with a purple grape, called a Mourvèdre grape. After filling all their glasses, he left to take care of other customers and promised to check back with them.

Sarah sat across from Jackie, Handsome by her side. "This is delicious. How do you like it?" She looked at Handsome.

"I'm not much of a wine guy, but this is tasty, goes down easy." He raised his glass. "Here's to our undercover agents Sarah and Jackie. You brought your criminals to justice."

They all clinked their glasses and took a sip.

"Okay, Handsome, let's hear how the criminals got their comeuppance." Jackie took another sip.

Handsome took a big drink and put his wineglass down. "We had a conference call last week with the Miami, Chicago, LA, and San Francisco PDs. You know where everyone was arrested and held, so I'll spare you those details. Because our local Miami detective was able to get a signed confession from the gang member Sergio hired, the evidence was so strong that Sergio was found guilty of first-degree murder. The judge sentenced him to thirty years to life in a California state prison. He's at San Quentin now, awaiting his transfer, and there's talk he may go to Pelican Bay, which is the worst prison in California. There's a slight chance he'll get paroled, but that won't happen for a long time. He also had to pay Maria one million dollars for child support. In addition, Sergio and Amanda were each fined ten million dollars, to be specifically allocated to creating a think tank that will increase awareness for organ donation and transplantation for Latino communities. Oh, and I forgot to tell you, Sarah—I heard that Bower's wife may be heading up the think tank and might want you involved, for real."

Sarah looked at Handsome. "No, thanks. I'm staying as far away from her and this whole thing as possible. Not interested."

"Holy shit. Do they just have that kind of cash sitting around?" Jackie asked.

"Let's just say they had to find it fast, so most, if not all, of their assets were seized and sold. Amanda will likely be renting an apartment if and when she gets out."

Sarah added, "Jackie, wait'll you hear Amanda's deal."

Handsome continued, "Amanda was convicted as a co-conspirator in first-degree murder and is currently at the Central California Women's Facility, in Chowchilla. She has lawyered up big-time, so her original sentence of twenty years is currently being appealed. Still, she'll be calling that place home for a while."

Jackie poured the rest of the wine into their glasses. Mark walked up just as she finished. "What would you like to try next? We have some great reds."

Jackie said, "Why don't you surprise us? I love a tasty, robust red."

"I've got the perfect one." He quickly returned with one of Cline's best sellers, Carignane. "This is my favorite red wine. It has some good fruit when you first taste it and a spicy finish. It's our house red because my wife loves it so much." Mark uncorked the bottle and poured a little into the new glasses he'd brought.

Jackie took a sip and said, "This is yummy. Pour on, my man." He filled the other glasses halfway and, just as before, promised to check back with them shortly.

They spent a few minutes nibbling the various cheeses and dried fruit quietly; then Jackie broke the silence. "What's it take to get put away for life in this country? Seems like a light sentence, if you ask me."

Handsome set his glass down and said, "They both hired top attorneys, so they were able to do some serious negotiating. I'm sure they'll be in the lowest-security sections, with lots of privileges. Money talks, but it doesn't get you off murder. I thought the fines the judge leveled on both of them were brilliant."

Sarah cut in, "It just sucks that they can practically buy their way out of this. Did you hear Bower's name mentioned at all?"

"No, there was no evidence that led to him or his wife, except that she was friends with Amanda. I think the judge spoke with some bigwig in transplant when he was figuring out the fines and where they should be directed," Handsome said.

Jackie leaned in toward both Sarah and Handsome. "How in the hell did they keep this out of the media? I was watching the news every day, waiting for the shit to hit the fan."

Sarah shook her head. "That's way above my pay grade. I sent Bower a note as soon as I knew Amanda and Sergio got arrested, and I never heard anything back."

Jackie's eyebrows furrowed as she said, "You mean he didn't share anything with you off the record at work?"

"Nope. Nothing. Sometimes it's best to leave it alone. Of course I was dying to know, but he just went along like nothing happened, working his ass off and running the show."

The three of them sat and enjoyed the rest of the wine and snacks, then Handsome followed Mark so he could order some wine to be shipped to his place in Miami. When he was out of earshot, Jackie reached over and touched Sarah's arm. "So, Mrs. Handsome, what's the deal with your new boyfriend? Are you going to try to have a real relationship, or are you going to keep running from love the rest of your life? I don't care either way; I'm just noticing that you two look pretty comfortable together."

Sarah glanced over at Handsome. He was still at the outside counter, talking to Mark.

She let out a big sigh and looked Jackie directly in the eye. "I'm scared shitless, but I do have feelings for this guy. I really tried not to like him too much, but he saw right past that the first night he was here. He stayed in a hotel for the first three nights."

Jackie smiled. "Quite the gentleman."

Sarah felt Jackie looking straight into her soul, as only Jackie could do. "I'm going to give love one more try, but if this bombs, then that's it. Never again. We'll try it long-distance, and then I may move to Miami. Who knows? The jury's still out."

"This is serious, Golden. I'm proud of you, buddy. Stay in the ring. You just never know."

"Thanks, Jack. By the way, any chance at all that we can reschedule our Cuba trip?"

"Don't push it. Laura and I are on good terms. I promised her that you and I would not ever go on any more undercover adventures. I'm thinking I can bring up a girls' weekend in Calistoga after my leg is healed. Just you and me. She said she's not letting me out of her sight, or the state, for a while."

Sarah thought about that. "I'll do Calistoga in a minute. I can't blame Laura. We'll get to Cuba someday."

Jackie laughed. "Yeah, maybe you can plan a destination wedding in Miami, and then we can all go to Cuba together for your honeymoon."

Before Sarah could protest, Handsome came back. "Did I hear someone say 'Cuba'? I have a good friend who lives there. We can go anytime."

Sarah and Jackie smiled at each other.

Handsome looked at both of them. "Just what are you two cooking up? I can't even begin to imagine. Anyway, I'm hungry. Let's go eat. You can tell me all your crazy ideas over lunch. My treat."

Author's Note

As of October 14, 2016, 119,712 patients are waiting for an organ transplant, according to the United Network for Organ Sharing.

Every day twenty-two people die waiting for an organ transplant, according to ORGANIZE.

Please, discuss organ donation with your family, and if you decide you want to contribute to the betterment of the lives of others even after you move on from this life, go to www.donatelife.net and sign up to be an organ donor. Organ donation is the most generous gift any of us can give.

Acknowledgments

I am forever grateful to my first writing teacher and mentor Guy Biederman, a gift to any writer who is fortunate to cross his path. To my writing tribe, Bella Quattro—Betsy Graziani Fasbinder, Linda Joy Myers, and Christie Nelson. Betsy looked at me over three years ago when I first came up with the idea of *Cut* and said, "That's your next book." She was right, and she has been a close writing soul mate and generous, loving friend, while Linda Joy and Christie have always encouraged me through my writing journey.

To Brooke Warner, for her clear and honest coaching and her leadership in creating She Writes Press so *Cut* could proudly take its place next to all the other professionally published books in most bookstores throughout the US.

To Annie Tucker, for her professional partnership from development through copyediting. Thank you for loving my story and characters as much as I did, and for polishing the manuscript so thoroughly. To my publicist, Kris Verdeck, for introducing *Cut* to the world.

To Detective Frank Falzon, for his insights into the world of law enforcement and my research assistant and sister, Kerry Peele, for finding all the perfect details that enriched my story.

To my loving and patient husband, Mark Schatz, who supported me through writing another book. To Gracie and Bennett, who always try to keep things funny and real and are the best kids a mom could ask for.

Lastly, to Elaine Petrocelli, co-owner of Book Passage, a large, successful, independent bookstore in Corte Madera, California. I attended three murder mystery conferences at Book Passage and was inspired by the professional and generous faculty.

About the Author

Amy S. Peele has been an RN since 1974. She discovered her passion for organ donation and transplantation when she started as a transplant coordinator at University of Chicago in 1976. She enjoyed a thirty-five-year career in transplantation before retiring in 2014 from the University of California San Francisco, which has one of the largest and most successful transplant programs in the US.

Peele has a love for comedy and improv and graduated from Second City Players Workshop in 1985 in Chicago. She has been writing for over fifteen years. In addition to killing people and using their organs in her murder mysteries, she enjoys meditating, teaching yoga, swimming, and pursuing her spirituality by studying the teachings of Deepak Chopra.

Amy invites you contact her at www.amyspeele.com.

Author photo © Charles Bearden

Selected Titles from She Writes Press

She Writes Press is an independent publishing company
founded to serve women writers everywhere.
Visit us at www.shewritespress.com.

A Girl Like You: A Henrietta and Inspector Howard Novel by
Michelle Cox. $16.95, 978-1-63152-016-7. When the floor matron
at the dance hall where Henrietta works as a taxi dancer turns up
dead, aloof Inspector Clive Howard appears on the scene—and
convinces Henrietta to go undercover for him, plunging her into
Chicago's gritty underworld.

The Great Bravura by Jill Dearman. $16.95, 978-1-63152-989-4.
Who killed Susie—or did she actually disappear? The Great Bravura, a dashing lesbian magician living in a fantastical and noirish
1947 New York City, must solve this mystery—before she goes to
the electric chair.

Just the Facts by Ellen Sherman. $16.95, 978-1-63152-993-1. The
seventies come alive in this poignant and humorous story of a fear-
ful rookie reporter at a small-town newspaper who uncovers a big-
time scandal.

Water On the Moon by Jean P. Moore. $16.95, 978-1-938314-61-2.
When her home is destroyed in a freak accident, Lidia Raven, a
divorced mother of two, is plunged into a mystery that involves her
entire family.

Murder Under The Bridge: A Palestine Mystery by Kate Raphael.
$16.95, 978-1-63152-960-3. Rania, a Palestinian police detective
with a young son, meets cheeky Jewish-American feminist Chloe
at an Israeli checkpoint—and soon becomes embroiled in a murder
case that implicates the highest echelons of the Israeli military.

The Black Velvet Coat by Jill G. Hall. $16.95, 978-1-63152-009-9.
When the current owner of a black velvet coat—a San Francisco
artist in search of inspiration—and the original owner, a 1960s
heiress who fled her affluent life fifty years earlier, cross paths, their
lives are forever changed . . . for the better.